THE EARTHBORN

Also by the author

Adventures in Godhood
Imaginary Friends
Weekends Can Be Murder

The Nash'terel books
The Earthborn
The Bloodstone (forthcoming)

SIC TRANSIT TERRA
(Edge Science Fiction and Fantasy Publishing)
Book 1: *The Genius Asylum*
Book 2: *The Otherness Factor*
Book 3: *The Relativity Bomb*
Book 4: *The Genome Rally*
Book 5: *The Cockroach Crusade*
Book 6: *The Identity Shift*
The Stragori Deception (forthcoming from Brain Lag)

THE EARTHBORN

A novel of the Nash'terel

ARLENE F. MARKS

Milton, Ontario

This is a work of fiction. All of the characters, events, and organizations portrayed in this novel are either products of the author's imagination or are used fictitiously.

Brain Lag
Milton, Ontario
http://www.brain-lag.com/

Copyright © 2023 Arlene F. Marks. All rights reserved. This material may not be reproduced, displayed, modified or distributed without the express prior written permission of the copyright holder. For permission, contact publishing@brain-lag.com.

Cover photo by Adam Wilson, https://www.fourcolourblack.com/

Library and Archives Canada Cataloguing in Publication

Title: The earthborn : a novel of the Nash'terel / Arlene F. Marks.
Names: Marks, Arlene F., 1947- author.
Identifiers: Canadiana (print) 20230159044 | Canadiana (ebook) 20230159052 | ISBN 9781928011965
  (softcover) | ISBN 9781928011972 (EPUB)
Classification: LCC PS8561.R2868 E27 2023 | DDC C813/.54—dc23

Content warnings: Car accident, death, gore

*In loving memory of my mother,
Mollie Lerman
(1925-2023)*

There is a legend on Rin Yeng, the fifth planet of the Gorna system. It concerns a mineral with mysterious properties, and a lost people called the Nash'terel, which in the Yeng tongue means "secluded ones".

The story goes this way: one day a curious young Nash'terel was exploring a cave deep in the mountains around the isolated valley where his people lived. He came across a strange and beautiful rock deposit in the cave wall. In his haste to break off a piece of it to study, he cut his hand.

He watched in fascination as the chunk he was holding absorbed the blood from his wound. Then the mineral changed colour, the milky white blossoming into an entire palette of vibrant hues. He named this mineral "dashkra", which in Yeng means "bloodstone".

When he shared his discovery with the other Nash'terel, they were struck by its ornamental beauty and began mining it. Nash'terel artisans ground and polished the stone and made it into jewellery that became incorporated into rituals and ceremonies. In the process, they created a fine dust that made its way into the air and the soil and eventually the bodies of the Nash'terel themselves, gradually turning them into an entirely different race of beings.

These new Nash'terel could shapeshift. They aged very slowly. They could recover rapidly from any kind of wound. They became excellent nocturnal hunters, needing very little sleep. However, there was a price to pay for these wondrous powers. The dashkra also gave them an obscene, unnatural thirst for the life essence of other creatures. Unable to slake it within their isolated valley, they were forced to hunt beyond its borders, finding their prey in nearby Yeng villages.

When the truth about "the secluded ones" came out, the Yeng were enraged and horrified. The emperor ordered his generals to assemble an army, but when the soldiers stormed into the valley, their quarry had vanished, along with all the dashkra. The Nash'terel had carved every last bit of the mineral from the caves and taken it with them. Only the dust was left behind.

In some versions of the story, the dust settled on the boots and uniforms of the soldiers and was thus carried out of the valley to infect other Yeng, over time turning them into shapeshifting vampires as well. In others, the Nash'terel escaped by killing the soldiers and assuming their shapes, hiding in plain sight among the Yeng and spreading the "blood sickness" each time they fed.

So the legend goes, at any rate. Whether the Nash'terel played a role in unleashing the epidemic on Rin Yeng is unknown. All that can be said for certain is this: if there ever were Nash'terel on that world, they aren't there any longer.

Chapter One

Bilyash crossed the parking lot in long strides, becoming more purposeful and determined with every step he took. He'd spent centuries listening to Uncle Maury's lectures about what it meant to be Nash'terel—a secluded one, in hiding on an alien world. But to one who had been born here, Earth wasn't an alien place. It was home. More to the point, it was Bilyash's home.

Throwing his shoulders back, he passed the final row of vehicles and headed toward the tall glass doors bearing the red, black, and white logo of the Toronto Academy of Film Arts. Bilyash—henceforth to be known among the humans as Billy Ash—was going to train as a movie makeup artist. After lurking on its margins in fascination for more than a hundred years, he had finally decided to follow his dream and join the film industry as a certified professional, no matter what Maldemaur thought of his "obsession with human culture".

They had had loud discussions lately about that. As far as Maury was concerned, the Nash'terel were a superior race. The very idea of an apprentice abandoning traditional learning paths in order to embrace the ways of a lesser species, he'd sputtered, well, it was worse than disgraceful. It was un-Nash'terel!

On RinYeng, Bilyash thought savagely as he reached the yellow brick building and hauled open the entrance to the foyer. This world was not RinYeng, nor was it merely a stopover on the way to somewhere else. And yet, after more than fifteen hundred years on Earth, Maury was still figuratively living out of a suitcase.

What was worse, he'd also made it clear that he expected Bilyash to do the same. Was it any wonder the younger being had insisted on moving out on his own some seventy years earlier?

Bilyash stepped inside and paused, grinning with anticipation as he surveyed the reception area. Considering what TAFA was, it wouldn't have surprised him to see a replica of a seedy hotel lobby from some noir film made back in the 1950s. In fact, that would have been much more interesting and *à propos* than the boilerplate office building decor someone had slapped in place here: the mustard-and-relish-coloured fake leather bench seating, the glass-topped end tables, the bubble-patterned industrial carpet parted by a terrazzo-tiled path to a pair of chrome-veneered elevator doors... No matter. He was finally where he wanted to be, with a three o'clock appointment for an intake interview, and nothing was going to dampen his mood.

He glanced at the clock mounted on the wall over the reception desk. He was ten minutes early. That was good. Administration was on the sixth floor. Bilyash nodded pleasantly to the receptionist (munching on bacon poutine-flavoured potato chips—her life essence was probably polluted as hell) and crossed to where one of the elevator cars had just disgorged its human freight.

Two females followed him into the car. The short, plump one with curly blonde hair stood to his left, nearest the control panel. She pressed the button for the sixth floor, then let her hand hover as she glanced a question at the other two passengers. Bilyash acknowledged it with a smile. The other female, taller and older with salon-styled dark hair, met her gaze briefly, then turned boldly appraising eyes on the shape he'd assumed for this new chapter of his life.

He'd waffled for a long while before selecting this appearance. The part of him that wanted to melt unnoticed into the student population had stridently disagreed with the part that yearned to stand out from the crowd. Ultimately, however, he'd realized that whatever shape he took, he would have to wear it—and keep it out of trouble—for at least the next fifteen to twenty years. That meant avoiding unwanted attention from his fellow students, both male and female. If he was too attractive, he might not be able to resist the temptation of easy prey. If he was too unattractive, he might become the object of pity or, worse, the butt of many jokes.

So, he'd sought the middle ground, combining features from George Clooney and Gary Sinise, with a bit of Keanu Reeves thrown in. Bilyash had patted himself on the back for creating an outward look that would be respected by his fellow students while at the same time discouraging their amorous attentions. And now, here he was, inside the building for less than a minute and already being inspected like a side of beef by a female giving off a pheromonal scent that threatened to ignite his groin.

He swallowed a sigh.

After a beat, the female ventured, "Are you the new administrator?"

He shook his head. "I'm here for an interview."

Her eyes lit up. "To be an instructor?"

"To be a student," he replied.

"Oh." The light instantly dimmed. She turned and for the rest of the ride faced silently forward.

Of course. An administrator or an instructor could be useful to someone climbing the professional ladder. But a late-blooming student? What help could he possibly offer?

The glass-walled Admissions office faced the elevator doors on the sixth floor. Bilyash stood back while the two females exited the car and turned left. Then he put them out of his mind and crossed the hall, primed and prepped for his interview.

"I apologize for the delay, Mr. Ash. The committee is ready to see you now."

Bilyash dropped the magazine he'd been reading onto the empty seat beside him and got to his feet. He'd been kept waiting for an additional fifteen minutes, long enough for a thorough mental review of everything he'd done (or forgotten to do) in preparation for this moment, and plenty of time for a feeling of dread to have taken root in his midsection. He'd been so focused earlier on avoiding problematic relationships with other students that he hadn't even considered the possibility of his application being rejected. What if the committee had no intention of admitting him to the Makeup FX program? What if they'd brought him here just to meet the person who'd lied so creatively on their downloadable forms?

More to the point, if his worst imaginings came true, how could he look Maldemaur in the eyes and tell him that he'd just let himself be humiliated by a bunch of... (shudder)... *humans*?

Bilyash drew a steadying breath and came to a decision: he was due for a feeding. If his application had in fact been turned down, then he would be following a TAFA administrator home tonight.

He hoped there would be a female on the committee. The life essence generated by the intense pleasure of an orgasm was so much purer and tastier than the stuff many other Nash'terel sucked out of their terrified or unconscious prey, and the human female orgasm could be kept going almost indefinitely.

Smiling to himself, Bilyash followed the clerk into the conference room.

Three humans sat facing him across a polished oak table, two of them female, none of them looking particularly happy. The one in the middle gestured to him to sit down. And the female beside her—

With a start, Bilyash recognized her as the dark-haired woman from the elevator car.

They began with introductions. The woman chairing the meeting was Jaymie Rosen, the Director of Admissions, and the man to her left was Anthony Allain, the Director of Student Services. The other woman had a name Bilyash instantly recognized, as well as an exalted reputation in the stage and filmmaking community. In fact, she was the reason he'd decided to study here: Cora Dolson, the creator and lead instructor of the Makeup FX program at TAFA.

Rosen opened a dark green file folder and read from the first page:

"Mr. William R. Ash. What does the 'R' stand for?" she asked.

"Roland," Bilyash replied, "as in Gilbert. But I prefer to be called Billy."

At this, the entire committee seemed to relax.

"It isn't often that we receive an application from someone your age with no previous experience in filmmaking," Rosen continued, scanning down the sheet. "Usually a mature student has been working in the field for a while and either needs the certification to move to the next level or wants to change specialties. But you seem to have done everything *except* make movies. So we're curious, Billy. Why, suddenly, at the age of 44, have you decided to train as a makeup artist?"

Suddenly? These people had no idea how long Bilyash had been preparing for this moment. He'd brought D.W. Griffith his morning coffee during the filming of *The Birth of a Nation*. He'd been on a first name basis with such actors as Shirley Temple, Buster Keaton, Marie Dressler, Mary Pickford, and most of the Keystone Kops. He'd worked as a gaffer, a props maker, a set painter, and at least a dozen other things on films produced in the 1920s and '30s, and had watched from the sidelines as movies grew from an interesting diversion to one of the mainstays of human culture.

Unfortunately, he couldn't put any of this on his application form and pretend to be just 44 years old. So he replied instead, truthfully, "I've always been a huge fan of the movies, but I've also been a lifelong student of the technical side, especially the fantastical elements, like creature design and monster makeup. I've watched every *The Making Of...* featurette I could get my hands on. And I recently got hooked on that reality television show, *Face to Face*. After binge-watching the first four seasons, I realized that I want to be more than a fan. I want a career in the industry, and if I don't take steps to achieve that goal now, I might never be able to."

Cora had straightened in her chair and was staring at him almost as intently as she'd done in the elevator.

"There's no doubt in any of our minds that you have a great deal of talent, Billy. The folder of makeup designs and before and after snapshots that you submitted with your application…? Most impressive," said Allain. "When Ms. Dolson saw them, she asked to sit in on your interview. I believe she has a few questions of her own to ask you."

Bilyash swivelled his head and met her steady gaze. From the expression on her face, it was clear that she was undressing him with her eyes. He could practically feel them plucking at his shirt buttons. And he was sure he hadn't imagined the disapproval that had momentarily cracked Rosen's official demeanour.

So that was the way things were around here? Interesting.

Cora cleared her throat, then said, "I run a very intense first year program, Mr. Ash. I expect my students to be available and focused not only during the day, but also for night work and on the weekends. How's your stamina?"

"I don't need much sleep," he assured her. "And I work out. You'll find I'm up for pretty much anything."

Allain barely suppressed a snort of laughter. Meanwhile, Rosen's natural scowl deepened.

"Good. Because moviemaking isn't a nine-to-five, five-day-a-week job," Cora said stiffly, more for their benefit than for his, Bilyash suspected. "Also, there's more to learning about movie makeup than just how to select and apply cosmetic product. My course isn't going to be easy. It includes elements from other disciplines. Facial reconstruction. Anatomic analysis. Even some physics and chemistry. There's a lot of theoretical study in addition to the practical aspects, and you'll have to pass written exams. Are you prepared to handle that kind of workload?"

He leaned forward, stared deeply into her eyes, and replied, "Like I said, I'm up for anything you care to throw at me."

Wearing a decidedly feline smile, Cora turned to the other committee members and said, "I think he'll do just fine."

Anthony Allain pressed his lips together and rolled his eyes.

Jaymie Rosen closed the green file folder and jogged it on the table. "Welcome to TAFA, Mr. Ash," she said dryly. "And good luck. You're likely to need it."

Maldemaur's naturally dark complexion was mottling. In his true form, he had brown skin, two broad, bony ridges that sprang upward from his temples and dropped to hug the curve of his ears, and a scar on his left cheek, resembling the wind-blown surface of a muddy pond. Now, leaning over the corner of the shiny metal table in his basement laboratory, he reminded Bilyash of a dragon in its lair, about to breathe fire.

The older Nash'terel was a light lord, not a flame lord, but Bilyash wasn't taking any chances. He scooped his brand new student ID card off the table and slipped it into his jeans pocket, just in case.

"Are you out of your damn mind?" Maury sputtered. "Have you any idea what you're about to do?"

Bilyash had been expecting a negative reaction. He replied firmly, "Yes! I'm about to do something I've always *wanted* to do. Listen, I came here to share my good news, not ask for your permission. I've been accepted into the program, and they even told me how impressed they are with my talent. You should be happy for me, Maldemaur."

"If by happy you mean terrified, then rest assured that I am. You'll be joining a segment of human society that specializes in drawing attention to itself, in turning private lives inside out as if they were pockets. This is exactly what I've spent the last five hundred years trying to shield you from, Bilyash. We're Nash'terel. We don't pursue fame, we shun it. We stay in the shadows. You're one of only a small number of young ones born on this side of the rift, and I promised when I took you in that I would keep you safe. On this world, even more than on RinYeng, we're safest when concealed. Since you've apparently learned nothing else from me, I would have hoped you'd understand that much, at least."

Nothing else? Not bothering to swallow the bitterness rising in his throat, Bilyash spat back, "So in order to be safe I have to give up everything else? Like trying new things? Like exploring my creativity and reaching for happiness? Is that how you lived before I came along? Scurrying through the darkness like a rat in an alley, darting from one hiding place to another and praying that no one would notice you?"

"Flying beneath the radar. Being quiet and unassuming. Not flaunting my abilities. Yes! It's how I survived," Maury retorted. "It's how I *thought* I was teaching you to survive as well. Evidently, I was mistaken."

"What makes you think I can't stay off the radar while training for a human career?"

"Because you're still quite young, and sooner or later you'll make a mistake. Listen, I've tried integrating myself into human society, tried it more than once, and each time, some nosy human spied on me, raised an alarm, and forced me back into hiding. No matter how carefully you tread in this world, humans will pose a danger to you. They're curious and they're stealthy. And their first instinct is to destroy what they fear. That's what happened to your parents."

"You told me they died in a fire."

"They did. It was set by a bunch of villagers who believed your family was devil spawn. Cottages went up like tinder in those days. The humans waited until you and your parents were all inside and then lit your home ablaze. I saw the flames and came running, but I wasn't able to save all three of you. One little slip-up was all it took to make those humans decide we were demons from hell. And you wonder why I'm so cautious?"

Silence fell between them then. For several seconds, the two Nash'terel stood facing each other, neither one willing to break it.

Maldemaur was the closest thing Bilyash had to a father. No matter how angry Maury became at times, he'd never turned his back on his young charge, and he'd never done anything to harm him. What he had done, for five hundred years and counting, was care for and worry about him. That was what Maury was doing now, Bilyash reminded himself.

"I'll take precautions, I promise. I'll follow all your rules, and I'll check in with you every day or two. But I have to do this."

Maury's shoulders sagged as the tension seemed to drain out of him. "You really need this to be happy?"

"I do."

Shaking his head in resignation, Maury replied, "You are the stubbornest, most—All right, then. I won't stop you. Go. Chase your dream. If you need me, you know where I'll be—hiding in a nearby shadow."

Maury's cardinal rule, the one he'd begun drilling into Bilyash from the moment he'd taken the youngster in, was never to hunt where he lived or where he worked.

Billy had already decided that where he learned fell under that rule as well. It was an easy one for him to follow, since the shape he'd chosen created a generational gap between himself and the human students, and Cora hadn't exaggerated the workload associated with her program. His days in the classroom kept him too busy even to think about anything else. So, not hunting at school was not a problem for Billy Ash.

On the other hand, *being* hunted there was.

He'd never had the tables turned on him like this. Being considered prey by a human was a decidedly discomfiting experience, especially since the one viewing him that way was the program instructor. He'd hoped that Cora's desire for him would wane once the courses began. However, several months into the academic year, the smouldering looks she regularly gave him made it clear that her appetite had only intensified.

"Billy, a word, please?"

As Cora bent to whisper this into Bilyash's ear, the male student sitting across the table from him fought to keep his expression neutral. They'd been drawing flayed heads, part of a study of facial musculature. Bilyash cast a glance at the other student's work and saw an unmistakable smirk on the sketched face.

It was January. He'd been wondering when the huntress would make her move. Bilyash closed up his sketch pad and met her outside the door to the studio. With effort, he kept his shoulders relaxed and his expression mildly curious.

"An opportunity has come up, and I think it might be of interest to you," she said.

"Oh?"

"An old friend of mine is looking for an intern for a summer shoot and has asked to meet my most promising student. Terrence Macy. Are you familiar with the name?"

"The current dean of horror movies? Of course, I am! I've seen every one of his films, most of them several times."

"He's coming to my place for cocktails tomorrow evening. Here's the address. Arrive at 7:30 sharp. Wear a suit." She handed him a slip of paper and watched as he tucked it into his shirt pocket.

"Thank you, Ms. Dolson," he said earnestly. "Is there anything I should bring?"

"Just yourself," she told him, looking like the Cheshire cat in *Alice in Wonderland*.

It took every gram of his self-control not to mirror that satisfied feline expression. Humans were so transparent. The invitation was probably sincere. However, Macy would be either tied up and unable to make it or on a tight schedule allowing for only a very short visit. Either way, that would leave Billy and Cora alone in her apartment for the rest of the night.

It appeared things were about to ratchet up a notch or two in Coraland.

To Bilyash's surprise, Cora Dolson had not overstated Macy's interest in meeting him. Following her instructions to the letter, Billy Ash had appeared at her door at the appointed hour, wearing a dark blue suit, a lighter blue shirt, and a blue and grey striped tie. The celebrated producer was already there, having brought a bottle of Yellow Tail Shiraz. The three of them sat in Cora's warmly decorated living room, drinking the Australian wine, snacking on water crackers and cubes of Gouda and Asiago cheese, and talking shop until nearly 2:00 a.m. When finally Macy glanced at his watch, feigned shock at the lateness of the hour, and took his leave, Bilyash waited with interest to see what Cora would do next.

The stage was set for a seduction. Would she follow through?

Cora put her back to the door she had just closed behind her departing guest and said thoughtfully, "He liked you, Billy, a lot. I don't remember the last time Terrence stayed this late while interviewing a prospective intern."

Bilyash shrugged and shifted his position on her moss green sofa. "It probably had something to do with the fact that there's only about ten years' difference in our ages."

"No, it's more special than that. A lot of people say that they're lifelong film students, but I think you really are. You're so knowledgeable about the minutiae of film history, it's almost as though you're channelling someone who was actually part of it. And there's something else about you. I sensed it the first time we met. You've got a lot of personal magnetism, Billy Ash."

She took a sinuous step in his direction. As he watched her glide across the carpet, Bilyash felt the temperature rise in his groin.

"In fact, it's pulling me towards you right now," she said.

Another step. More heat, spreading slowly upward to claim his belly.

"They say opposites attract, but I don't think that's true," she told him. "I think we have a great deal in common, you and I."

Now she was directly in front of the sofa, gazing hungrily down at him. In a throaty voice, she continued, "I'm seldom wrong about these things, but if I'm mistaken this time, tell me now and we'll say goodnight and never mention this part of the evening again. Trust me, there'll be no hard feelings."

...other than the ones he was experiencing at that moment, Bilyash added silently. And the second he got to his feet, she would know about them too.

Flames were now dancing across his chest. One way or another, he would be feeding tonight. They weren't at school, and she had made the first move, so it might as well be here.

Bilyash stood up and opened his arms, and in a heartbeat, Cora had leaped into his embrace, offering her lips for a kiss.

Not yet, he thought. She had to be in the throes of orgasm before he would take her essence, and at the rate his thirst was growing, she needed to get there quickly. Fortunately, he had a special talent for making that happen.

Gazing into her eyes, he sank back onto the sofa, pulling her down to sit beside him. Bilyash gathered her into the crook of his arm. The pulse at her throat was strong. He visualized it. All that blood being pushed through her veins and arteries. Waiting for his blood to summon it to and from the sensitive parts of her body. That was all the human orgasm was, after all: the sensation of movement as a tide of red corpuscles rose and ebbed. It was the brain that translated the sensation into pleasure. Judging from the dreamy expression on Cora's face, that switch was definitely turned on.

With practised skill, Bilyash commanded the *dashkra* in his body to concentrate in his hand, in his fingertips... to compress itself, becoming dense enough to attract the blood of the prey like a magnet, drawing it first down, then back up to her chest as he dragged his fingers along the fabric covering her torso...

Cora's entire body tensed. The back of her head pressed into the curve of his elbow, and soft, inarticulate sounds escaped from her mouth. She was ready. Bilyash covered her lips with his own and began to drink her life essence. Several long swallows later he broke off contact.

It wouldn't do to drain her entirely. She was famous, after all, the kind of prey whose death always attracted public notice and a thorough police investigation. On a more practical note, she was also his instructor, and there remained more than three years in the program.

Perhaps, after graduation...?

Bilyash looked down at Cora, asleep on the sofa with that Cheshire cat expression on her face again. Something told him this wouldn't be his last visit to her apartment. He straightened her clothing and draped a throw blanket over her. Then, scanning the room one last time to make sure he wasn't leaving anything behind, Billy Ash put on his overcoat and let himself out, locking the door behind him.

Chapter Two

———•◆•———

Four Years Later

Madison's face was falling off, and doing it beautifully, Bilyash thought. Not lumpy and bunched together as skin tended to be after it was ripped away from bone and muscle, but rather the elegant droop and slide that occurred when the anchoring tissue beneath the skin had gradually decayed away. The actress's cheeks and forehead looked like an ancient silk curtain falling slowly into tatters. It was even the same shade of grey. Decrepitude in motion.

It was his best makeup application yet.

From his usual spot behind the lights, Bilyash watched as the brain-thirsty pack of zombies closed in on the survivors of their previous attack, huddled in terror in the burned-out remains of a chapel. On the first day, there had been only two walking dead. Now there were twenty, many of them lurching and staggering, their leg muscles falling in shreds around their ankles. Tomorrow there would be a couple more, and then a couple after that, until the whole busload of tourists were literally dead on their feet.

Only the driver—an A-list actor who'd insisted on having a survival clause in his contract—would get out of this alive. Him and his Chihuahua. Terrence Macy's yappy dog got a part in every movie he produced. It was his trademark, like Hitchcock's cameo.

"Cut! Stay where you are, people, till we've reviewed the take," bellowed the assistant director.

The Chihuahua wasn't people. He'd known from the first day of filming four years earlier that Bilyash wasn't people either. Poochie had taken one look at the figure looming in the shadows and run yelping to the far end of the set. A week into that first summer shoot, he'd become brave enough to stand his ground. Now he just stared and growled, daring the monster to make a move.

"Okay, that's a final," the assistant director hollered. "Zombie extras, you're done for today. Report to Makeup to be normalized before you hit the street, please."

One of the other two makeup artists stopped on his way to the trailer and punched Bilyash playfully on the shoulder. "You did a helluva job on these designs, Billy. I love the way you gave each zombie a name. Uncle Frood, Aunt Mastra, Uncle Maury. And that burn scar on Maury's face is pure genius. It's like you've given each of them a backstory."

"It's just my way of keeping track," said Bilyash with a shrug.

"Ash!" Macy called out. They turned and saw the producer, struggling to keep Poochie O'Bark from leaping out of his arms as he hurried across the set toward them. "I want to talk to you about directing makeup design for my next film as well. Have you got an agent yet?"

"Not yet, Mr. Macy."

"Well, for heaven's sakes, get one! You're not an intern anymore. You're a pro. You get screen credits now, which means you get noticed. Your work on my films has been outstanding. Once *Zombies Take Graceland* is released, other producers will want to snap you up for their projects, and you'll need someone to help you negotiate the best deal. Like I've been telling you all along, you have a great career ahead of you in horror movies."

"Thank you, sir," said Bilyash. "That's very high praise."

He couldn't help grinning as he visualized Maldemaur's reaction to this news. Uncle Maury had practically spat fire when Bilyash had registered for the Makeup FX program at TAFA. He'd sunk into sullen acceptance when Billy Ash had graduated with honours and immediately been hired by Macy to work at the film studio in Richmond Hill, just north of the city. What would he do if the younger Nash'terel decided to move back to Hollywood to pursue his career? Move with him? Oh, lord, he hoped not!

It took the better part of an hour to dezombify the extras and prep the trailer for the afternoon makeup call. By then, the caterer had set up a lunch buffet under a long tent outside the sound stage door. A welcome change from March's brisk air and overcast skies, today's early spring sunshine was giving them their first chance to eat *al fresco* since filming had begun two weeks earlier. Cast and crew were already lined up with disposable plates in their hands, happily chatting as they moved slowly past an array of dishes purporting to be food.

Even after all his time spent among the humans, it still made Bilyash queasy just looking at some of the things they consumed. With all the healthy and interesting sources of nutrition that existed on this planet, they still insisted on filling their stomachs with pasta and vegetables coated with tasteless white slime, beans soaked in colourless acid, and little triangular sandwiches with mystery fillings. Not to mention the globs of cake fried in fat and coated in sugar waiting on the dessert table. Honestly, the stuff these creatures put into their bodies! It was no wonder their essence was so polluted. If he didn't know better, he might believe they did it purposely, to discourage Nash'terel from drinking it.

Though largely ignorant of the presence of his kind on their world, humans obviously realized they were part of a food chain. They broadcast that awareness each time they put a cartoon animal into an ad for a restaurant. Nothing says, "I'm on the menu and loving it!" like a smiling pig wearing a chef's hat and holding out a platter of spareribs.

Bilyash wasn't particularly hungry, having consumed half a beef heart for breakfast before coming to work, but appearances were important among the humans, so he pried a plate off the stack and went to stand at the end of the line. As he'd done every day for the past two weeks, he would take a drib of this and a drab of that and move them around with a plastic fork while he sat alone somewhere for a while. People always assumed that he'd originally taken much more and was simply throwing away leftovers when he dropped the plate and its contents into the trash bin. Unfortunately, that was all he saw on the table, day after day: garbage. And he was growing tired of pretending that it was anything else.

Over the years, Bilyash had sampled nearly every kind of raw meat on the planet: human flesh, of course, as well as the animals humans bred or hunted for their own consumption and, out of curiosity, a few they tried to avoid putting in their mouths. His favourite, it turned out, was beef. Humans ate beef all the time, including some of the organ meats. Admittedly, raw liver might be too much to ask for as part of a luncheon buffet, but with all the money Macy was paying these caterers, would it have killed them to put out some steak tartare occasionally?

"So, you're the incomparable Billy Ash."

The voice had come from directly behind him. Bilyash pivoted and found himself face to face with a tall, curvy brunette wearing a deep V-neck top and a pair of skin-tight jeans. Her hair was pulled back in a ponytail. She had a dimple in her left cheek, and her brown eyes were sparkling with laughter.

"Excuse me?"

"There's an instructor at Ryerson who can't stop talking about you," she went on breezily. "She says you're not only a genius makeup artist, you're also an amazing lover."

Those last two words paused every conversation within earshot. Bilyash glanced around at a crowd of faces, all turned toward him and wearing amused and expectant expressions. Some of them still wore zombie makeup as well. For an unsettling moment, he felt like the next *nosh* in a Terrence Macy movie.

"I think we should take this meeting indoors," he said, firmly replacing his paper plate on the table.

"Oh, yes, let's," she purred, widening her eyes and licking her lips suggestively.

You think you're going to eat me, sweetheart? he thought. *You're in for a surprise.*

"Ah, I see you found him!" The sudden nearness of Macy's voice startled them both. The producer was smug-faced and, for the first time that day, empty-handed, having evidently found a place to park Poochie the Yap. "Billy, this is Angelina Fiore. She's an intern from Ryerson who'll be working with us in makeup and special effects until we wrap up post-production."

"You can call me Angie," she told him, and made another circuit of her lips with that small pink tongue. He visualized himself biting it off and imagined how it would taste. Oversalted, no doubt, like all raw human flesh.

"Angie has come up with a brilliant idea," gushed Macy. "A zombie dog. Wouldn't that be amazing? You could design a makeup to turn Poochie into an undead Chihuahua."

Bilyash was speechless. The concept was impractical at best, laughable at worst. This dog was not an actor. Even if they could find a way to make the obstreperous animal sit still for the application, he'd be ripping and scraping everything off within seconds. Ditto for the sensors they would have to stick all over his body if they opted for digital motion capture.

Angie piped up, "And I could translate it digitally, using computer animation programming to enhance his recorded image."

By then Bilyash had found his voice again. "Sounds interesting," he conceded. "I'd like to see how you do it."

"Is there a computer inside the makeup trailer?" she asked.

"Yes. I use it for designing and storing specific characters."

"Perfect!" She interlocked her fingers, turned her hands palm outwards, and stretched her arms out in front of her. "Take me to it, Billy Boy, and prepare to be impressed."

Billy Boy? In truth, he was already impressed with Angelina Fiore, and glad that the trailer would give them privacy over the lunch hour. She wasn't steak tartare, he decided, but she would do.

Angie had come prepared. She pulled a flash drive from her jeans pocket and inserted the device into the side of his computer.

As he leaned over her shoulder, sensing the essence that

practically oozed from her pores, a familiar thirst began stirring warmly inside him. However, he reminded himself sternly, first things first. A dangerous loose end had apparently been left dangling, and he would have to take care of it as soon as possible.

"So, Cora Dolson is at Ryerson now?" he asked quietly.

"She started teaching there about eight months ago." Angie's fingers flew over the keys as she spoke. "We bonded over coffee one day in the Timmy's across the road from the university, and... the floodgates opened. You were all she could talk about. How you took her to the moon and back, actually made her pass out with ecstasy every single time you made love. Left her feeling physically drained for days afterward, but yearning for more."

And alive, he thought grimly. He'd liked Cora. Respected her contributions to the film industry too much to remove her from it. Clearly, that decision had been a mistake.

"And she spoke only to you?"

"About how much she misses her weekly space flight? I'm pretty sure I'm one of a select few to hear about that. About your magical makeup mojo, however, she wants everyone to know. You were her star student, her pride and joy. Billy Ash gets held up as a shining example in every class she teaches."

"Magical mojo? That's an exaggeration," he assured her.

"Once I knew you'd been sleeping with her, that was what I thought too," she assured him back. "So, when Cora mentioned this internship opportunity to me, I jumped on it, hoping to meet you. I wanted to see for myself whether you were everything she said you were."

Everything?

Heat was spreading through his groin now. His thirst was growing stronger. With effort, he kept his hands clamped on the back of her chair and asked, "How did you know I'd be working on Macy's film?"

"It wasn't hard to find you. I just asked Cora. She's opened a file on her computer dedicated to following your career."

And she was telling others about him. Telling the whole damned world. Bilyash cursed inwardly. Maldemaur had been right. He should have drunk that woman dry the day he graduated from the program. Well, better late than never, as the humans were fond of saying.

Angie finished typing and leaned back to give him a better view of what was happening on his computer screen. She'd looped an action scene from one of the *Expendables* movies, then used digital animation to morph Stallone, Statham, and Lundgren into three-week-old corpses as a banner faded in on top of them—*The Expendables 35: Nothing Stops These Guys*.

"This was my audition piece to secure the internship," she told him.

All right, he had to admit, he was impressed. Poochie McArfArf would almost certainly emerge from post-production as the first undead Chihuahua in movie history. And with luck, Angie's talent would glow brightly enough to claim Macy's full attention, freeing Bilyash to do what he should have done earlier.

Abruptly he became aware that she had turned her upper body and was staring at him with bold appraisal. "I can see why she was attracted to you," Angie remarked. "You're tall, well-built, handsome in a rugged sort of way. You're definitely Cora's type."

His thirst had become strident. He wasn't sure how it had occurred, only knew he didn't dare ignore it any longer. Its heat had raced upward, touching his belly and chest with fire. Soon it would envelop his brain, triggering a feeding lust. And then,

Bilyash would mindlessly glut himself on the essence of the nearest living creature, draining it completely, regardless of the consequences. Angelina Fiore would die, and he would have broken one of Maldemaur's cardinal rules: Never hunt where you live or where you work.

He mustn't let things go that far. Besides the fact that nastiness ensued whenever the police became involved—something else Maury had drilled into him over the past five centuries—Bilyash had a strange, untethered feeling in his gut every time he and Angie made eye contact. It was something he wanted to explore, and another reason to keep her around.

Leaning over her, he murmured sultrily, "I guess the question is, am I *your* type, Angie?"

He bent forward and brushed his lips against the side of her neck, then raised them a little to tease the lobe of her left ear.

An instant later he got his answer. She gasped in and let out a breath. Then, in a single, sinuous motion, Angie rose to her feet and wrapped her arms around his neck, tilting her head for a kiss.

Not yet.

There was a sleeping area with a cot thoughtfully supplied at the back of the trailer. This was where he carried her, laying her down on top of the blanket. He checked his watch. They had thirty minutes of privacy left. Not quite enough time for a trip to the moon, but sufficient for a suborbital launch. Maury might disagree, but technically, this wasn't a hunt, not when the prey had come to him so willingly. In any case, all he needed was a snack, just a swallow or two of essence to keep the thirst at bay until tonight.

He had to leave some room for Cora, after all.

* * *

Bilyash left Angie asleep on the cot and hurried to log her out and disconnect her flash drive from the computer. The humans' lunch break was over, and actors and crew were wandering back to the makeup trailer. Her presence wouldn't come as a surprise, given the conversation everyone had overheard at the buffet. Some eyebrows might be raised, some snickering heard as makeup was being applied or refreshed for the afternoon shoot, but no one would suspect what had really happened while the humans were downing their swill. He hoped Macy hadn't been expecting her to begin work yet, because Bilyash was certain that Angelina Fiore was done for the day.

As it turned out, using his blood talent had boosted an unexpectedly powerful natural orgasm into a climax of seismic proportions. She would probably be aching for days from all the muscles and ligaments she'd strained. He'd had to clap a hand over her mouth to muffle her screams so that people outside wouldn't hear them and think he was... well... doing exactly what he *was* doing, which was slowly taking her life.

Nobody would believe she was enjoying herself while he did it. Orgasms never looked like fun to those who were only witnessing them. When he'd finally covered her lips with his own, essence had rushed into him like water from a broken spigot. Bilyash had no idea how much he had drunk, only knew it was more than he'd intended, and that it was the purest essence he'd ever tasted. Anxiously checking for a pulse afterward, he'd been relieved to discover that she was still alive.

Of *course* she was done for the day. How could she not be exhausted after all that?

As it turned out, he was wrong, on both counts. A couple of

hours later, as the last camera-ready actor was leaving the trailer, Angie sat up and stretched, as though waking from an ordinary nap, then got carefully to her feet and came to stand beside his makeup chair. "My flash drive?" she asked.

"Check your right front pocket," he told her. He glanced around to make sure they were alone, then added, deeply curious, "How do you feel?"

She gave him a sly smile. "Like an astronaut, post-flight. Cora was right about you. And it's interesting... I'm still fully clothed. Can I assume that you did all that without actually—?"

"You can."

The smile broadened. "Wow! Until next time, Billy Ash. There... will be a next time, right?"

He shrugged. "You know where to find me."

"Trust me, I will."

And with that, she stepped down gingerly from the trailer and headed toward the sound stage.

Watching her through the window, he saw a sway, a slight stumble, but then a squaring of her shoulders followed by a series of slow, deliberate steps. All by itself, his head began to shake. By rights, she shouldn't even be able to stand up. Angelina Fiore would definitely bear further watching. She was unlike any human female Bilyash had ever encountered.

Speaking of human females... he needed to pay a final visit to Cora Dolson. Send her on a one-way trip right out of the solar system. But Uncle Maury had rules for a reason. Her bedroom mustn't look like a crime scene, or the hunter would become the hunted. He didn't relish the thought of living in hiding; he and Maury had done enough of that already. So, Bilyash would have to keep his mind clear and his senses sharp. It would be an assassination, not a feeding. That meant he would need a receptacle to draw out Cora's life essence.

Bilyash reached for his phone and punched up a familiar number.

"Listen, I've got better things to do than run back and forth every time this goddamned thing goes off, so leave a message and maybe I'll call you," grumped the greeting on Maldemaur's answering machine.

It was an improvement over the previous one he'd recorded. Maury did love his expletives. Bilyash waited for the beep, then said, "It's me, and you were right about Cora. I'll be stopping by later today to borrow one of your special containers."

Maury had been listening. He picked up. "Be careful when you get here. The rift opened a couple of days ago and at least five separate teams of assassins came through it. Word is, one triad just landed in North America. I've set traps around the house, in case they come looking for us."

"For us? You're using the royal 'we' now?"

"No, *ristim*, I'm talking about you and me."

Stifling his irritation at being called a halfwit—even when delivered with affection, the insult stung—Bilyash focused on the rest of the message. "You think I'm a target? That's ridiculous. I was born on this world. The 'powers that be' on RinYeng shouldn't even know I exist."

"And yet, somehow they do. It's not just you they're targeting. Two other Earthborns were murdered yesterday, one in Iceland and one in Australia, and I don't want you to be number three. I promised to protect you, and that's what I intend to do."

"Children need protection, Uncle Maury, and I'm not a child anymore," Bilyash reminded him. "I've been living on my own for seven decades now."

"Well, you weren't on your own the last time the rift opened, and it was a damn good thing. By the time the assassins had been identified and disposed of, we'd lost four of our most promising adepts."

"That was the year you insisted that we move to Hollywood."

"For protective coloration. Everyone and their brother-in-law wore a disguise down there. It made us harder to find."

"It's where I got hooked on the movies," Bilyash pointed out.

"I know, and I've been kicking myself for that ever since. But the past is past, and things are different now. As you say, you're not a child. I can't force you to put a defensive perimeter around your apartment, but I can tell you this: watch your back. From now on, trust no one. And remember, it isn't paranoia if someone is actually trying to kill you."

The line went dead. Bilyash stared at his phone thoughtfully for a moment, then slipped it back into his denim jacket pocket.

Chapter Three

———◆———

Built in the 1940s amidst what had then been nothing but scrub and woodlands north of Toronto, Maury's secluded bungalow had eventually been overtaken by a rising tide of suburban development. Now he had neighbours. Now, almost seventy years later, his was the only wood-and-siding structure in an area of established brick homes.

The house was showing its age but still looked pretty solid, Bilyash thought. He was standing across the road, on a patch of grass beside a fire hydrant. At this hour of the night, the residential street was enveloped in shades of darkness, but dark was just another colour to Nash'terel eyes. Those were the ones Bilyash wore now. Reverting only his eyes to their original shape while keeping the rest of his body human hadn't come naturally to him. He'd had to work at it. But it was a good skill for a hunter to have on this world.

Nash'terel eyes enabled him to steal quickly and confidently through a maze of pitch-black alleys and find his way along obstacle-strewn paths in parts of the inner city that had long ago been claimed by shadows and decay. And, on the chance that Maury was right about himself and Bilyash being the targets of assassins who had recently come through the rift, Nash'terel eyes could be the key to keeping the two of them alive.

Right now, however, Bilyash's main concern was to get himself safely from the street to the bungalow's front door. It wouldn't be easy.

As he'd warned on the phone, Maury had set up a security perimeter around the house to foil the current cohort of Yeng assassins. He'd had centuries to perfect his traps and alarms, and to learn how to conceal them even from Nash'terel eyes. Fortunately, Bilyash had spent five of those centuries learning how to spot them. Tonight, he saw alarm triggers disguised as clumps of dry grass and tripwires that looked like spider silk, lurking all over the property and all but invisible in the dark. There was a pit trap as well, crude but effective, its outline betrayed by a slight drop in ground level. And every second paving stone of the narrow walkway leading to the tiny porch was just a little paler than the ones in front and behind. This was new. Maury had probably painted them with something whose unpleasant properties Bilyash preferred not even to guess at.

Mercifully, there wasn't an election coming up. After all the years he'd spent discouraging unwanted company, door-knocking political canvassers were pretty much the only uninvited visitors Maldemaur had to worry about anymore. If one of them should end up in that hole in the ground...? Bilyash shuddered to imagine the consequences.

He pulled out his phone and tapped in Maury's number. The answering machine cut in after two rings. "Listen, asshole, I've got a million better things to do than chew the fat right now," it snarled. "So leave a fuckin' message. But don't hold your breath waiting for a call back."

After the beep, Bilyash said, "It's me. I know you're listening. Deactivate the trap at the front door, because I'm damned if I'm crawling through your basement window again."

He heard male laughter—not Maury's—just before the connection was broken.

Bilyash froze, staring at his phone in disbelief.

It isn't paranoia if somebody's actually trying to kill you.

Great. Maury never let guests into his home. If he wasn't alone in there, then he was almost certainly in trouble. He might even be dead. Maldemaur was the closest thing Bilyash had to family right now, so walking away wasn't an option. But he'd just announced his intention to enter by the front door. There would no doubt be an assassin waiting there to greet him. A giggling assassin, he amended. That would also make him a stupid assassin.

All right, then, the front door it is.

Hesitating for only a moment, Bilyash slid the phone back into his jacket pocket, dragged in a lungful of air, then began what must have looked like a strange dance to anyone watching him as he negotiated his way through the temporary minefield that was Maury's front lawn. When he reached the walkway he paused, mentally flipping a coin. Which would be safe, light or dark? Neither, he decided, and took a long diagonal stride, planting his feet on opposite sides of the stone at the base of the three concrete steps leading to the front porch. He examined them carefully. Maldemaur was too smart not to give himself multiple escape routes from the building. There had to be a safe way to get up and down those stairs.

Bilyash crouched, putting the top step at eye level, and found what he was looking for: a slight upward bowing in the middle. He gripped the railing uprights on either side and crouched lower. The other two steps bowed as well. All right. If the centres were booby trapped, then the sides were probably safe. Or maybe they weren't. Maybe that was the conclusion Maldemaur *wanted* intruders to draw.

Bilyash cursed inwardly. He didn't have time for this. Clearly, the steps were too risky. He'd have to take his chances on the wrought iron railings that flanked them. Carefully placing his hands and feet and moving with deliberate caution, he climbed the right-side railing as though its uprights were the rungs of a ladder laid on its side. After a couple of anxious minutes, he was standing on Maury's front porch with his pulse pounding in his ears.

There was a brown, coarse-fibred mat bidding him welcome. Right. No way was he putting his foot on that.

For another long moment, Bilyash stared at the doorknob, debating with himself. Maury might or might not have heard his message. In either case, he might or might not have been able to deactivate the trap Bilyash was about to step into. If it was still active, it might or might not kill him. If it didn't, there might or might not be a Yeng assassin waiting inside to finish the job. That was a lot of ifs, and a daunting amount of danger. Common sense was telling him to run away, as far and as fast as he could. But the older Nash'terel had always been there when Bilyash needed help. He wasn't about to abandon Maury now that their situations were reversed.

Just as Bilyash reached for the knob, the door flew open, and a huge figure wearing a white fedora and a pinstriped suit with outlandishly wide shoulder padding took its place. He was all straight lines and angles and looked as though he'd stepped out of a comic strip from the 1950s. Bilyash's jaw dropped.

"Get in here, kid," growled the man. He thrust out a hand the size of a six-pound roast, grabbed Bilyash by the front of his jacket, and yanked him through the opening.

The house was dark and quiet inside. These days, Maury kept the upstairs space furnished for show. He'd even shaped himself into a middle-aged retiree for a few months and hired a decorator to make sure the place would look lived-in to anyone who peered through a window.

As the hulking intruder wordlessly propelled "the kid" ahead of him through the hallway, Bilyash glanced around for signs of a struggle and saw none. Unfortunately, that didn't mean there hadn't been one. A faint light was showing under the door that led to the basement. That was where Maldemaur spent all his time, where he actually lived. His laboratory could be a shambles right now, and Maury could be lying in the middle of it, bleeding.

Bilyash's heart was racing. As the basement door swung away in front of him, he half-expected to be thrown down the stairs; but the intruder released his grip and took a step back, letting him make his own unsteady way to the bottom.

The lab had never been what Bilyash would call tidy, but it wasn't the ruin of broken glass and overturned furniture that he'd been visualizing. And standing, not lying, in the middle of it was Maldemaur, wearing the shape that always reminded Billy of Albert Einstein.

"I see you've met Gershred," he said. "He's our new bodyguard."

It took several heartbeats for the meaning of his words to sink in. *Our* bodyguard?

Maury misinterpreted his silence. "You can talk freely around him, Bilyash. He's one of us."

"And by one of us, you mean...?"

"He's Nash'terel."

"My *hainbek* is heat," said the bodyguard, wearing the opposite of a reassuring grin on his face. "Your talent?"

"Magnetism," Bilyash replied distractedly. Then he turned to Maldemaur and reminded him, "You hardly ever leave the house. How did you end up with—?"

"Gershred," Maury supplied. "I warned you earlier about the assassins coming through the rift. Well, that information was given to me in a meeting with the Council of the First, at the Riftgate Club."

"You're kidding! The Oh-So-Important Ones? The Not-Really-First to Arrive on Earth? Those big-shot Yeng actually summoned you to a meeting at their Very Private Club? And you *went*?"

"There's a first time for everything," he pointed out impatiently. "Now listen: the First apparently have agents on RinYeng who sneak signals through the rift each time it opens and update them about what's happening on the other side. When the Council heard about the emperor's purification campaign, they contacted every Yeng and Nash'terel they knew on Earth, to warn us."

Bilyash frowned. "A purification campaign? That doesn't sound good."

"It's not. Unless we can figure out a way to seal the rift permanently, every infected Yeng who comes through it from now on will be a trained assassin. It seems the emperor smelled a revolution brewing and needed a scapegoat. So, he resurrected the old stories about us and told his subjects that the filthy Nash'terel who'd contaminated their planet with the blood sickness were all living happily ever after on our side of the rift. Unfortunately, that happens to be true."

"So they're coming to wipe us out? Again?"

"Not just us this time," said Gershred. "We're still the primary targets, but we're not the only ones they'll be hunting."

"He's mounting a campaign to purify both sides of the rift," Maury continued. "Simply banishing the infected to Earth each time the rift opens has done nothing to stop the spread of the disease on RinYeng, so that tactic has been abandoned. Any infected Yeng not able or willing to be trained as an assassin is being euthanized and cremated instead. Meanwhile, the assassins who have completed their training are being sent here with orders to destroy every being who shows symptoms of the sickness—Nash'terel first, then Yeng."

"Every being?" said Bilyash. "Including themselves?"

"Yes. It's a suicide mission," Gershred assured him.

"Until now, we've kept ourselves apart from the Yeng on Earth," Maury continued. "The first ones to follow us here from RinYeng took every opportunity to become wealthy and powerful in human society. We've done our best to stay out of their way, and they've been quite happy to ignore us. However, with a threat now looming for every exile on this world, including the First, they've come to appreciate how important our unique Nash'terel skills could be to their own survival. Hence, the summons from the Council. The First want to bring all the elemental masters together under their protection."

"In exchange for the Nash'terel protecting *them*," said Bilyash. "That's rich. I hope you told them where they could get off."

"I detected the trap and decided to turn it to our advantage. I may not require protection, but you do. So, without naming you, I insisted that my apprentice's talent was essential to my work,"

Maury replied, "and they agreed to treat us as a unit. I also explained, in words of one syllable, that the only effective protection for a Nash'terel master was another Nash'terel master." He gestured toward the hulking being filling the laboratory doorway. "In addition to being a heat lord, Gershred is a trained warrior, a veteran of many human battles. Like you, he has a fondness for human culture, so the two of you should get along famously."

"I appreciate the thought, Uncle Maury, but I don't want a bodyguard hovering over me," said Bilyash. "Besides, I have my own place, and not even..."

"Call me Shred," said the bodyguard quietly. Everything about him implied menace. Bilyash had to repress a shudder.

"Not even Shred can be in two places at the same time," he concluded.

"Quite true," Maury agreed. "And that's why I think you need to move back in with me, at least until the immediate threat posed by these assassins has been neutralized."

"No. You don't understand. I've met someone."

The words had just spilled out. Now he paused, belatedly realizing that this might not be a wise thing to reveal in front of the First's appointed bodyguard, Nash'terel or not.

"And?" Maury prompted him. When Bilyash remained silent, Maury said with a sigh, "Let me guess. She's human."

Bilyash took a moment to choose his words. "I'm not sure what she is. All I can tell you is that she's no ordinary human female."

Shred was instantly attentive. "Oh? In what way is she special?"

"She arouses my thirst, even if I've recently fed. She overflows with essence, and it's hardly polluted at all. And she intrigues me. She's..."

Maury and Shred exchanged a significant look.

"She's what?" Maury wanted to know.

"I'm not sure how to put this. I feel a strange connection to her, something I've never felt with any human female before. It's almost as if we're alike."

"And you're absolutely certain that she's human?" said Shred after a beat.

"Yes! I know the difference between Yeng and human essence. What exactly are you suggesting?" Bilyash demanded.

"I'm reminding you that essence can be chemically altered, and not all assassins will present themselves as male," Shred pointed out evenly.

Bilyash struggled to swallow a sudden lump in his throat. "She's not an assassin," he blurted.

"Modified Yeng essence emanates an unpleasant odour that only Nash'terel can detect. It varies in intensity, depending on the chemical that's been used. Have you noticed anything like that coming from her?"

"No. The only scent rising from her skin is a floral perfume."

"Then you may be right about her not being an assassin. But she could still be an assassin's bait. Consider, Bilyash. She is already influencing you to reject my protection. You're insisting on continuing to live alone because you want to have somewhere private to be with her. Privacy is ideal for an assassin. It means there can be no witnesses or interference. It also ensures that there will be enough time to clean up afterward and leave unseen."

"You seem to know an awful lot about how assassins operate," Bilyash challenged him.

"I should," Shred returned. "I've hunted down enough of them."

"What do you really know about her, Bilyash?" cut in Maury. And because it was Maury asking the question, Bilyash replied.

"Not much yet. We met earlier today. Angie is a film student at Ryerson University. She's interning on the set of Macy's current production—"

"—and she already knew who you were when you were introduced. Or maybe she introduced herself. Told you she'd heard all about you from a mutual friend and just had to meet you in person," said Shred, nodding with grim satisfaction when Bilyash fell uncomfortably silent. "A good assassin always researches the target," he concluded.

Bilyash's memories of that short time with Angie began twisting in his mind, distorting themselves like the images in a series of funhouse mirrors. Everything she'd said, everything she'd done, suddenly had two meanings, one innocent, the other deadly. He would need some time alone to sort through it all and decide what made the most sense. But first, he had a loose end to take care of.

"What are you going to do, Bilyash?" Maury inquired.

He squared his shoulders. "What I came here to do in the first place. Pick up an essence receptacle and then pay a final visit to Cora Dolson."

Maury gazed a question at Shred.

"He'll be all right," came the reply. "I'll make sure of it."

Chapter Four

———◆———

Driving home from Maury's place in his zombie car, so named because he'd rescued the bright yellow Volkswagen Super Beetle from a wrecking yard and brought it back to life, Bilyash considered his transportation options. Cora lived in the east end of the city, a good eight kilometres from his apartment building on Davisville Avenue. Normally, he would take public transit to Victoria Park and walk the three blocks to her home, but tonight's visit was going to be the furthest thing from normal. In any case, it was now past one o'clock in the morning, too late for the buses and streetcars to be running, and at this hour the subway system was about to shut down as well... which didn't really matter, since Bilyash made a point of avoiding the subway, having learned the hard way how that electrified third rail on the track could interfere with his senses. (Out of curiosity, Bilyash had ridden one of the trains on the brand new Bloor line in Toronto and had exited the car nearly blind. Fortunately, the effect had been only temporary. Terrifying while it lasted, but eventually it was gone.)

He could drive to Cora's, but even if he stayed on the side streets and parked blocks away from her apartment, he would still have to cross main roads to get there. Those intersections were camera-monitored and the zombie car was distinctive, making it easy to track. Or he could call for a cab—not a bright move for an assassin now that taxis were equipped with security cameras and every ride was digitally documented.

There was only one safe and sensible way for him to get where he needed to go. Bilyash drove himself home, parked in his numbered space in the below-ground garage, and exchanged his jeans and denim jacket for a dark blue hoodie and sweatpants from the suitcase in the trunk of his car. He remembered to zip the whisky flask Maury had given him into an inside pocket, along with a multi-head screwdriver from his emergency toolbox and an extra pair of socks. Then he sneaked out the service door into the alley behind the garage and began the run to Cora's place.

He'd done it before, covering the distance in just about an hour. However, tonight would be different. Tonight he was an assassin, not a lover. Tonight he had to be careful not to arouse any suspicion, neither on his way there nor on the way back.

Bilyash kept to the shadows as much as possible, pulling his hood forward to further conceal his face, and maintained an easy pace. A hunter, he knew that humans jogged at all hours in this city. It was foolhardy of them but they did it anyway, even in places like the Don River greenbelt and the underpasses below the Parkway, where a predator like himself might be lying in wait. Tonight, Bilyash needed to look like a jogger. A faceless innocent just passing through the phenomenal field of anyone who happened to be awake and looking out a window. Nothing out of the ordinary. Nobody to be alarmed or curious about.

It would have been a lot easier if there hadn't been a seven-foot-tall shadow pounding the pavement right behind him. Cursing silently, Bilyash ducked into the mouth of an alley and waited for Gershred to catch up.

The big bodyguard was wearing his Nash'terel eyes. He veered unerringly into the alleyway and stopped. No longer cartoonish, his features now reminded Bilyash of a bulldog. He half-expected Shred to roll his tongue out of his mouth and pant.

"What do you think you're doing?" Bilyash spat at him. "And how the hell did you manage to latch onto me so fast?"

"I tailed you until I knew you were heading home, then took a few shortcuts. Beat you there by about five minutes and staked out the building. And what I'm doing is keeping you safe, kid."

"Not like this, you're not. You're drawing attention to us," he hissed. A second later the penny dropped. "I get it. You're going to screw me up at every turn until I agree to do things your way. And were you planning to follow me into her bedroom as well?"

Shred just stood there. The look on his face did the talking.

With effort, Bilyash kept his voice low and urgent. "Forget it, big fella. Maury may have sold the Council on the idea of our being a matched set, but he's the light lord who can turn day into night and convert a toaster into an essence receptacle. He's the one who can actually protect them, and he's the one you should be with right now."

"Funny, he said something similar about you, only he referred to you as a power source."

Bilyash cursed inwardly. He tried not to think of his talent in such cold scientific terms, orgasms being so much more fun to generate. However, Maury might have been right. Since childhood, Bilyash had demonstrated an aptitude for creating magnetic fields.

So maybe he was important to Maldemaur's experiments, and maybe that did increase Bilyash's value to the Council of the First. But, dammit, he had a kill to make tonight, one that was necessary in order to avoid future complications, and it was going to be hard enough without a well-meaning bodyguard getting in the way.

"Look, I'll make you a deal," he said, exasperated. "Go back and guard Maury for tonight. This mission I'm on is only dangerous for me if I'm noticed before or afterward, and I'm really good at not being noticed, but only if I'm alone." When Shred hesitated, Bilyash added, "Please! I promise, if an assassin shows up, I'll take a rain check. I won't let the games begin without you. But right now, I need you to back off and let me do what I have to do."

"And when you're done...?"

Bilyash checked his watch. "I'm supposed to report to the set in about five hours. You can meet me there. Maury will give you the address of the studio. I'll tell Macy that we're cousins or something and get you a visitor's pass. And then you can guard me to your heart's content. Okay?"

Shred considered him thoughtfully. "Okay, kid. Deal."

Cora lived on the ground floor of an older building, part of a double row of quadplexes on a side street that had been waiting patiently for gentrification for at least the past thirty years. The building was turned ninety degrees, its front door facing the driveway it shared with its neighbour, and Cora's apartment sat on the side farthest from the street, its windows deep in concealing shadow.

Bilyash stole across the back of the building, ducking under and around each window, then flattening himself against the brick wall for a moment as he listened for movement inside before going on.

When finally he'd turned the corner and was crouching beneath Cora's bathroom window, he set his hands to feeling around the wooden frame. This was an old-fashioned casement window, and it had been no more than a couple of years since his last visit. With luck, the landlord hadn't yet gotten around to modernizing the building's locks and fastenings.

There it was: the faint sensory blip of metal on the other side of the sash. The lock hadn't been changed; it was still a sliding bolt assembly. Holding a strong enough magnet against the glass at precisely the correct angle, Bilyash should be able to work the bolt from this side of the window and let himself in. That was why he'd brought the screwdriver set. A chubby plastic handle that stored eight different-headed shafts, all aligned around a central metal core, it would be more than suitable for his purposes.

With rapid movements, he uncapped the container, selected a shaft at random, and plugged it into the bottom of the handle. Then, holding that shaft with his right hand, he overturned the handle into the palm of his left. When he could feel the ends of all the remaining shafts touching his skin, he began the process of magnetizing them.

A *hainbek* was, literally, an understanding, so deep and complete that it gave one the ability to control a natural force. An elemental master like Maury could exercise that control over a distance. He could turn light bulbs on and off in houses a block away and sometimes did, for fun. By projecting some of his essence into it, he could also turn light solid, and on more than one occasion had foiled a pursuer at night by temporarily trapping him inside the cone-shaped glow of a street lamp. Such were the powers of a master.

Controlled essence projection took centuries of training to

become instinctual. For an apprentice like Bilyash, still in his first thousand years of life, projection was possible but forbidden, due to the dangers it posed. Bilyash couldn't just conjure a magnetic field around a metal object by thinking about it; he first had to be touching it with some part of his body. Only then could he consciously imbue the object with some of his essence. That was what he was doing now, to the screwdriver.

Under Maury's tutelage, Bilyash had learned through tireless (and exhausting) practice how to control the flow of his energy in order to determine the size and strength of the magnetic fields he created. He'd also figured out through trial and error what the maximum capacities were of a variety of everyday metal objects, and for how many minutes the charge would hold before the field around them collapsed, dissipating the magnetic energy (and with it his borrowed essence) into the air. The denser the metal, the more essence he needed to transfer, and the more would be lost if his timing was off.

This investment of his life force was always a calculated risk, made riskier than usual tonight by what he had come here to do. Once he'd loaded up the metal parts of the screwdriver in his hand, he would have approximately ten minutes to slide the bolt aside and let himself into Cora's apartment. After that, the essence would be irretrievable, leaving him physically depleted until the next time he fed.

Fortunately, as long as the lock was his sole concern, only the magnet needed to be strong. After three minutes of fumbling, Bilyash was finally able to start teasing the metal bolt aside, a couple of millimetres at a time. The process seemed to take forever, but at last he felt the latch release, permitting him to drag the window partway open using the still-attached magnet. Expelling a shuddering breath, Bilyash checked his watch. Four minutes left. That was plenty of time for him to retrieve his essence. Was it enough time for him to get through the window and close it again first?

It would have to be. Quickly, he unplugged the screwdriver shaft and replaced it in its slot inside the handle. As long as the casement remained open, there was a chance someone might notice it, and there mustn't be any visible sign that Cora might have had a visitor tonight.

That meant no shoeprints in her bathroom sink and no grass cuttings on her carpet. Bilyash unlaced his runners. Then he took the clean socks out of his pocket. Wearing them like mittens, he reached up and pulled himself through the window and into Cora's bathroom. He paused halfway to heel-toe out of his shoes as close to the wall of the building as possible. Carefully, he dragged himself the rest of the way inside and swung his legs around so that he was sitting on the edge of the countertop. He reached back with a sock-clad hand and closed the window, then checked his watch again.

Two minutes. Tearing the socks off his hands, he brought the screwdriver set out of his pocket, popped the cap, and spilled the ends of the shafts into his palm. He collapsed sideways against the medicine cabinet as the icy sting of Nash'terel essence flowed up his arm and back into his body, carrying with it a renewed feeling of strength.

Ten minutes later, Bilyash was ready to proceed with the rest of his mission. Before he set foot on Cora's vinyl floor, however, there was one last thing to do. Balancing on his butt on the countertop, he pulled the clean socks on over his sweaty ones. No sense risking the possibility of damp footprints giving him away.

Silently he eased himself past the partly open bathroom door and moved through the darkened apartment, making his way to the bedroom. Cora loved the seashore. Just as he remembered, there was a beach scene pattern in the wallpaper and the ceiling was ocean blue. And there she lay, softly snoring in the middle of a double bed, tangled in beige sheets and wearing a lacy aquamarine-coloured nightgown. Bilyash padded across the carpet to the nightstand and set Maury's flask down between a conch-shell lamp and an empty wine goblet. So she'd had a bit of the grape at bedtime? Good. She always slept heavily after a glass of Beaujolais.

This was going to be a two-handed job. First, he needed to draw the blood from her core into the extremities of her body. Then he would pull it all back in a tsunami-like wave, overwhelming her heart and inducing fibrillation followed by cardiac arrest. It would take a prolonged and powerful compression of *dashkra* in his fingers to accomplish that, requiring a great deal of energy and concentration on his part. He'd done it just once before. Not well—he'd never been comfortable with the idea of using orgasm as a punishment—but effectively enough.

Cora, he'd decided, had raised his expectations and accepted his trust, only to betray him. She'd broken his heart. It was poetically fitting that he do the same thing to her.

Bending over her, he turned his hands into blood magnets. Then he placed his fingertips on her wrists. The rush of blood into her upper limbs darkened her hands and forearms. He deposited some of his essence beneath her skin to slow the return of blood to her core while he quickly tended to her other limbs.

Cora awoke with a gasp and turned in confusion to look into his eyes. His slanted, glowing, Nash'terel eyes.

"Did you miss me?" he murmured.

"Billy? What—? How did you—?"

"Ssh. It's time for your space flight, Cora. All the way to Alpha Centauri."

"My arms and legs feel strange. What—? What are you doing to me?" A note of fear had crept into her voice.

"This." He stroked her tenderest parts with two fingers, and a gasp escaped her lips. "Cora," he said, putting his lips close to her ear, "I'm going to give you the orgasm to end all orgasms. And then you'll never see me again." *Or anyone else, for that matter,* he added silently.

With that, he placed both his hands flat on her rib cage and turned them into a single, powerful blood magnet. A moment later, it was pulling all her blood toward her heart, drowning it in a torrent of red corpuscles and creating five orgasms at once. Well, maybe not orgasms. Maybe they were death throes. When the whole body spasmed like that, it was hard to tell the difference.

He withdrew his hands and stood back to watch. Cora clutched at her chest, her eyes wide and bulging, a stream of inarticulate sounds issuing from her mouth. Her body bucked and her head thrashed from side to side. He made no effort to hold her still. Bruising would raise suspicions, which would in turn lead to a police investigation, a complication that he would rather avoid if possible. Finally she lay motionless, her eyes darting desperately, her breath coming in brief ragged gasps.

"Billy... something... wrong... call... 9-1-1..."

Actually, he had a better idea for ending her pain. He opened the flask. Then he leaned over, enveloped her lips with his own to begin drawing out her essence, and set the mouth of the flask in place. It grew warm to the touch as the specially treated *dashkra* inside it continued to drink her life force, and as Bilyash waited for the sound and smell of human death.

At last, Cora Dolson uttered a short, cawing syllable and fell silent. In that same moment, her bowels and bladder relaxed. Bilyash replaced the cap on the flask. His job here was done.

He left the same way as he'd entered, remagnetizing the screwdriver and using it to slide the bolt back into place behind him. Thinking about all the information Cora had gathered on him and stored in her computer made him uneasy, but he'd quickly realized that using his talent to corrupt her files would only raise unwanted red flags in some cop's brain, resulting in the very sort of unpleasantness he'd just gone out of his way to prevent.

When all his essence was back where it belonged, Bilyash laced up his runners, checked to make sure the flask and screwdriver were safely tucked away in their zippered pocket, then stole through the shadows and onto the street.

Chapter Five

———•———

Shortly after dawn, Bilyash was cruising through light traffic, eastbound on Elgin Mills Road, and watching for the series of barrier-equipped entrances on his left that marked the location of the Alpha Dog Film Studio.

Like Maury's bungalow, the facility had originally been built out in the country on a tract of land that, over time, had been surrounded by industrial development as the city of Toronto expanded northward. Alpha Dog sprawled over a hundred and fifty or so acres of real estate. Its groomed lawns and cluster of large, green-roofed pavilions had served first as a fairground, then a farmers' market, a sports complex, and finally as warehousing for a major furniture and appliance store before Terrence Macy had bought it some twenty years earlier. He'd converted it into a collection of individual sound stages for rent, each with its own private driveway and unpaved parking lot.

The sound stage housing Macy's latest project was located nearest the main road and therefore had the shortest driveway and the greatest visibility in daylight to any passing traffic. The dark green sound stage door was clearly marked. As was the black and white police cruiser now sitting beside it, rotating roof lights flashing a warning.

At the sight of that car, Bilyash nearly drove past the entrance, his thoughts racing, his hands and jaw tightly clenched as he mentally reviewed the past few hours, trying to determine where he could have slipped up. A second later, he was certain he hadn't. And yet the police were here, waiting for him. Had he been betrayed? And if he had, what would be the safest course of action?

Bilyash had arrived back at his apartment building at the exact time he would normally be leaving for work. Today especially, he knew, he mustn't be late. Unaccustomed lateness drew notice, and that was the last thing he needed right now. So, he'd gone directly to the trunk of his car and exchanged the hoodie and sweat pants for the first clean items that came to hand: the jeans and denim jacket that he'd worn the day before. In retrospect, this was probably a mistake, but only if anyone noticed. Jeans were common attire among the film crew, so maybe it wouldn't matter.

Maury's flask was another issue. Filled with essence, it was noticeably warm to the touch. Humans expected containers like this to hold hard liquor. If the flask were discovered, either in his car or on his person, and a human twisted off the cap, there would be questions, the kind every Nash'terel dreaded. The kind that had sent him and Maldemaur into hiding more than once in the past.

So, as he approached the driveway, Bilyash's first instinct was to speed up and keep going.

Then common sense cut in. It wasn't even seven o'clock in the morning. Cora's body couldn't possibly have been discovered yet. In any case, an innocent person wouldn't run from a scene like this. An innocent person would be drawn by curiosity to approach it.

Forcing himself to present a calm exterior, Bilyash made the turn, pulled into his usual spot, and parked. As he deliberately strolled along the driveway and toward the police car, the sight of yellow tape barring the door to the sound stage brought him to a bewildered halt.

"There you are! Thank goodness!" said a familiar female voice. He looked to his left and saw Angie hurrying toward him from the direction of the makeup trailer. Her eyes were red-rimmed and welling with tears.

"What's going on?" he asked.

"It's Terrence Macy. He's dead, Billy," she told him in a choked voice. "Murdered. The security guard found him about an hour ago and called 9-1-1. I overheard him talking on the phone. He told the operator it happened on the set, so I went inside to see for myself, and—oh, God!" Her voice caught on a sob. Angie shook her head hard, as though trying in vain to clear her memory of the nightmarish image clinging to it. When she spoke again, it was in a wide-eyed, horrified whisper. "He was lying on the floor in pieces, just ripped apart, and there was blood everywhere. Billy, he was the sweetest man. How could something like that happen to him?"

Bilyash went cold all over. Outside of a Terrence Macy movie, he knew exactly how something like that could happen. Maury was right. They were being hunted by Yeng assassins, and hunting consumed energy. And, much as he hated to admit it, Shred was right too. The assassins would have researched their targets. If they'd come to Bilyash's workplace, it was because they'd been unable to find him where he lived; and if Macy had surprised them as they were preparing their ambush, he could have triggered a feeding lust.

Angie let out a moan and laid her head on Bilyash's shoulder. Reflexively, he put his arm around her.

Then a racket exploded off to his right, and, like a yapping missile, Poochie came arrowing across the grass toward him. Bilyash thought for a moment that the dog was attacking him, but he was wrong. With a uniformed police officer in close pursuit, the Chihuahua darted around him to take shelter, shivering and growling, behind his jeans-clad legs.

"Great," Bilyash muttered. "*Now* you've decided I'm the good guy?"

"Excuse me, sir," said the officer, pulling a spiral-bound notepad from her shirt pocket. "The victim's dog seems to know you. Would you show me some identification, please, and tell me what your relationship was with Terrence Macy?"

At the sound of his master's name, Poochie wrapped his front legs around Bilyash's ankle and began to howl.

"He may have witnessed the murder," Angie explained. "His paws were all bloody when I found him earlier." She bent down and scooped the dog into her arms. The Chihuahua struggled for a moment, then lay limp and panting in her embrace. "Poor thing. He'll probably need treatment for post-traumatic stress."

"Your identification, sir?" the officer repeated politely, her hand outstretched to receive it.

Bilyash pulled his wallet out of his pants pocket and extracted his driver's licence. Handing it over, he replied, "I designed most of the makeup for Mr. Macy's latest film. The one we've been shooting here," he added, jerking his head in the direction of the sound stage door.

"William Ash," the officer read from the licence. She quickly compared his face to the photo on the card. Then, satisfied that they were identical, she copied down Bilyash's current name and address before returning the licence to him. "So, you've been working for the victim, Mr. Ash? For how long?"

"About four weeks in total."

More scribbling in the little pad. "And where and when was the last time you saw him?"

"Yesterday evening, on the set, at about eight o'clock. We'd just wrapped up shooting for the day." Bilyash stole a glance at Angie. She was cuddling Poochie and nodding her agreement.

"And what did you do after that?" continued the officer. Her voice sounded a little monotone. Bilyash wasn't surprised. He was probably the fiftieth person she'd interviewed since arriving on the scene. She had to be bored as hell.

"I went to the makeup trailer. It took a couple of hours to normalize all the actors and—"

"Normalize?"

"It's a horror film. Zombie makeup is complicated to apply, and we have to be careful when taking it off. Anyway, by the time we'd finished doing that and setting things up for this morning's call and I was able to lock up the trailer and go home, it was well after ten o'clock."

"Did you hear or see anything unusual between eight and well after ten o'clock?" the officer wanted to know.

The temptation to jolt her out of her tedium by reporting a werewolf sighting was powerful, but common sense was stronger. "No, sorry," he told her sadly. "The trailer is well-insulated, and the three of us were mainly concentrating on getting done and getting out of there."

She perked up. "The three of you?"

He gave her the names of the other two makeup artists. She

copied them into her pad.

"And you were the last to leave?"

"Yes."

"And you locked the trailer behind you?"

"That's what I said," he replied, unable to keep all the annoyance out of his voice.

She drew herself up a little. "I'm asking if that's what you *did*, Mr. Ash."

"Yes. I locked it up tight." *And swallowed the key,* he wanted to say, but restrained himself.

As though reading his thoughts, she asked, "You have your own key?"

He pulled it out of his pants pocket by its orange plastic fob and showed it to her. She grunted a syllable of acknowledgement and made a notation in her little pad.

"Who else has a key to the trailer?"

"There's more than makeup in there, so we're pretty careful. Just Macy, the security guard, and me."

Scribble, scribble.

"So, you left this location after ten o'clock," she resumed. "And where did you go from here?"

"I stopped to pick something up at my uncle's house. From there I went straight home."

"Can anyone corroborate that?"

Bilyash's patience was wearing thin. "Corroborate what? That I left here, that I went to my uncle's, or that I arrived home? And why are you asking that? Am I a suspect?"

"Quite the contrary, Mr. Ash. We ask these questions so we can eliminate you as a suspect. I'll need the name and address of your uncle."

He paused, thinking of all the traps Maury had set. Then he gave this officer precisely what she was asking for.

"Is there any way to prove what time you arrived home?" she asked.

"There are security cameras at the entrance to the parking garage under my building."

"Mm-hmm," she said to herself, the top of the pen making jerky little motions in the air as she recorded the information on her spiral-bound pad. "And that's your vehicle over there?" she added, pointing at the Volkswagen.

"It is," he told her.

She copied down the licence plate number. "One last question: where were you between one o'clock and four o'clock this morning?"

Killing Cora Dolson. The words had leaped immediately into his mind. Fortunately, they stayed there. Bilyash hesitated, struck by the double irony of his situation. The first was that his alibi for Macy's murder was that he'd been murdering someone else at the time. The second was that even though it was true, the alibi probably wouldn't be believed, simply because he'd done such a good job of making it appear Cora had died alone and of natural causes.

"Sir?" the officer prompted.

"I was in bed," Bilyash replied at last, with a lack of conviction in his voice that made him want to kick himself.

The officer had picked up on it. No longer bored, her expression now became skeptical. "Uh-huh. And can anyone corroborate that?"

"Yes. The woman who shared that bed," Angie cut in. "That was me." Bilyash's surprise must have shown on his face, for she patted him on the arm and told him, "It's all right, darling. The whole crew knows about us. It's the worst-kept secret on the film set." Addressing the officer once more, she declared, "We spent the night together at his place."

"And you are...?"

"Angelina Fiore. The other officer has already taken my contact information."

"Hmph. I'll bet he has," she muttered, only half to herself.

Bilyash repressed a smile. Angie made no such effort.

"How about giving it to me as well, just in case?" said the lady cop, her grip on her pen noticeably tightening.

Angie reached into her pocket and handed over her driver's licence.

Scribble, scribble.

"So, you spent the night together. And you know for a fact that he didn't go out again once you'd fallen asleep?"

Angie's cheeks dimpled. "I never said we slept, just that we shared the bed."

More rapid scribbling. Then, "You arrived separately this morning," the officer pointed out.

Bilyash decided to go with the flow. "Just trying to keep up appearances," he said with a sigh. "But I guess we don't need to worry about *that* anymore."

"Okay, that'll do for now," the officer told them, closing up her little pad and putting it back into her pocket just as Bilyash's phone went off.

He recognized the ring tone. The two women stood quietly by while he answered the call.

Maldemaur was on the other end of the line. He wasted no time on social amenities. "You'd better get over here right away," he said, in a voice so taut Bilyash thought it might snap. "Those people we were talking about just paid me a visit." Wherever Maury was, it was noisy. Bilyash heard shouting and a sound like a waterfall in the background.

"Are you all right?" he demanded. "Is Gershred? What's going on over there?"

"Not much. I'm just standing on the street watching my house burn down," Maury informed him. "They were expecting to find you with me. They even asked for you by name. So if you know what's good for you, you'll drop everything and get your ass over here, *now*!" With that, Maury broke the connection.

Two kills and a house fire in less than six hours, Bilyash mused. This day was definitely heating up.

"Well?" said the officer.

"I'm sorry, but I have to go. That was my uncle. He needs me."

"All right," she said. "If we have any further questions, we'll contact you."

"And me?" Angie piped up hopefully. "And Poochie?"

The dog was an actor after all. Right on cue, he turned large, liquid eyes on the officer and gave her a piteous look.

She melted. "I don't think he'll be crucial to our investigation. You're free to go, for now. Just don't leave town."

Not until Angie and Poochie were in the car with him did Bilyash notice that, like him, she was wearing exactly the same outfit as she'd had on the day before. Maybe it was significant. Maybe it wasn't. And maybe, by giving him an alibi, she'd given herself one as well.

Chapter Six

———◆———

There were police cars blocking the road two streets from Maury's house in every direction, and a billowing green and yellow cloud hanging over the area. This had to be Maldemaur's worst nightmare. All those volatile substances in his basement, feeding the flames and poisoning the air. All his carefully-prepared essence receptacles either melting or exploding like grenades, sending centuries of dedicated research literally up in smoke—along with a huge quantity of *dashkra* particles. And all that media attention as a neighbourhood was evacuated and the hazmat team was called in to help fight the blaze. The Nash'terel generally tried to avoid publicity. If Yeng assassins were responsible for this fire, then they might be playing a much larger game than Maury had suspected.

Bilyash parked as close to the scene as he could, just across an intersection from one of the police barricades. A strong and unmistakable rotten-egg smell struck him like a collapsing wall the moment he opened the driver's side door.

"Pee-yew!" declared Angie, her nose wrinkling with disgust as she stepped out onto the sidewalk, and Poochie noisily agreed. "What is that godawful stink? Sulphur?"

Bilyash took in the gas-masked uniformed officer hurrying toward him. "That's sulphur," he confirmed, "among other noxious things. Maybe you'd better stay here while I try to locate Uncle Maury."

Wordlessly, she got back inside the car.

"I'm sorry, sir," said the officer, sounding like Darth Vader with a head cold. "You'll have to move your vehicle. There's a chemical fire—"

"It's my uncle's house that's on fire," said Bilyash, reaching for his driver's licence for the second time that morning. "I just want to find him and make sure he's all right."

The officer scanned his identification, uttered a grunt of satisfaction, and handed the card back to him. "Thank you, Mr. Ash. And what is your uncle's name?"

"Doctor Malcolm de Maur. That's M-A-U-R."

"He's a doctor?"

"The doctorate is in chemistry."

A figurative light bulb went on over the officer's head. "Of course. Are you his next of kin?"

Bilyash swallowed hard. Maury had told him earlier that he was watching the fire from the street, but it was possible that he'd gone back in to try to save some of his work. "Have you found a body?" he asked quietly.

"Not yet, but we'll know more once the fire is out. The neighbour who called 9-1-1 described Doctor de Maur as a reclusive old man who almost never left his house. By the time first responders arrived, the building was fully involved. At this point, it's probably all they can do just to keep the flames from spreading.

I'm sorry to say this, Mr. Ash, but if your uncle *is* inside, then it's doubtful that he's alive. Are there any other family members that we may need to notify?" And out came another of those spiral-bound notepads.

Bilyash felt numb. "No," he murmured sadly, "there were just the two of us."

He felt a tug at his elbow and turned to find Angie standing beside him. "Billy, we need to go," she told him. "We need to go *now*."

Over her shoulder he saw shadows moving around inside his car. Instantly, he knew who they were.

"Thank you, Officer," he said. "You'll keep me informed?"

"Of course, Mr. Ash."

They wheeled and hurried back to the car, where Maury and Shred were crouched down in the back seat, partly concealing the large brown leather briefcase that sat on the floor between them. Poochie, meanwhile, was having apoplectic fits in the front seat. He calmed down considerably when Angie gathered him into her arms, but still continued to glare and growl at the two non-people hiding behind her.

Bilyash put the car in gear and headed west, toward Dufferin Street.

Once they were out of sight of the police barrier, the passengers in the back could sit up straight. Or straight*er*, anyway. His head seeming to rest directly on his shoulders, Shred tucked himself into the corner, as far away from Maury as possible. In the Volkswagen, for someone the bodyguard's size, that amounted to about seven extra centimetres of space.

Meanwhile, Maury had assumed a shape that made him look like Peter Capaldi, the twelfth Doctor Who. Bilyash managed not to react. A light lord modelling himself after a time lord? Apparently, some of that inferior human culture had rubbed off on him after all.

"Unbelievable," Maury spat. "Simply un-fuckin'-believable. You know twenty-three different ways to kill and *that* was what you came up with? In a laboratory full of accelerants?"

At this, Poochie reared up, put his front paws on Angie's shoulder, and yapped loudly into the back seat, as if to say, *You tell him, Maury!*

"I said I was sorry," Shred replied. "It was a reflex. And it seemed like a good idea at the time."

"So, the body they're going to find...?" said Bilyash.

"They won't," Shred declared flatly. "I disposed of it before the fire trucks showed up."

"...and it's one of the assassins, yes," said Maury. "There were two, but the other one got away."

"I think I know where the third one went," Bilyash told him. "Terrence Macy was found murdered earlier this morning, at the studio. This is his dog," he added, raising his voice to be heard over the Chihuahua's growl-barking.

"And he's in your car because...?" said Shred.

Before Bilyash could reply, Angie cut in briskly, "He's a murder witness and we're his protective custody detail."

In the rear-view mirror, Bilyash saw Maury and Shred exchange an *Aha!* look. Then they both faced front, and he saw something else in their eyes, something that caused a primal response to stir inside him.

The thirst.

No, you don't, he thought grimly. *This one is mine.*

"So!" said Maury, pinning on his own version of a charming

smile. "I gather this is the young woman you were telling us about last night? The one simply bubbling over with energy?"

"When I stopped by to borrow your flask, yes," he replied. Bilyash dug into his jacket pocket, found the receptacle, and tossed it into the back seat for Maldemaur to catch.

"And you've topped it up for me," the older being observed. "Very considerate. Now, how about introducing us to your new friend?"

There was no way around it. His midsection tightening, Bilyash said, "Angelina Fiore, meet my Uncle Maury and his... associate, Gershred."

"A pleasure, my dear," said Maury, widening his smile to reveal a mouthful of teeth that instantly cowed Poochie into silence. The dog was perceptive, Bilyash mused. His own mind had shown him an image of Angie carrying a basket and wearing a red hooded cape.

"Likewise," she replied over her shoulder. "So, why are people trying to kill you? Are you secret agents or something?"

Startled, Bilyash nearly drove his car onto the sidewalk. He had to spin the steering wheel hard to avoid hitting a lamppost, and spin it again the opposite way to avoid smashing into a parked orange Neon sporting a whole row of bumper stickers. Tires squealed and Bilyash cursed as he fought his way out of the skid. Luckily, there was no other traffic to contend with on this residential side street. Better still, he'd heard not a peep out of any of his passengers, including the dog. When the Volkswagen was once more under his control, Bilyash let out the breath he'd been holding and told her firmly, "It's complicated. I'll explain it to you later."

Angie sat pressed back against her seat, eyes wide and cheeks flushed. Wordlessly, she nodded to let him know she'd heard him.

Then, addressing the two passengers behind him, he went on, "We're almost at Dufferin, Uncle Maury. Where am I taking you? North or south?"

"South first, to my bank. After that, north, to a gentleman with connections who can set me up with a used car. I'm leaving town until this situation is resolved, and for your own safety—and hers—I advise you to do the same. Do you still have the keys I gave you for the cabin on Georgian Bay?"

"In the glove box."

"Good. You should be safe there. And your travel bag?"

"In the trunk, mostly. The rest is in the makeup trailer. We'll pick it up right after we've dropped you two off."

Maldemaur said nothing, just made a disapproving face. Shred, however, piped up, "Not too bright, kid."

As he made the left turn onto Dufferin, Bilyash pressed his lips together, refusing to rise to the bait. He and Maldemaur had had this discussion numerous times before. Maury always argued that Nash'terel had to be ready to drop everything and disappear at a moment's notice, no matter where they happened to be at the time. Then Bilyash would explain patiently that while he understood where Maury was coming from, the two of them lived vastly different lives, and there was no one-size-fits-all solution to every problem.

Billy had no desire to go over that same ground yet again, especially with Angie and Poochie both sitting there listening attentively to every word that was said. (As if she hadn't heard too much already!) "Don't you worry about us," Bilyash called over his shoulder. "Just make sure Uncle Maury gets away all right."

Maldemaur's bank was a brick structure about the same size as his former home, planted like a guardhouse beside the entrance to a large shopping mall parking lot. At this early hour, most of the lot was empty. Bilyash pulled into a spot directly opposite the bank's front entrance, turned off the engine, and got out to let Maury exit the rear seat.

As he got back behind the wheel, Bilyash felt a large hand clasp his left shoulder. Poochie tensed and began to growl.

"A word, Billy?" came Shred's murmuring voice in his ear.

"Sure." He pocketed the car keys in case Angie was tempted to bolt, and stepped out onto the pavement again. Shred followed him, moving with surprising agility for such a large man.

"You were right about her," Shred said. "She exudes enough essence to trigger the thirst at a distance."

"I noticed."

"We can't all stay together, not as long as she's around."

Reluctantly, Bilyash had to agree.

"With two assassins on our tails, it appears splitting you and Maldemaur up is the best way to handle this. I'll go with Maldemaur. At best, we'll draw both the Yeng away from you and the human. At worst, they'll split up as well. If they do, Maury and I will take out ours and come help you with yours. If we turn up on your doorstep, it will be because a second member of the triad is dead. If I turn up alone, you'll know Maldemaur is.

"For the record, kid, it's not a plan I like, particularly, but it's the best I can offer at the moment. The Council may have agreed to treat you and Maury as a unit, but they also instructed me to give priority to keeping Maldemaur safe."

Bilyash couldn't very well argue with that. It was what he himself had urged Shred to do only a few hours earlier.

"I understand," he said.

"You've been lucky so far, but from now on you'll need to be careful as well. Speaking as your long-distance bodyguard, I'm going to give you some good advice. You're being hunted, and cockiness will get you killed. So, stay aware of your surroundings and never underestimate a trained assassin's ability to find you. At the first opportunity, trade this car for something newer and nondescript. Pay cash for everything. And keep that human female with you, by force if necessary," he added, lowering his voice. "She has essence to spare. You can feed on her indefinitely without having to hunt, and that's important in a sparsely populated area. Do I need to explain to you why?"

"No. We've lived in small villages before. I know how to keep a low profile. But does this mean you've changed your mind about her being an assassin's bait?"

"Not entirely. I now think it's unlikely, but it could still be possible, so I wouldn't be too quick to drop my guard around her. If she *is* working with a Yeng, you'll find out soon enough."

The "gentleman with connections" that Maury knew lived in the heart of an aging housing development west of Dufferin and dealt in more than just cars, it turned out. In exchange for a large envelope full of cash, he was also able to provide them with untraceable phones for making emergency calls to each other, security systems for both their safe-houses, four taser guns, two parabolic microphones, and three handguns, with ammunition.

Maury had cleaned out several bank accounts in order to pay for all this gear. Bilyash had no clear idea of how wealthy Maldemaur was. He only knew that the indirect manipulation of matter, which the humans had once called alchemy and now referred to as chemistry, had always been a lucrative profession on Earth, and that the money the older being had spent today was but a small fraction of what he was worth. So, when it became evident that he was buying for both of them, Bilyash had accepted Maury's gifts with an earnest thank you. He might never use them, but it was the thought that counted.

After Maury's travel bag had been moved to the trunk of his newly-purchased dark green Mustang, and the carton of "insurance" had been crammed into the trunk of Bilyash's car, the three Nash'terel said their goodbyes. Bilyash and Angie watched through the idling Volkswagen's windows as the Mustang pulled out of the driveway, turned left in front of them, and peeled away to the west. Then Bilyash put his own vehicle in gear and headed in the opposite direction.

He needed to retrieve his makeup kit. With luck, the police would all have gone elsewhere, film production would be shut down, and the trailer would be empty. There would, of course, be at least one security guard on duty, hopefully one Bilyash knew. Security's job was to keep rubberneckers and media types out of places they didn't belong. It was even more crucial—and the guard would be that much more vigilant—now that the sound stage was a sealed crime scene.

Not a problem, Bilyash reckoned. His business was inside the makeup trailer, fifty metres away from the yellow-taped door. He had a key to the trailer, he was authorized to be inside it, and the only things he would be removing from it would be his own personal belongings. And he was innocent, he reminded himself firmly, of this particular crime, at least. Not so innocent if he were asked by a police officer to pop open the trunk of his car.

Noticing how quiet it was in the front seat, Bilyash cast a curious glance sideways. Poochie had evidently barked and growled himself into exhaustion. He now lay sound asleep on Angie's lap. And Angie sat staring straight ahead, her back rigid, nervously gnawing her lower lip.

"Are you all right?" he asked, realizing even as he heard himself utter the question that he already knew the answer.

Keeping her gaze directed at the windshield, she replied in a faint and weary voice, "You said you would explain why people are trying to kill you. I'm not sure that I want to hear the reason."

She was afraid. He could understand that. Her day had begun with carnage and proceeded from there to a hazmat emergency, followed closely by an under-the-table deal with a criminal, and she probably hadn't even had breakfast yet. Too tired and hungry to keep pretending to herself that she was enjoying a romantic adventure, she had to be wondering what the hell she had gotten herself into, and whether she would come out of it alive. Bilyash sifted his mind for a way to reassure her without letting on that he had no intention of parting company with her, because Shred had been right—keeping Angie Fiore near him could well tip the scales in favour of his own survival.

Bilyash hated the idea of using constraint against her. He was a lover of females, not of physical violence. But if charm and deception both failed... No, he decided, thinking furiously, there had to be another way.

This wasn't the first time he and Maury had found themselves having to cut ties with human friends and go into hiding. Bilyash recalled a half-true story Maury had once told to satisfy the curiosity of a female that he had been fond of. With a little tweaking, perhaps it would work here as well.

"Listen," he said, "I can't go into detail, but you weren't far off the mark when you mentioned espionage earlier. Those assassins who were sent after us are agents of a foreign government."

Angie turned in her seat, instantly attentive.

Encouraged by her reaction, he went on, "Uncle Maury and I escaped here, years ago. Maury is a scientist. He developed a process for—No," he said emphatically, "you're better off not knowing."

Her eyes widened. "It's dangerous?"

"Extremely. Just talking about it puts you in someone's crosshairs," he replied, warming to his subject. "It scared the hell out of Maury, so he destroyed his lab and all his work before we left to come to Canada. When the Canadian government found out who he was and what he'd done back home, they made him an offer he couldn't refuse. He warned them that it had to be kept top secret, and that his former government must never find out."

"But somebody talked," she supplied grimly.

Matching her expression, he said, "They must have."

"And that's why your uncle had all those chemicals in his house? And why he's got that big hulking guy—Shred?—with him all the time?"

"I guess so."

"And the other government felt cheated out of its secret weapon and will do anything to stop him from giving it to anyone else?"

"I never said it was a weapon," he reminded her.

"You didn't have to," she snapped. "So, you're a target as well?"

"Unfortunately, yes. I was his lab assistant for a while. I guess they figure I know too much about his work."

She stared at him incredulously for a moment. "Billy, you are a very attractive man and, from what I've seen of your work, a true makeup artist... and you've shown me that you're every bit the lover that Cora says you are. But you can't lie worth a damn.

Seriously? Stealing the plot of a B movie from the fifties? I know we've been acquainted for less than a day, but—do I really strike you as being that dim?"

His jaw dropped. Whether he could have replied or not, Angie clearly had no intention of letting him speak, for she continued, in a stage whisper that made every word feel like a slap, "If you didn't want to answer my question, why didn't you simply say so, instead of handing me a load of fictitious crap?"

He waited, hoping the question was rhetorical.

It wasn't.

"Well?" she prompted him, her brown eyes filling with storm clouds.

She'd left him no choice but to give her an honest answer. "I didn't think you could handle the truth."

"You didn't think I could handle the truth," she echoed incredulously. "After all the truth I've already handled today? And damn well, I might add! How's this for fucking truth?" She thrust her hand out in front of her and began counting on her fingers. "This morning I saw parts of Terrence Macy scattered all over the sound stage and the floor of the set pretty much painted with his blood. Then, while chasing his hysterical dog around, I slipped in a puddle of gore and nearly ended up with a mouthful of something that had been ripped out of Macy's chest. And, in case that wasn't enough of a shock, the chest-morsel had already had a big bite taken out of it.

"Then I learned that your uncle is some kind of mad scientist, with a really creepy assistant named Shred who knows twenty-three different ways to kill someone but his first choice is to set them on fire. Lovely. From their conversation in the car, I found out that you and your uncle are both being hunted by assassins, one of whom is probably responsible for Macy's grisly murder. And since there was no blood on Poochie other than what he stepped in while careening around the set howling with terror, I'm assuming that the killer was also the one who snacked on the corpse. It feels like I'm living in one of Macy's movies, only it's real blood, not cherry syrup, and death is a permanent condition."

Angie's urgent whisper had risen continuously in pitch. Bilyash winced as it became a quiet shriek.

"How *dare* you tell me I can't handle the truth when I've been processing *that* all morning? I know there's more to this story. So what is it, Billy? How much worse can it possibly be?" she demanded.

Lady, he thought, staring stolidly ahead, *you have no idea.*

Aloud, he said, "It wasn't completely fictitious. But you're right: I did underestimate you, and for that I apologize. I'll try not to do it again."

In the silence that followed, thickening the air between them, Bilyash thought he could feel her reproachful eyes boring into the side of his head. Not even Poochie stirring to wakefulness on Angie's lap distracted her gaze. After what seemed a very long time, she finally sank back against her seat. "You're not going to tell me, are you?"

"Angie, you will know everything, I promise, just not right now. Right now we have to follow Maury's example and get the hell out of Dodge. After I've removed my stuff from the trailer, I'll drive you home to pick up yours, and—"

"That won't be necessary," she said uncomfortably.

He hoped he'd misheard. If she'd decided not to come with him, this scene could turn ugly very fast. "Why not?"

"Because my stuff isn't there."

Now it was his turn to stare at her.

"My roommate kicked me out," she told him with a shrug. "I ran out of money and couldn't pay my share of the rent. And when I saw that there was a cot in the trailer, and a wash basin, and curtains for privacy, it just seemed like the perfect solution. So, after you locked up last night, I snuck into Macy's on-set office and borrowed his key to let myself back in. That's where I spent the night."

"And the contact information you gave that cop earlier today…?"

"No longer current. As they'll find out if they have more questions and come looking for me." She sounded remarkably unconcerned.

They were driving north on Dufferin Street, a four-lane thoroughfare that spawned residential, industrial and commercial development by turns as it both fed and channelled the outward-spreading growth of the city. Dufferin was busy at all hours of the day, but especially so during the morning rush hour.

As they sat in backed-up traffic, waiting for a red light to turn green ten cars ahead of them, Bilyash considered Angie's "chicken and egg" situation. The police would only find out she'd lied if they decided to contact her with further questions. And having already taken her statement, they'd only want to question her if they suspected that she'd lied to them. So far, so good. If they searched the makeup trailer, they would discover where she'd actually spent the night. But the trailer was nowhere near the murder scene, so to do that they would need a search warrant, which would require them to show probable cause, which in turn they wouldn't have unless they knew that she had lied about where she had spent the night.

Or, he abruptly realized, unless they found evidence to suggest that the killer might have gone inside the trailer at some point. Like drops of Macy's blood on the ground nearby.

Bilyash glanced at the Chihuahua on Angie's lap. The dog's paws were clean.

Seeds of dread sprouting in his midsection, he remarked, "I thought you said Poochie had blood all over his feet."

"He did. But once I'd finally caught him, I cleaned him up. Had to. The smell of it was driving the poor little guy nuts."

Oblivious to the growing tension in the car, Poochie chose that moment to give an enormous yawn.

"And where, exactly, did you wash his paws?"

Her eyes widened with sudden comprehension. "In the basin inside the trailer," she whispered. "Oh, my God..."

"Was he dripping?" When she didn't answer right away, he repeated sternly, "Angie, was Poochie dripping blood when you took him to the trailer?"

"I—Maybe. I'm not sure."

"Let's assume the worst. So, there's a trail of blood drops leading from the sound stage to the trailer, and a bloody towel waiting to be found inside. I told the police that the trailer was locked, and that only three people have a key. Macy's is missing, because you borrowed it—"

"No, I was able to return the key to his desk drawer before the police arrived. It was close, but I made sure no one saw me do it. I didn't want to get in trouble for sleeping in the trailer."

Or for the murder? Bilyash sighed inwardly. With Macy's key back in place, suspicion would naturally fall on himself and the guard.

So, he'd been right earlier. Angie had given him an alibi because she needed one herself. In fact, she'd probably alibied them both before he even pulled into his parking spot in the sound stage lot. That would explain her rush to greet him. She needed to be with him when he was approached by an officer taking statements, to ensure that their stories matched.

"In some ways, it would have been better if someone *had* seen me," she mused aloud. "Then at least there would be a witness to the fact that my clothes got bloodied *after* the murder had been committed. I'd still be liable for trespassing, but—"

"Where's your blood-stained clothing right now?" he cut in.

"Wrapped in a clean towel and stashed in my backpack, inside the trailer."

Of course, it was. Now they were *both* incriminated.

Angelina Fiore was trouble on two legs, sloppy and meticulous at the same time. She was also, he reminded himself, the purest and most abundant source of human essence that he had ever encountered.

"I was going to sneak the backpack out to my car before anyone else arrived," she continued, "but Poochie was having conniptions, so I had to catch him first and calm him down. Then I had to wash myself up and put yesterday's clothes back on. By that time, it was too late to do anything but lock the trailer, return the key, and keep my fingers crossed."

Bilyash was barely listening. A single fact had leaped out at him, capturing his imagination.

"You've got a car," he informed her.

She gave him a curious look. "Yes."

"Parked in the sound stage lot?"

"No, I parked it on the street. I didn't know whether the driveway would be barred overnight and I wanted to keep my options open. Why are you so interested—?"

"Because my car will be too easy to track. If we're going to make a clean getaway, it will have to be in yours."

"Can we at least stop for breakfast first? My stomach's been growling for an hour."

"Right after we've switched vehicles," he promised her, hoping that whatever she drove, it would be newer than the zombie car and completely forgettable.

Chapter Seven

———◆———

Bilyash took the shortest route possible to the studio. Forty-five minutes later, the Volkswagen was headed eastbound along Elgin Mills Road, approaching the driveway that led to sound stage number 5. As he made the left turn, no longer facing directly into the bright mid-morning sun, his eyes could finally relax from what had been threatening to turn into a permanent squint. The parking lot was off to his right. He counted only three cars in the lot, none with black and white markings or roof lights. A promising sign.

Even more promising was the absence of yellow police tape around the makeup trailer. If there were homicide detectives on the scene, they'd apparently found no reason to investigate the south side of the building.

Bypassing the entrance to the parking lot, Bilyash continued to the end of the driveway, where the police car had been sitting a few hours earlier. As expected, there was a uniformed guard perched on a folding lawn chair beside the sound stage door. Bilyash waved when he saw who it was.

"Hi, Henry," he called out as he and Angie piled out of the Volkswagen.

The guard heaved himself to his feet, looked both ways as though crossing a road, then strolled over to meet them. "Mr. Ash! I wasn't expecting to see you again today. Some kind of family emergency, I heard."

"An emergency for my uncle. Not so much for me. He's getting on in years, and doesn't handle change as well as he used to."

"I hear you loud and clear, sir. My dad's the same way. And what can I do for you today?" the guard asked pleasantly.

"I gather the production has been shut down?" said Bilyash, gesturing at the yellow-taped door.

"Yeah, until the police have finished inside. Processing the scene, they call it. I won't tell you what I call it. Mr. Macy took out insurance so production could be completed if something happened to him, but we're stalled until the set can be cleaned up. It'll be a couple of weeks at least."

Bilyash pulled out his key and dangled it by the plastic fob where the guard could see it. "Ms. Fiore and I left some personal belongings in the makeup trailer. Is it okay if we go get them? I'll turn this in to you when we're ready to leave."

Henry frowned suspiciously. "What kind of personal belongings?"

"My makeup kit's in there, and I have a rent payment due. I'm going to see if I can get another gig to tide me over until production resumes. You're welcome to inspect whatever I bring out." He assumed his most disarming demeanour and waited for the human's response.

"The police have instructed me to keep everything exactly as it was..." Bilyash drew a breath and held it until the guard finally continued, "...but there's no tape across that trailer door, and if it's your own personal stuff, I guess it'll be all right."

"Thanks, Henry. We won't take long."

"Take as long as you need, Mr. Ash. I'm not going anywhere."

"By the way, Henry," Angie piped up, "has anyone been looking for Poochie?"

"Macy's dog? Not really. When it got quiet, we figured he must have run off. Why?"

She shrugged. "Just wondering whether Mr. Macy had any family who might want to adopt him."

Henry let out a snort of laughter. "Not likely, Miss. I've been keeping my eyes open for Alpha Dog for a lot of years, and I can tell you for certain that there are no Poochie fans in the Macy family. That spoiled little mutt broke up both of Macy's marriages and drove his kids to distraction. If someone did agree to take him, it would probably be straight to the pound."

"That's a shame," she said. "He's kind of cute. Loud, but cute."

The guard arched a knowing eyebrow. "Sounds like he's already found a new home," he observed. "If anyone asks, I think that's what I'll tell them."

"Thank you, Henry," she replied warmly.

Once they were inside the trailer, Bilyash asked her, "What was that all about?"

"I figure it's bad enough that you're being hunted by assassins and I lied to the police. The last thing we need on top of that is to be charged with dognapping. If nobody else wants him, no one will care that we have him."

He paused and shot her a look. "You do realize that two people with a Chihuahua will be a lot easier to track?"

"True," she admitted. "But the way he reacts to strangers, it will also be damn near impossible for anyone to sneak up on us."

She was right. In fact, Bilyash reflected, Poochie's barking was probably the reason Macy had been drawn to investigate the sound stage last night. It might also have alerted the night shift guard to the presence of an intruder, forcing the assassin to leave before he'd finished feeding.

Had Poochie saved Bilyash's life? It was a thought worth keeping in mind.

Tucked under the counter at his makeup station, Billy's kit was a moderately large metal trunk set on end, with a pair of wheels at the back and a retractable handle on top. He swung open the lid, revealing an array of sliding compartmented trays and racks, and set about packing them with the various jars, brushes and appliances from the counter. Meanwhile, Angie went straight to the rear of the trailer and slid a black and blue zippered backpack out from under the cot.

Definitely not a dollar store knock-off, the pack looked durable and made of quality material. That had to be her overnight case. Like him, she probably carried the rest of her portable belongings in her car.

Bilyash reached into the cupboard under the sink and found a white plastic garbage bag. He snapped it open and offered it to Angie. "Put everything that's got blood on it in here."

She unzipped her pack, pulled out a towel-wrapped bundle, and dropped it wordlessly into the bag. As she watched, he carefully removed the liner from the lid of his kit, revealing a shallow compartment, then pressed the bag inside it. With some adjustment and a little pressure, Bilyash was able to replace the liner, reposition the lid rack with all its pots and jars, and easily close the kit.

"Anything else?" he asked. "Any dried blood spatter from Poochie's paws that we need to clean up?"

She gave him a startled look. "Gawd, I hope not!" she declared. Then, apparently reconsidering her tone, she explained, "There shouldn't be any in here. My clothes were already a mess, so I wiped him off with the hem of my jersey before bringing him inside."

"What's left in your pack?"

"Hardly anything." She spread it wide open to show him a yellow nightgown, a transparent plastic zippered case filled with toiletries, a wooden-handled hairbrush, and an e-book reader. With a forefinger, she stretched the expandable lip of a pocket inside the pack to reveal something pink and shiny that he guessed must be underwear.

"No purse?"

"For overnight? Not needed," she replied. "My purse is in the car, and the car keys are in here." She gave her right front pants pocket a proprietary pat.

He studied the backpack for a moment. It would be tight, but, "I can fit in everything except the e-reader. That's okay. Henry will be expecting you to have something personal with you when we leave, and that's the item least likely to arouse suspicion. I need you to keep watch out the window. Tell me the second he starts coming this way."

Wordlessly, she took up her post.

Meanwhile, Bilyash busied himself removing the drawers from the bottom half of his kit. He'd had the makeup case custom-made in anticipation of a day like this; but never in a thousand years could he have foreseen that he would be travelling with a human female companion. Well, he thought wryly, at least she knew how to pack light.

Bilyash uncovered the second hidden compartment in his makeup kit, folded the backpack and its contents as flat as he could make them, then pressed them against the rear wall of the case and snapped the false lining in to hold everything snugly in place. With the loaded drawers back inside and the kit closed and locked—not quite as easily as before, but still not threatening to burst its hinges—they were ready to go.

He turned querying eyes to Angie, still standing at the window.

"He's pacing in front of the door to the sound stage," she reported. "Looks like he's getting impatient."

No surprise there. The guard was probably having second thoughts about letting them enter the trailer. "Then let's not keep him waiting any longer. Make sure you wave to him with the hand holding the e-reader."

The makeup kit was awkward rather than heavy. Bilyash swung it down to the ground with ease, then extended the handle so he could pull the case along behind him to his car.

Henry strode over to them the second they emerged from the trailer. "See you in a couple of weeks?" he said, reaching for the key. His fingers closed tightly around it as it dropped onto his palm.

"I certainly hope so," Bilyash replied.

He opened the driver's side door of the Volkswagen and settled the case into the space behind the front seat. Then, as casually as they could, he and Angie got in and fastened their seat belts. Bilyash started the engine, executed a three-point turn, and managed to restrain himself from flooring the gas pedal as he drove back to the street.

"That's my car," Angie told him, pointing to a bronze-coloured

Buick even older than the vehicle they were in, parked about ten metres west of the driveway.

They were too close to the studio, with too much traffic and too many potential witnesses around, to risk making the switch yet. Bilyash knew he would probably regret it, but he told her, "You want breakfast? There's a pretty good family restaurant in the strip plaza at the next traffic light east of here. Mom and Pop's Place. Follow me into the receiving area behind the plaza. We'll empty my car into yours, and then you can drive the Buick around to the front, leave Poochie in the back seat with the window cracked open, and walk in like any other customer. I'll meet you inside. Order whatever you want. Breakfast will be on me."

What Bilyash liked best about Mom and Pop's Place was the location of its single-user washrooms, right next to the service entrance at the rear of the restaurant. Carrying his own version of Angie's overnight bag, he hauled the steel door open and slipped unnoticed into the women's washroom, locking himself inside.

The half-tiled walls and worn metal fixtures dated back to the 1980s, and there was no countertop around the wash basin, but none of that mattered. All he cared about was the mirror mounted on the wall beside the light switch and having fifteen minutes of privacy. The assassins would be looking for Billy Ash. It was past time he reinvented himself.

With rapid movements, he stripped off his clothes and dropped them in a pile under the sink. Then he closed his eyes and consciously relaxed the part of his mind that had kept his Nash'terel form confined in this particular human shape.

The transformation began almost immediately, with a profound, encompassing sense of relief. Skin melted, allowing muscles to lengthen and expand. Bones grew denser. Joints refashioned themselves. Scales rose to the surface, hardening to protect his neck and shoulders, the backs of his hands, the tops of his feet. He felt his skull shift and flow, returning to its familiar configuration of ridges and channels.

When Bilyash next opened his eyes, the face looking back at him from the mirror belonged to a Nash'terel with olive-green skin and slanted golden eyes. Iridescent scales shielded his nose and cheeks and armoured the roots of the three long ridges of bone that rose from the top of his forehead and reached backward, hugging the contours of his head like the fingers of a clasping skeletal hand.

He checked his watch. Angie would be sitting at a table by now, waiting for her breakfast to arrive. There was no time to spare.

Bilyash unsnapped his tote bag and pulled out a change of clothing and a clear plastic pocket containing a black and white photograph. He hadn't used this identity in over fifty years. With luck, the assassins wouldn't have researched that far back.

He stared at the photo for a full minute, reawakening the part of his mind where that human shape was stored. Remembering what it felt like to occupy that form. Giving his body permission to assume it once again. Waiting for the familiar icy sensation to trickle along his bones, signalling the beginning of the transformation. It was never easy.

Gripping the sides of the wash basin with both hands, Bilyash braced his feet, closed his eyes, and hoped, as he always did in this situation, that his brain would get it right the first time.

Bilyash left the washroom and sailed across the dining area to the table where Angie was sitting, watching the 24-hour news station on the wide-screen television mounted on the opposite wall. She did a double-take when he plopped himself down on the chair facing hers.

"There now, that's better," he declared, dropping his Bargello-decorated tote bag beside her purse on the extra seat between them and running both hands down his lap to smooth out his ankle-length daisy-printed skirt.

She frowned warily at him. "Excuse me? Have we met?"

Leaning as far across the table as his ample bosom would permit, he lowered his voice and asked pleasantly, "Is this enough magical makeup mojo for you, Angie?"

With a gasp, she jerked upright as though stuck with a pin. Her eyes widened, then narrowed as she looked him up and down. Searching for seams or edges around the sharp, stern features of his new face, no doubt. Staring at his steel-wool hair and suddenly generous cleavage. Speculating on the source of all the extra padding. "Billy?" she whispered. "That's amazing! How did you do that so quickly?"

"Trade secret," he told her. "And that's Aunt Minerva to you, girlie."

Angie's cheeks dimpled. "Yes, ma'am. This one's yours," she added, pushing a glass of ice water across the table toward him. "I didn't know what you wanted, so—"

Right on cue, the server appeared with a heaping platter of food and two empty plates. "Here's your Super-duper Lumberjack Breakfast," she announced.

Bilyash glanced uneasily around the room. Only two other tables were occupied, one by three men in business suits who appeared absorbed in an earnest discussion about some papers that they were passing back and forth. The other was taken by a very young family of four. Both groups had obviously sat down and ordered long before he and Angie had arrived, and neither group was now paying them the slightest bit of attention.

All right, then, he thought. *No assassins here. Not yet, anyway.*

Then he noticed what was sitting in the middle of their table and blurted out, "You're not really going to eat all that, are you?"

There was enough food for three healthy human adults on the Super-duper Lumberjack Breakfast Platter. Angie had already helped herself to the scrambled eggs and some of the hash-browned potatoes, leaving him to choose from pancakes, peameal bacon, sausages, toast, and a strip of something that might have been beef before it was ruined on the grill. There were also several chunks of cantaloupe and watermelon in a small glass bowl.

Angie made a wry face and replied, "Of course not, silly. I'll eat what's on my plate, you'll eat as much as you want, and whatever's left we'll take in a doggy bag for Poochie." Misinterpreting his silent pause, she added, "He'll be okay with it. I saw what Macy fed him, and, trust me, it didn't come off the pet food shelf at a grocery store. What's the matter, Auntie Min? Aren't you hungry? Not even for the fruit? It looks really good," she coaxed.

"The water will be enough for me," he assured her. "I usually skip breakfast." *Human-style breakfast, anyway,* he added privately, *and those terrible catered lunches, and sometimes dinner, too, depending on what's available. Unless it's steak tartare,* he amended. He could eat that three times a day.

"You missed an interesting news story," said Angie between mouthfuls, "about a house fire in a North York neighbourhood. Two firefighters were injured when they fell into a sinkhole in the front yard of the building."

"A sinkhole?" he repeated, with effort maintaining a mildly surprised expression.

"That's what they're calling it. Apparently, one of the firefighters landed on top of the other, dislocating his own shoulder and breaking his partner's leg. I don't know what your uncle had in his lab, but they showed some aerial footage of the fire, and it looks like the inside of a blast furnace."

Hot enough to be a cremation chamber, perhaps? Maybe Shred wasn't so stupid after all.

For the next few minutes Bilyash sat quietly, sipping his water and watching Angie eat. He couldn't help marvelling at her body's ability to generate unpolluted essence on a diet of sugar, fats, starches, and protein, most of it loaded with chemical preservatives. Then she glanced up at the television. Angie's jaw and fork both dropped as the glance became a disbelieving stare and her next intake of breath a horrified gasp.

Bilyash turned in his seat in time to catch the final sentence of a breaking news story crawling along the bottom of the screen: *Award-winning makeup designer Cora Dolson found dead of apparent heart failure at age 59.* As the meaning of those words sank in, his skin began crawling as well. This was not right. It was far too soon for her body to have been discovered, let alone for the story to have hit the news media. Cora was known to be a late riser, sleeping in until at least ten o'clock every morning. Nobody should even have missed her until well after noon, unless...

Wait a minute. What day of the week was this? Macy always started his interns off on a Monday, and yesterday had been Angie's first day on the set, so today had to be—

Damn! Cora's cleaning service arrived at eight o'clock sharp every Tuesday morning. The 9-1-1 call would have been made right away, and the police would have been on the scene within minutes. They never dawdled when a major entertainment figure was involved.

Gripped by a sudden restlessness, Bilyash spun on his chair and reached for his tote bag. He fished a couple of bills out of his wallet, dropping them deliberately in the middle of the table. "We need to leave, now," he said in a low, tight voice.

Angie gulped hard and tore her gaze away from the television. "Yeah, I don't think I can eat any more either. Let me just get a container for these leftovers—"

"There's no time for that."

As though seconding the motion, Poochie began barking hysterically, loudly enough to be heard all the way inside the restaurant. A moment later, a heavy-set man with a greying goatee walked through the doorway, and paused. He was wearing denim pants and steel-toed boots. A casual observer might take him for a road worker on a break. However, as the man stood blocking the exit and surveying the room with cold, dark eyes, Bilyash knew better.

This customer wasn't planning to order from the menu. He was a hunter.

Angie had apparently caught his vibes as well. She and "Auntie Min" exchanged a meaningful look across the table.

"Maybe we should stay here," Angie suggested quietly. "We're in a public place. There are witnesses."

"That won't help. Macy was a witness, and look what happened to him," he whispered back. "We'll have to move quickly. Give me your car keys. Make sure he sees you do it."

"Why?"

"Because I want to see how he reacts. The keys?"

Reluctantly, she pulled them out of her pocket and placed them on the table in front of him, just as the man appeared at Bilyash's elbow.

"Excuse me," he said in a voice slick as grease. The Yeng smelled very faintly of rotting fish and looked even more cruel and calculating when he smiled. "You seem awfully familiar. Have we met?"

Bilyash decided to be hard of hearing. "I'm sorry, young man. Were you saying something?" he replied, loudly enough to draw the attention of everyone in the dining area.

There was a flicker of doubt in the hunter's eyes, just for an instant. Then the man's expression set even harder than before. He bent from the waist and said, for Bilyash's ear alone, "I know who you are and you know what I am, and what I'm capable of. Come with me now and I won't kill everyone in this room."

No, not all. Just the ones who are old enough to talk, Bilyash added silently.

Poochie had resumed barking at the top of his lungs, prompting the other diners to begin sending disapproving glances to their table.

"Oops! Sounds like Frankie's losing it out there, Aunt Min," Angie pointed out brightly. "I'd better go calm him down before someone calls the police about the noise." Then, pausing only to wrap a couple of sausages in a paper napkin and stuff them into her purse, Angie got to her feet, scooped up the car keys, and hurried toward the exit, watched by seven pairs of eyes.

Still playing the hard-of-hearing card, Bilyash said in a loud, stern voice, "So, young man, you think you know who I am? It's very possible that you do. I was the principal teacher at a juvenile detention centre for seven years. If that is where you got your education, then it shouldn't surprise you that I look familiar." With that, "Auntie Min" heaved herself to her feet.

Bilyash had chosen this identity for a reason. As Minerva Pennington, he had been a matron in a women's prison for several years, and a psychiatric nurse for several more. Nearly six feet tall, with a sturdy build and an imposing manner, Min had been a formidable figure in her day. As she now rose to her full height, standing eye to eye with the assassin and with a regal tilt to her chin, she was clearly still someone to be reckoned with.

The Yeng, however, refused to be impressed. "Allow me to walk you to your car," he said, and reached for her arm.

Abruptly, Bilyash realized that Poochie was still barking, sounding a little hoarse but just as frantic as before. A glance out the window showed him that the Buick hadn't budged from where they'd left it. Angie was nowhere in sight. He could have sworn she was making her escape before the bloodshed began. So where was she?

If she had conceived some crazy plan to rescue him...!

Bilyash had no choice now. He had to make a scene, to keep the assassin distracted until Angie made her play, whatever it was. Snatching up his tote bag, he stared directly into the man's eyes and thundered, "Do I look like an invalid to you, young man? Or is it your habit to walk around insulting women with grey hair? Perhaps you should count yourself fortunate that I *don't* remember who you are."

There was scattered applause at the end of his pronouncement. And there was something else: the screeching of tires in the parking lot just outside the entrance of the restaurant.

Bilyash stood frozen in amazement as the zombie car screamed to a halt, then peeled off again, out of the parking lot and headed north.

The assassin cursed loudly and raced outside.

After emptying the Volkswagen of all their belongings and gear, Bilyash had left the keys in the Super Beetle's ignition, hoping aloud that someone would steal it. Evidently, someone had, and was drawing the assassin away by convincing him that he'd accosted the wrong person. Angie's plan was gutsy, and ultimately suicidal if Bilyash didn't catch up to her before the Yeng did.

"Honestly, the way some people drive!" he declared to the room. Then Bilyash sailed through the door like the dignified matron Minerva Pennington had always been, hoping that he wouldn't have to break character and hot-wire the Buick in order to join the pursuit.

His hopes faded when he reached the car and saw what Angie had done. She'd tossed the sausages in the back seat and the keys in the driver's seat. Then she'd locked the doors. Sloppy and meticulous at the same time. Bilyash shook his head in disgust.

Behind him, the assassin's black minivan roared out of the parking lot and took off after the Volkswagen. Meanwhile, Poochie was ignoring the sausages (thus demonstrating unexpectedly good taste, Bilyash thought) and was leaning on his front paws against the side window, yapping at him as if to say, *They're getting away, you idiot! Do something!*

Extending his right index finger in front of him, Bilyash stared through the window at the door key. It generally took a minute or more before he felt the icy sting of a shape change, but this was one that he'd practised many times before, during an earlier, more reckless period of his life. Maury had been scandalized when he'd found out, and had made him promise never to do it again; but Maury wasn't here, and Bilyash needed to get inside this car before Angie and the assassin got too far away.

In ten seconds, "Auntie Min" had a finger shaped exactly like the door key to a 1993 Buick Regal. Bilyash inserted his finger into the lock and magnetized them both. A moment later he heard the soft *click* of the tumbler mechanism moving, and he was able to open the driver's side door and slide behind the wheel.

It was good to know that he hadn't lost his touch.

"Shut up, Poochie. I have to drive," he said in Minerva Pennington's most authoritative voice. Miraculously, the dog obeyed.

Chapter Eight

———◆———

Once he was northbound, Bilyash floored the Buick's accelerator. The road crossed open countryside, and he was soon whipping past a succession of farmers' fields and treed lots, and crudely lettered signs advertising fresh eggs and home-baked pies. Farther north, the terrain turned to rolling hills, offering him an unfettered view of the next several miles of roadway each time he topped a rise; and what he saw ahead of him made him curse in every language he knew.

The minivan was a kilometre in front of him and rapidly closing on the Volkswagen. They were racing directly toward a two-lane bridge with concrete abutments and iron railings, and a couple of klicks beyond that, a fair-sized town. To either side of the road, thick stands of old-growth forest made a near-impassable wall.

Angie didn't dare slow down, not with the assassin right on her tail, but that meant she couldn't risk making a left or right turn either. Each time the Buick headed down a slope and he lost sight of the other two vehicles, Bilyash's heart rate increased. Each time he crested a hill, the minivan had gained another few metres and the Buick's chances of overtaking it seemed to slip further away.

Clearing the final rise before the long, straight, downhill run to the bridge, Bilyash saw the minivan pull out to pass, just as Angie swerved left to block it. In nightmarish slow motion, the Volkswagen seemed to bounce off the right front fender of the assassin's car, sending both vehicles careening in opposite directions. The Volkswagen glanced off the edge of the abutment to the right, flipped onto its side, and skidded down the embankment beside the bridge with a harsh metallic scream.

No-no-no don't roll. DON'T ROLL, Bilyash commanded the zombie car. It paid him no heed.

Meanwhile, the speeding minivan had demolished the abutment on the left and ripped through a section of railing. Concrete exploded into a cloud of dust that rained down on the car as it dived nose first off the bridge, into the ravine below.

It was deep. Slamming on the brakes, Bilyash brought the Buick to a halt on the shoulder of the road, just in time to watch the minivan drop out of sight. A second later he heard a sickening crunch, a screech of tortured metal, and then a very loud, very hollow groan as the wreck finally came to rest. After that, there was silence.

Bilyash scrambled out of the car, struck by the deathly stillness that now surrounded the scene of the accident. He was all alone on the road, with no traffic coming from either direction. Nothing was moving. Even the air seemed to be holding its breath. He ran first toward the Volkswagen, which lay on its roof halfway down the bank of the ravine, its roll halted by a clump of sturdy bushes. To his immense relief, Angie was conscious and struggling to free herself from her seat belt. She was cut and bleeding, but gave him a weak smile and a thumbs-up sign when she saw "Auntie Min" peering anxiously through the driver's side window.

Instantly, Bilyash's focus narrowed to a single goal: getting Angie safely out of that car. Bracing one foot against the side of the Volkswagen and marshalling all the strength Minerva's body possessed, he managed to muscle the door open. Then he reached in and unlocked Angie's seat belt, carefully easing her down and out of the vehicle. He knew from experience how fragile most humans were, and what a long time they took to heal.

Only when he had set her down on the grassy slope a safe distance away from the car and assured himself that all of her external injuries were minor did it even occur to him to think about the driver of the minivan. Bilyash cursed inwardly. He could practically hear Shred's voice scolding him. *Not too bright, kid.*

"Stay here," he told Angie, and hurried to the other side of the bridge.

The assassin's car had landed on its wheels at the bottom of the ravine and was up to its door handles in scrub. And its windows were tinted. Damn!

Bilyash hitched up his skirt, knotted it above his knees, and began making his way down the steep bank, watching for movement in and around the vehicle. There was none. That could be very good or it could be very bad. As he cautiously picked his steps through a dense tangle of roots and coarse foliage, grateful to be wearing Minerva's sensible low-heeled shoes, he noticed a splash of darkness on the inside of the windscreen—blood, most likely—and felt a surge of satisfaction, alloyed with caution.

The assassin was hurt, certainly. Incapacitated, perhaps. Dead? Unlikely. And that was a problem. Like the Nash'terel, the infected Yeng were shapeshifters with strong recuperative powers. With luck, however, this Yeng would be unconscious, and Bilyash could use his talent to induce a fatal cerebral hemorrhage.

The driver's door had unlatched on impact and now hung partway open. Warily Bilyash sidled up to it, pressing himself against the minivan's flank. Then, in one swift motion, he stepped away from the car and flung the door wide, bracing to receive an attack.

There was none. The driver's seat was empty. In fact, the whole minivan was empty. Bilyash's flesh crawled as he realized where the assassin must have gone. Where he'd given him time to go by tending to Angie first.

Not too bright, kid, Shred's voice repeated in his mind, just as Poochie began urgently barking again.

A sharp popping sound erupted twice on the other side of the bridge.

Gunfire.

Bilyash tumbled out of the minivan and hurried along the bottom of the ravine, doing his best to ignore the grisly images now parading through his mind and the sick, twisting feeling they'd planted in his stomach. Angie couldn't be dead. She mustn't be!

She wasn't. As Bilyash emerged from beneath the bridge, he saw her standing beside the Volkswagen, ashen-faced, tightly gripping the handle of a small-calibre pistol. It was pointed directly at his chest.

"Angie," he said softly, "what are you doing?"

She blinked a couple of times, as though waking from a dream. Her hands began to shake. Her eyes went wide as saucers, and her lips visibly struggled to form words. "It was—" she finally managed to gasp.

"Put the gun down," he instructed her, taking a deliberate step toward her, and then another.

Her eyes welled with tears. "It was a—" she repeated in a

tremulous voice. "I shot it and it disappeared. It had horns, and bright red skin, and—" She swallowed hard before continuing, "—and a snout like a bear. And its eyes glowed yellow."

Bilyash had been slowly walking toward her. As soon as he was close enough to reach for it, he wrapped his fingers around the gun and gently took it from her hands. In that instant, she shuddered and collapsed backward against the overturned Volkswagen.

He glanced at the gun. It wasn't the one Maury had purchased for him earlier. "Where did you get this?" Bilyash demanded.

"From my purse. When I saw you headed for the minivan, I thought you might need it. I was about to bring it to you when that—that *demon* lurched toward me from under the bridge. Don't tell me I imagined it," she warned him. "I used to have nightmares about creatures like that and I know what I saw, Billy."

"All right, I won't tell you that," he said. "But I will tell you that the assassin got away. He's hurt but still alive, and he'll keep coming after us until either he's dead or we are. So we need to take the Buick and get as far away from here as we can, right now, before some good Samaritan comes along and offers to call 9-1-1."

"We need a different car," Bilyash muttered.

Dozing beside him in the front seat, occasionally wincing as she shifted position, Angie murmured back, "You want to trade this one in somewhere?" When he didn't respond immediately, she opened her eyes and stared at him in disbelief. "You want to steal one?"

Admittedly, the thought had crossed his mind. Shaping his finger into a key earlier had brought back memories of his short-lived life of crime, and of the rush he'd always felt as he drove away unseen in someone else's vehicle. But back then, he hadn't had a target painted on his back, nor two pistols in his possession, one of them illegally obtained, the other recently fired. For just an instant, he was seized by the urge to open the Buick's glove box and make sure Angie's gun was still where he'd stuffed it.

"Listen," he pointed out, "we're makeup artists. All we need to do is change the look of this one. A paint job and a couple of swapped-out licence plates will do it. We'll pick a dark colour that can't be identified exactly if we're spotted driving at night. What do you think of midnight blue?"

She thought for a second. "I like it. But where are we going to get the licence plates?"

"We're on our way there right now," he told her.

Maury wasn't the only one who knew "gentlemen with connections". Armin was the owner of The Crash Pad, the wrecking yard west of Aurora where Bilyash had found the zombie car. A moonlight entrepreneur, Armin provided a full range of products and services for the discerning cash-carrying customer in need. He was also a fellow Nash'terel, something he and Bilyash had tacitly agreed never to speak about.

The Chihuahua was not party to that pact, however. His hackles went up and he started to growl the second the Buick passed through The Crash Pad's tall iron gates. Bilyash pulled up beside the door of Armin's office and turned off the engine.

"Shut up, Poochie," he commanded. Grudgingly, the dog subsided into silence.

"Is there a problem?" Angie asked softly.

"Shouldn't be," he assured her.

Bilyash looked her up and down for a moment. They'd stopped at a gas station so she could go into the washroom and clean herself up after the accident. She'd changed her clothing, but soap and water had only accentuated the angry red marks and bruises on her face, neck, and hands. If anyone saw her in that condition there would be questions, and he preferred not to have to answer any right now.

"You'd better stay in the car," he told her. Visibly relieved, she leaned back against the padded headrest.

Bilyash fetched his tote bag out of the rear seat and approached the office door. It looked ready to fall off its hinges. In fact, the entire building looked as though it had been thrown together by a team of drunken carpenters, all getting in one another's way. But outward appearances could be deceiving, especially when they were manipulated by an adept with the appropriate *hainbek*. That was why Armin was the perfect person to help them.

A short, balding man with hawk-like features and a huge cigar hanging off his lip stood behind the counter, inspecting a printed list that had been folded, spindled, and mutilated. He glanced up briefly, then returned his attention to the badly abused piece of paper in front of him. "What can I do for you, lady?" he asked.

Bilyash changed his eyes to their Nash'terel shape and colour and replied, "I was wondering if I could use your washroom, Armin. I don't seem to be myself today."

The other being looked up, startled, then nodded with recognition as he met Minerva's slanted golden gaze. "It's just down that hallway, on the left."

"Thank you," she said primly, and went in the direction he'd pointed.

Fifteen minutes later, Billy Ash strolled back around the corner, wearing his denim jeans and jacket, gripping the handles of the tote bag in one hand and patting his pockets with the other to make sure he hadn't left anything behind.

"Bilyash?" Armin ventured.

"The one and only," he replied.

They traded smiles.

"Thought so. It's been a while, kid. What can I do for you?"

"There's a Buick outside that needs a colour change and new licence plates. And different tires, so the tread can't be matched."

Armin's grin faded. "You're back to stealing cars?"

"No, but I'm going to ground, and I need your help to get there."

Bushy brows knitted. "I've heard rumours about assassins. Are you being pursued?"

"I'm trying to avoid that. I've got cash." Bilyash reached into the tote bag and pulled out the thickly stuffed envelope he'd transferred there from his suitcase while waiting for Angie to finish washing up.

Armin hesitated for only a moment. "Bring your chariot around back and I'll see what I can do."

"One more thing," said Bilyash. "There's a human in the car. She thinks you're going to paint it and physically replace the tires and licence plates."

Armin gave him a look. "Subterfuge will cost you extra."

"And there's a dog."

The look filled with disgust. "Trying an exotic new diet, are we?"

"He's our alarm system. He goes nuts around Yeng and he's got a loud bark, but the human can control him."

"So that's why you've got her? To turn off the dog? No, don't bother, I don't want to know. Honestly," he added with a sigh, "the things I do for old times' sake…"

Two hours later, Bilyash's envelope was lighter by three thousand dollars, and he was at the wheel of a car that the assassin had never seen, headed west under a clear blue sky along a series of concession roads and side streets. All he needed now was to come across a small town with an even smaller motel where he and Angie could hole up until nightfall.

Maury's safe-house wasn't that far away. Going north on Highway 400, they could stop in Barrie for groceries and pet supplies and still be there by mid-afternoon. Under normal circumstances, that would have been the plan. But nothing was normal right now. The assassin had already found them once and had been foiled by recklessness and sheer dumb luck. Once he'd recovered from his injuries, he would be right back on their trail. Eventually he would find them again. It was inevitable. However, the inevitable could be delayed if Bilyash could sneak Angie and Poochie up to the cabin in the dark.

So, he took the scenic route through rural Ontario, past signs pointing to places with names like Palgrave and Mono Mills, while both his passengers dozed. Bilyash knew what he was looking for, and just south of Alliston he found it: an older, family-run motel less than a kilometre from a hospital.

An ER visit could draw the assassin to them, but it was a risk he'd decided to take. Humans were a fragile species, and Angie had endured quite a beating when the Volkswagen had flipped onto its roof. The longer Bilyash sat behind the wheel, watching her drift in and out of wakefulness beside him, the more certain he became: before they went any further into hiding, she needed to be seen by a doctor.

First, though, they had to talk things over and come up with a plausible explanation for her condition. It would have to be thought out and utterly convincing—some types of injuries were automatically reported to the police, and the ER staff would be difficult to fool.

The Shady Spot Motel was off the main road but in sight of it, and while obviously cared for, it was just nondescript enough to go unnoticed by anyone not actually looking for it. Best of all, there was parking space behind the building and a back entrance to each of the rooms.

Pulling into a spot beside the motel office door, Bilyash turned the rear view mirror and aged Billy Ash's face about twenty years. Angie was slumped against the passenger-side door, her chest rhythmically rising and falling. Behind him, he saw Poochie raise his head and stare curiously at the shape-shifting reflection in the mirror.

As though they were being sculpted out of clay by invisible fingers, jowls sagged, pouches popped, skin folded into creases. From the back seat meanwhile came a series of doggy throat-mutters. When Bilyash was satisfied that the transformation was complete and convincing, he turned to face the Chihuahua and signalled him to be quiet. Then 70-year-old Billy went into the office to register two guests and a pet.

After paying cash in advance for one night, Billy drove around to the back door of their room and began unloading the car, beginning with the makeup kit. By the time he was ready to move Angie, she was sitting up wide awake with Poochie on her lap, gazing uncertainly around her.

She leaned away from Bilyash when he opened the passenger side door. It took him a second to realize why.

"It's me, Angie," he assured her.

"Billy? But when did you—?"

"Let's get you inside. Then we'll talk."

Chapter Nine

———◆———

There was just one chair in the motel room, and Bilyash took it, motioning to Angie to sit on the bed. As though sensing that this wasn't going to be a pleasant discussion, she chose to perch on the edge of the dresser instead.

"Tell me about the gun you used earlier," he said, getting in the first word. When dealing with Angie, he'd learned, that was important. "I asked you where it came from and you ducked the question. Why?"

Her expression hardened. "You may be the right age for it, even if you don't look it, but you're not my father, Billy," she informed him, and crossed her arms over her chest.

"True. And before we leave here tonight you're going to look old enough to be your mother," he told her, gesturing toward the makeup kit. "For now, though, I just want to make sure there won't be any more surprises coming out of that handbag of yours. You don't happen to have a machete in there, do you?"

Her lips quirked in a smile.

"Or a set of brass knuckles?" he continued. "Or maybe an ice pick? Because we need the ER staff to believe us when we tell them—"

"No!" She leaped away from the dresser and stood in the middle of the room, her hands clenched and gripping the air in front of her.

Bilyash stifled the urge to get to his feet. In his calmest, most placating voice, he said, "Be sensible, Angie. You've just been in a serious car crash—"

"I can't be seen by a doctor," she declared. "There can't be any paperwork on me, anywhere. If they find out—!"

Bilyash was suddenly and intensely curious.

"What can't the doctors find out, Angie?"

Her lips pursed as though holding back a torrent of words. "Not the doctors," she finally told him. "The others. They're bad people, Billy." She sank down onto the bed, tears percolating into her voice. "I should have said something earlier, but I was afraid. I thought that if you knew, you would consider me a liability and leave me behind. And between Cora's death and Macy's murder, I just—" She shuddered, then looked up at him with a different kind of fear in her eyes. "Billy, please tell me you had nothing to do with what happened to Macy."

He paused. Technically, he'd had everything to do with what had happened to Terrence Macy, but now was not the time to be splitting that hair.

"If you're worried that you might have alibied his killer, don't be," he assured her. "I was nowhere near the sound stage that night."

"That's good," she said, visibly relieved.

"Who's after you, Angie? Start at the beginning. And give me the unabridged version. I want to know exactly what we may be facing."

"Okay," she said, "from the beginning. I was born in a town in the foothills of northern British Columbia, called Middlevale. You won't find it on a map. It's an isolated community—everything has to be flown in—and it's owned by a religious cult called The Church of Human Purification. This cult has been around for a long time. I'm the eleventh generation of my family to grow up in it."

Human purification. It wasn't the first time Bilyash had encountered that expression. Now, hearing Angie speak the words so matter-of-factly sent a chill down his spine. Not trusting his voice, he waved at her to continue.

"The cult leaders enforce a set of very strict rules. One of them is that only they can pick which couples will be allowed to marry and procreate."

"And this purifies...?"

"Our souls. That's what they told us, anyway: the purer the life force, the closer it is to godliness. When I came of age, a mate was chosen for me and a wedding date was set. And the boy I loved and had already given my virginity to was banished. Well, not right away," she amended. "First he was thrown into a cell. I was devastated. Godliness meant nothing to me. We were just fifteen, and I was unshakably convinced that Brendan O'Connor and I were soulmates, destined to spend the rest of our lives together.

"So, I begged my father to go and ask the cult leaders to make an exception for us. He refused at first, but I kept at him until he agreed. When he came back from the leaders' compound later that afternoon, his face was ashen. And the look in his eyes—! When we asked him what was wrong, all he would say was, 'It isn't banishment.' He ordered my mother and me to pack up whatever we could carry. We didn't question him. As soon as it was dark, the three of us slipped out of town.

"Nobody saw us. We headed for the landing strip. The supply plane had been unloaded and the pilot was getting ready to take off again. My father approached her and talked her into flying us out of there. By the time anyone missed us, we were already in hiding, halfway to Montreal, in a town even smaller than the one we had left behind. We stayed in several places like that, each time for no more than a couple of years, under assumed names. If any of the residents got nosy, we 'let slip' that we were in a witness protection program. In the meanwhile, we concentrated on losing ourselves in the local community. We learned a lot, especially about working with computers and the internet, and we used that knowledge to acquire new identities."

"...and guns to go with them?"

"No. We didn't dare fill out any paperwork that could be used to track us down, so I picked one up on the street after moving to Toronto. I thought it would be expensive, but the man only wanted ten dollars for it. I was surprised."

Bilyash wasn't. His first instincts about that pistol had been correct. Guns weren't sold that cheaply unless they were stolen or had been used in a crime and were being disposed of.

He gave his head a firm shake to get his mind back on track. "So, these 'others' that you're afraid of are the leaders of the cult?"

"Yes."

"Is one of them named Vincent, by any chance? Or Victor?"

"No, but when we left there was a woman, Victoria Spears, who'd been running things ever since I could remember. Why?"

He batted away her question and threw one back at her. "How do you know they're still looking for you?"

"I've been monitoring them online. Every once in a while they send out feelers. Early on, they even put out an Amber alert. We thought we'd have to spam them with false leads, but about a thousand other people saved us the trouble, and they never repeated the exercise.

"My father saw something that day that he wasn't meant to see. He never told me what it was, only that the cult leaders were monsters, and that we mustn't ever let them find us again. I came to Toronto two years ago to reclaim the life I felt had been stolen from me by the cult and by my parents' fears. I wanted to be creative and have fun, and I wanted to be part of the movie industry—but I knew I had to be careful about it. So, I reinvented myself as Angie Fiore, then stayed off the grid and under the radar so no one would have a reason to look beyond the ID that I carry in my purse. And it worked, until today."

"The statement you gave the police. The incorrect contact information." As their eyes met, he knew: "You've never had a roommate, have you?"

She shifted uncomfortably. "I tried it. I needed an address to register for Ryerson and didn't dare get a place on my own, even if I could have afforded it. But I had a lot of anxiety at first, and trust issues that made it hard for me to live with someone else. So, I moved out after the first couple of months of classes. She was probably glad to be rid of all my 'tics and fetishes', as she called them. But I was living in my car and had no fixed address, so she let me go on using hers for official purposes. And now she's dead, and the Toronto police are going to be tracking down everyone who knew her. That's what it means, you know, when they use the word 'apparent' with a cause of death. It means they'll be investigating the hell out of it."

Bilyash was speechless. He'd been wondering how things could possibly get any more complicated. Now he knew: Angie's roommate had been Cora Dolson.

"Now do you understand why I have to stay out of that ER?"

Unfortunately, he did, with crystalline clarity. It hadn't been lack of concern that he'd heard in her voice earlier. It had been resignation. And now he was on the run with Cora's absentee roommate, putting them both on the police radar as well as in the sights of at least one Yeng assassin. All his painstaking care to avoid leaving evidence at the scene of Cora's killing, all his precautions to avoid being seen while breaking into her apartment—all of it had been for nothing.

Misinterpreting his silence, Angie leaned forward and said earnestly, "I know how bad this must look to you, but please believe me, Billy, I had nothing to do with Cora's death."

"I know," he told her.

"And you mustn't worry about my health. It'll be all right. I just need to get some sleep. I've checked, and nothing seems to be broken. Ever since I was a kid, I've been able to bounce back from just about anything after a good night's sleep or two. My father used to say that I had India rubber in my genes."

No, thought Bilyash, not in her genes: in her essence, in its purity and abundance. That was why the "cult" had been established. And that was why he and Angie had to stay together, for both their sakes.

"Okay," he said, moving to sit beside her on the bed and putting his arm around her shoulders. "I'll believe you're all right until there's a reason not to. For now, I'm going to go out and let you sleep. Poochie must be getting hungry—I know I am—and I think we passed a grocery store on our way here."

She looked up gratefully at him, and he bent over her, placed his lips on hers... and drank. It had been a stressful day. A depleting day. He took her essence in long swallows, feeling renewed strength wash through him in an icy wave, not stopping until she lay limp in his arms. He made sure she was still breathing, then laid her down gently on top of the bedspread and pulled the spare blanket over her. Yesterday she'd recovered enough to walk after a two-hour nap. It would be interesting to see how long it took her to reach that point while her own body was healing.

Poochie stood near the door, making small, uncertain sounds.

"No, I'm not taking you with me," Bilyash told him. He lifted the Chihuahua onto the bed as well. "Your job is to watch over her while she's sleeping. Understand?"

Doggy brows furrowed and the doggy head tilted, as though Poochie was wondering, *What are you up to now?*

"If you're good, I'll bring you back some dinner," Bilyash said. Then he headed out the back door, closed it quietly behind him, and took the burner phone out of the trunk of the Buick.

Maldemaur answered on the third ring. "What do you want?" he demanded. "Don't tell me you're in trouble already!"

"I think I know where your old nemesis Vincaspera is right now."

"Vincaspera? That scheming, traitorous—?"

"The very one," Bilyash confirmed. "If I'm right, she's been out in British Columbia for the past two or three hundred years, most recently calling herself Victoria Spears."

"She's reverted to her birth gender form?"

"If you say so. I can tell you that Vincaspera's human shape is currently female, and she's fooled a large sampling of humans into following her to an isolated part of B.C., where she's set up a community for them and has been keeping them happy and ignorant while manipulating their bloodlines. Angie and her parents escaped from there, I'd guess about eight years ago. Vincaspera is purifying human essence through selective breeding. And Angelina Fiore is walking proof that the method works."

A stream of profanity issued from the phone then that made even Bilyash uncomfortable, followed by an audible sigh.

Ever wary of assassins, the Nash'terel had gone undercover on Earth, spreading out over the planet and seldom making contact with one another, even within family groups. Nonetheless, news had a way of travelling around, and, as the humans were fond of saying, leopards didn't change their spots.

One leopard in particular, Vincaspera, had been Maldemaur's bitter scientific rival back on RinYeng, constantly finding out what Maury was working on and then setting out to discredit or overshadow him. Evidently, she'd just done it again, beating Maury to the finish line with an abundant supply of almost pure human essence. No wonder the light lord was ready to spit fire.

"So what do you want to do with your human?" Maury asked.

"With Angie? Just what Shred recommended. I'm going to keep her close, drink from her when I need to, and stick to our original plan. I only called you because I thought you'd want to know about Victoria Spears. And what are *you* going to do now?" Bilyash returned.

There was a pause. "It's better if you have deniability, kid," came Shred's voice over the phone. "And this conversation never took place." A second later, the line went dead.

Bilyash had lied earlier about driving past a grocery store, but in fact there was a Back to Basics, proudly displaying its trademarked green and yellow sign, just a klick or so north of the motel. As he strolled up and down the aisles in search of something Angie could have for dinner before they set out on the last leg of their trip, Shred's final words kept bouncing around inside his brain.

Why would Bilyash need deniability? So the Council of the First would still agree to protect him after Maury had done something unsanctioned or even egregiously wrong, perhaps? Like tracking down and destroying a fellow Nash'terel scientist? It ought to be an easy enough kill for an elemental master. In fact, assuming that the First were aware of Vincaspera's little experiment, their decision to bring Maury onside might have been prompted by that very fear. Hadn't a human strategist once advised keeping one's friends close and one's enemies closer?

In the meat department of the store, Bilyash paused to look over a selection of fresh cuts of beef. The steaks looked appetizing. Should he get one or two? Poochie ate people food—Angie hadn't been the only one to notice what Macy put into that personalized bowl for his pet—but the pampered Chihuahua would probably turn his nose up at anything raw, and Bilyash had no intention of cooking this evening. One nicely marbled rib steak, then, for himself. And for Angie? She would need protein, he decided, and headed for the deli counter.

Ten minutes later he was standing in the express check-out line with the steak, a tin of gourmet dog food—*boeuf bourguignon* for small breeds, *ooh, là là!*—and a thick corned beef sandwich on a kaiser roll. He'd popped three bottles of water into his basket as well. It wasn't until he was setting them up in a row on the conveyor belt that the final pieces fell into place in Bilyash's mind.

Back in the 1950s and '60s, humans had begun installing bunkers in their back yards, to protect them while they waited out the aftermath of a possible nuclear war. They had equipped these shelters with several years' worth of supplies and provisions, including drinking water. Now the exiles from RinYeng were facing a similar threat. In about a hundred years, an army of trained assassins would be coming through the rift, bent on annihilating every Yeng and Nash'terel on Earth.

According to Maury, the First wanted to harness the unique abilities of "the secluded ones" in order to ensure their own survival. Bilyash had assumed he was referring to the Nash'terel arsenal of fully-trained *hainbeka*. But what if that was wrong? What if the First were actually planning to barricade themselves underground while the massacre was going on, like the humans in their bunkers, and they were looking for a way to stockpile human essence?

Essence purification had been Maldemaur's primary goal for as long as Bilyash could remember, but first, he'd had to create leak-proof containers for storing samples. After experimenting for a full century, he'd finally developed a way to make *dashkra* absorb and release essence instead of blood. Now, properly treated and aged, a chunk of raw *dashkra* could be crushed and placed inside any enclosed space to create a serviceable essence receptacle. Maury had brought a generous supply of stones with him through the rift. In fact, every Nash'terel master on the planet had a portion of the rare and dangerous mineral in their possession.

And the First were proposing to bring all the masters together, claiming it was in order to protect them? *Yeah, right.*

Meanwhile, Victoria Spears was quietly farming humans to produce pure or nearly-pure human essence, in quantity.

It all made sense now—the First were probably planning to bottle human essence, either for their own use when they went into hiding or to sell at exorbitant prices, like fine wine. Or maybe both. The Oh-So-Important Ones were notoriously self-serving.

And Bilyash had just given Maury the information he needed to scuttle their crass little scheme.

This conversation never took place.

Bilyash handed the cashier two bills, a twenty and a ten. She blushed, evidently misinterpreting the expression on his face.

He stopped at a dollar store to pick up two plastic bowls, a spoon, and a cheaply-made leash before heading back to the motel. Angie and Poochie were sound asleep when he returned, Angie under the blanket and the Chihuahua on top of it. Quietly, Bilyash emptied the tin of dog food into one of the bowls, filled the second one with water, and set them both down on the floor near the foot of the bed. Then he took his steak into the washroom and closed the door, looking forward to eating this slice of beef in the time-honoured Nash'terel way.

First, he took off his shirt. Raw meat was messy, even the supermarket variety. As he unwrapped the parcel on the counter beside the wash basin, the familiar pungent aroma of wounded animal flesh drifted into his nostrils. His fangs itched in response and then emerged, upper and lower, ready to sink themselves into the prey. Grasping the steak with both hands, he lifted it out of a growing pool of sticky red and held it over the sink. Blood dripped down onto the white porcelain, each drop painting a scarlet stripe as it raced toward the drain. Bilyash clamped his fangs on a corner of the steak, locked his jaw muscles, and wrenched off a mouthful of meat, closing his eyes to maximize his enjoyment of its taste and smell as he chewed.

Juice was dribbling down his chin. He bent lower over the sink and took a second bite, and then a third. Soon, the entire inner surface of the basin was red, along with his hands and the bottom half of his face, and nothing mattered except the chunk of meat that he was devouring and the warmth that it kindled in his belly. Although Earthborn, he was Nash'terel, and this felt right. It was the way things were done.

Then Bilyash raised his head and saw his image in the mirror—the bloodied fangs, the fierce expression—and deep inside he knew what Angie's father must have inadvertently witnessed that day, what must have become of Brendan O'Connor and anyone else the cult leaders had "banished". In human eyes, that would be enough to make Victoria Spears and her associates monsters, to be avoided at all costs.

With equal certainty, Bilyash knew something else as well—he never wanted Angelina Fiore to see him that way, ever.

Angie slept until just past six o'clock. By then, Bilyash had already cleaned up the washroom, using the dumpster behind the motel to dispose of anything that might raise questions about the middle-aged couple who had checked in that afternoon. He'd also fed Poochie and walked him around the block a couple of times. It hadn't been a leisurely stroll for either of them. The dog had scampered after any small thing that moved. He'd repeatedly criss-crossed Bilyash's path and woven between his legs, forcing him to step carefully in order not to trip on the leash.

Now, worn out from the fresh air and exercise, Poochie lay dozing on the carpet near the front door, while Bilyash opened his kit and converted the motel room desk into a makeup station.

He was glad that he'd thought to bring along a full set of facial applications. The sculpted transfers sat beside the highlight and shadow tones that he would need, along with his palette of reds, browns and purples. Brushes, sponge wedges, pencils and fixing powder shared the rest of the desktop with a bottle of isopropyl alcohol and a spray applicator of sealant. It was everything he would need to add thirty years to Angie's face. It was also, he reflected ironically, a welcome break from zombies.

Hearing Angie stir behind him, Bilyash turned in his chair. She sat up and stretched, the blanket falling unnoticed onto her lap. Then their eyes met, and his mind filled with memories tinged with thirst. He filed them away. Now was not the time to be scratching that itch.

"Is it my turn?" she asked. He was momentarily confused. "To age," she added, indicating the improvised makeup chair. Wearing an impish grin, she added, "You gonna use your makeup mojo on me, Billy Ash?"

"Dinner first," he told her, handing her the corned beef on a kaiser in its brown paper wrapper, followed by one of the bottles of water.

She accepted it, then paused expectantly. "You're not eating?" she asked after a moment.

"I had a bite while I was out getting that. If you're still hungry later, we can pick something up at a fast food place on our way north."

That seemed to satisfy her. Relieved, he watched her tuck into the generously-filled sandwich.

He wasn't the only one paying attention. Poochie's head had come up at the first crackle of the paper. Now he sat on the floor beside the bed, making pathetic little noises and staring up at Angie with huge, soulful eyes.

"Don't give him any of your dinner," Bilyash warned, rising from his chair. "He's a glutton. He's already had a whole tin of beef *bourguignon*." He scooped the Chihuahua up and deposited him back at his post near the door.

Angie's cheeks dimpled. "So that's the way it is? The dog gets French cuisine and I get deli on a roll? Oh, we are definitely stopping for something else, Billy, and it won't be fast food."

"You want something French? Like snails?" he teased.

"Nope. Like an eclair. Topped with chocolate and filled with lots of custard."

"First the sandwich," he told her sternly. "Then we'll talk about dessert."

"Now you really do sound like my father."

There was a note of sadness in her voice, prompting him to ask, "Do you know where your parents are?"

"No. We parted ways when I realized that cleaning houses for minimum wage was slowly killing me inside. So, I told my parents that I would be safer melting into the crowd in a large city like Toronto than trying to hide out in a series of small towns. They disagreed with me, but in the end they had to let me go. My father gave me the car, and money for gas. He said it was so I would have freedom of movement, but I think he was just worried about who else might be riding the bus or the train. It's been a couple of years, so I'm pretty sure my parents will have moved again, but wherever they are, they're living in constant fear, and that's not a life, Billy. It's barely an existence."

"And yet you feel the need to carry a gun," he pointed out quietly.

"To defend myself in case the cult ever finds me again. And now, to defend *you* from whoever or whatever is trying to kill you. What was that creature, Billy? And don't tell me I imagined it. I know what I saw."

He uttered an exasperated syllable. "If I tell you, will you eat the damned sandwich so that I can do your makeup and we can get on the road?"

"Yes."

Knowing that the truth would drive a wedge between them, Bilyash paused, sifting his thoughts for a plausible lie. "All right, then," he said at last. "The man who was chasing you in that car isn't just an assassin. He has a special mental ability. It's like instant hypnosis. He can make you see whatever he wants you to see."

She gasped with recognition. "'I know who you are and you know what I'm capable of.' That's what I overheard him say to you in the restaurant."

"Yes. He must have seen the Buick in his rear view mirror, figured out that I was driving it, and realized that he would eventually have to take me on. But after being injured in the crash, he knew he didn't have a chance against me. He needed to escape. Just one problem: when he emerged from under the bridge, there you were, holding the gun. So he decided to paralyze you with fear, giving himself a chance to get away. That's why he put that terrifying image into your mind."

"But I wasn't paralyzed," she protested. "I put two bullets into him, I *know* I did."

"And then you saw him disappear, or thought you did, instead of what was actually happening."

"I. Shot. Him," she said through gritted teeth.

"There was no body, Angie. I looked. Whether you hit him or missed him, he got away. And now he's somewhere, healing, and we need to go to ground, just like you and your parents did, before he recovers sufficiently to come looking for us again. This is for a short time, I promise. We aren't going to live in fear. We just need to be safe while we come up with a plan."

Chapter Ten

———————◆———————

Compared to the hours-long zombie transformations he'd performed in the makeup trailer at Alpha Dog Studios, aging the human face was a quick change. It was also the culmination of the entire first year of study at the Toronto Academy of Film Arts.

Cora Dolson had been a perfectionist, insisting that her students have a thorough understanding of facial anatomy. Bilyash knew where every muscle lay, and how and where it was attached. He could analyze at a glance how much fat lay beneath the skin and how it would behave when bones and fibrous tissue were in motion. He could furrow a brow, coarsen a nose, crepe up a neck, and create and deepen lines, and have it all look perfectly natural on high definition video.

What he had to do today, however, was for higher than high def. Angie's face would have to fool the human eye in three dimensions from less than a metre away. What was even more important, her aged look would have to be realistic enough to convince her that the changes to his own face had been a makeup job as well. So, he took his time, paying meticulous attention to detail. Imagining that Cora Dolson was standing behind him, wearing her "impress me" expression.

When he was sure that even Cora would have been pleased, he removed the towel bib from around Angie's neck with a flourish and said, "Go check it out in the mirror."

Looking as excited as a small child opening a birthday gift, she jumped up and raced into the bathroom while he set about packing up his kit. A moment later he heard an exhilarated whoop.

"Magical makeup mojo rocks!" Angie declared. "Is it waterproof like yours?"

Bilyash nearly dropped the palette he was holding. Had she seen him wiping his face earlier? Had she seen the blood he was washing off it? Thinking fast, he called back, "It will handle perspiration and you can eat and drink with it on as long as you're careful, but that's about it."

"So I can have my chocolate eclair? And some Lady Grey tea?" came the wheedling voice from the washroom. "Sitting down in a restaurant?"

He paused with the bottles of alcohol and sealant in his hands and glanced at Poochie. The Chihuahua was grinning from ear to ear. *You're done, pal,* he seemed to be saying. *May as well surrender now and get it over with.*

Stop for tea and pastry while running for their lives? Sure. What could possibly go wrong?

"That one."

Bilyash looked where Angie was pointing and saw a café-curtained window tucked in between a flower shop and a variety store in a tiny strip mall. All three businesses sported the same large, glowing green signs with their names spelled out in identical longhand script. He read the middle sign aloud:

"*La Pâtisserie*. It's probably closed," he told her. "This place barely qualifies as a village, and it's after ten o'clock on a weeknight."

"Maybe you're right. But I see lights on inside and there are cars parked in front of it. Come on, Billy," she coaxed, "take a chance. Let's live dangerously."

She had no idea. Nonetheless, he signalled for the next right-hand turn, found an entrance off the side street, and pulled into the lot. Lying on the back seat, Poochie poked his head up and muttered inquiringly the moment the engine was turned off.

"Okay," said Bilyash, "here are the ground rules. First, we're a middle-aged couple, and 'Billy' and grey hair don't go together. So from now on I'm Bill and you're Lina. All right?"

"As long as Lina gets an eclair, it's fine by me," she told him.

"Second, if Poochie starts barking while we're in there, or if either one of us gets a bad feeling for any reason whatsoever, we drop everything and head for the exit immediately, with or without your pastry. I don't want a repetition of what happened at Mom and Pop's Place."

"Agreed," she replied without hesitation.

Now for the big one. He made his expression as stern as possible and told her, "Third, we leave the gun in the car. We're in rural Ontario. All waving a weapon can accomplish out here is to get us noticed and remembered by the locals. And the last thing we want to do is leave a trail for the assassin to follow once he's recovered enough to come after us again."

She snapped him a mock salute. "Yes, *sir*. We be cool then. No heat."

Humour was one way to deal with danger. Bilyash had done it himself on occasion. Still, perhaps the only reason Angie was able to joke about their current situation was that he had decided to keep her in the dark about just how perilous it was. He could reverse that decision, tell her all about the cult that *he'd* been born into, but he'd seen how honesty had served Maury in the past, and Bilyash had no desire to put himself through that kind of pain. Only one truth mattered to him right now—he needed Angie and she needed him. And he would do whatever it took, tell whatever lies were necessary, to keep her with him.

"What's our code word?" she asked. "In case something goes wrong."

"We don't need one. Just give me a look and say, 'We have to leave.'"

"All right, then. Is there a fourth rule? Or can we go inside now?"

Premonition was already stirring in his mind, but if a French pastry was the price of peace for the rest of the trip, then he was willing to tempt fate and get it for her.

La Pâtisserie was a bakery with display cases on one side and a row of three small wooden tables on the other, providing seating for ten beneath a mural of Parisian landmarks. A young woman wrapped in a white bib apron large enough to fit someone twice her size stood behind the counter, watching expectantly as Bill and Lina stepped through the door.

Bilyash paused just inside the threshold and scanned the room. A tall, thin man, also clad in an apron, sat at the rearmost table, next to a depiction of the Eiffel Tower. Sipping something from a mug, he was engrossed in transferring information from a ledger book into a notebook computer. At the middle table, Notre Dame

Cathedral looked down on two more men wearing heavy cotton work clothes and playing cards around a carafe of coffee and a small plate with half a muffin on it. None of these men had looked up or paid the slightest attention to the new arrivals. This was good, Bilyash thought. And the vacant table was the one nearest the door, affording a quick exit if necessary.

"What can I get for you?" chirped the girl.

"You know what I want," Angie murmured to him, and went to plop herself down under the Arc de Triomphe.

The symbolism wasn't lost on him. Bilyash walked over to the counter, pulling out his wallet as he placed their order: "Two chocolate eclairs, please, and a cup of Lady Grey tea—"

"—to go," Angie's voice cut in, sounding higher-pitched than usual.

Surprised, he turned and saw a chilling tableau. Angie sat stiff and motionless in her chair, her tightly clasped hands resting in her lap, her expression tense beneath the makeup. And the two card players, both large and muscled and looking about twenty years younger than "Bill", had paused their game and were now turned in their seats, silently watching her with a familiar thirst in their eyes.

Bilyash cursed himself for thoughtlessness. He should have realized something like this might happen. All Yeng assassins possessed altered essence, but not all the Yeng on Earth were assassins.

The men at that table were Yeng wearing human shapes, and it didn't matter how long ago they had fed, or whether they'd already targeted the bakery owner and his assistant, both of whom were apparently oblivious to the scene being acted out before them. Just as Maury and Shred had done in the back seat of the Volkswagen, these Yeng had caught the scent of Angie's overflowing essence. Now, as then, it had triggered a primal urge. Unlike Maury and Shred, however, they were strangers, with no reason to control themselves in his presence.

Angie hadn't been able to see what Bilyash had noticed in the rear-view mirror of his car. This time was different. She was pinned to her seat by the hungry gaze of two pairs of eyes, and was probably imagining the worst a pair of human males could do to her. She had no idea how much worse the worst could turn out to be.

Not yet, anyway, he amended. But she would. Angie was sharp. She would figure it out and have questions for him, tough ones, and he would have to come up with satisfying answers or risk losing her. But first things first.

Bilyash stepped over to stand beside her chair. When both Yeng were looking at him instead of her, he hardened his features and said in a menacingly quiet voice, "Gentlemen, is there some reason you're staring at my companion?" Then, just for good measure, he showed them his Nash'terel eyes.

Their human eyes widened briefly in response. One of the men sat back slightly, acknowledging Bilyash's prior claim to the prey, but the other leaned forward and pointed out, "There's enough for three."

Bilyash glanced over at the baker's helper, who had wrapped the eclairs in waxed paper and was in the process of slipping them into a white paper bag. She halted, frowning uncertainly at what she'd just heard. Choosing to believe that they'd been talking about pastry. "You want only two eclairs, right?"

He nearly laughed. Ignorance was such bliss!

"That's right. And you can forget about the tea." He pulled a ten dollar bill from his wallet, slid the wallet back into his pants pocket, then cupped his hand around Angie's elbow and urged her to her feet. As she stood up, so did the two men, both glaring at him now.

"There's enough," the second man—the alpha, evidently—repeated in a voice like gravel tumbling down a chute.

Bilyash drew and expelled a deliberate breath. He hadn't wanted to resort to this, but there seemed no other way to get Angie out the door without bloodshed. "Yes, enough for one Nash'terel," he hissed fiercely, his eyes trained like lasers on the alpha male's face. "Think carefully about what you do next."

Bilyash was a lover, not a fighter. He thought for a second about the gun they'd left in the car. That had been a mistake, perhaps a fatal one. If either of these two males decided to call his bluff, Bill and Lina would have to make a desperate dash for safety.

Reluctantly, the two men broke eye contact, sank back onto their chairs and resumed playing cards. The bakery owner still hadn't looked up from his ledger books. The girl behind the counter stood watching uneasily as Bilyash dropped the money in front of her, picked up the bag of eclairs, said tersely, "Keep the change," and, with a hand firmly clamped on Angie's arm, backed them both out the door of *La Pâtisserie*.

The girl and her boss were probably doomed now that the Yengs' thirst had been aroused. Bilyash didn't care. Angie was safe, and that was all that mattered to him.

For the next half hour he drove in silence, with Angie sitting like a crash test dummy beside him and Poochie sound asleep in the back seat. Bilyash let his mind wander back over the events of the past twenty-four hours, flinching each time it tripped over something that didn't add up. Or that added up too neatly.

The Nash'terel weren't religious, but most of them believed in what the humans would call probability. Bilyash had grown up with a mythology in which the universe had been set in motion at the beginning of time by an unfathomable intelligence who'd then left it to run in order to see what, if anything, would develop. It was a gamble, like life itself, and the mission of every sentient being was to beat the odds and survive.

Fair enough. However, Bilyash was having difficulty shaking the feeling that in his case, something had skewed those odds, resulting in a whole series of strange coincidences. The fact that Cora's body had been discovered hours before it would have been on any other day of the week. Meeting Angie just before he had to go on the run from assassins, then learning about her past connection to Maury's archrival. And what about the scene in the bakery shop just now? What were the chances of their encountering a pair of Yeng on the hunt, in an obscure corner of Nowhere, Ontario?

Either the universe had begun taking sides in the struggle between the Yeng and the Nash'terel, or—

"I'm sorry, Billy." Angie's weary voice blew that thought right off its rails. "If I hadn't made such a big deal out of pastry, we never would have gone in there. Maybe I *am* a liability."

"Wrong place, wrong time," he assured her. "It happens. Fortunately, those men weren't assassins. They were just a couple of thugs who saw grey hair and thought we'd be easy targets for a robbery."

She uttered a mirthless laugh. "For robbery? Don't lie to me. I saw the look in their eyes, like hungry wolves sizing up a deer. And I think they saw the same thing in your eyes as well."

Something shifted in the pit of his stomach. "Oh?"

"'There's enough for three.' That's what he said. Please, tell me it didn't mean what it sounded like."

He had a good idea what she was probably imagining. Bilyash paused, carefully picking his words. "If you're thinking what I think you're thinking," he began, "then no, that's not what it meant." After a beat, he added, "But even if it were, I swear to you, Angie, I wouldn't have let them lay a finger on you."

Her eyes were boring into the side of his head again. "I know you wouldn't. And you didn't. You stepped right up and shut them down, with a word. 'Nash'terel.' It scared them. I could see it on their faces. What's a Nash'terel? And how did you know that they would be frightened by it? William Ash, I want to know what the hell is going on with you, and I want to know it now!"

From the instant the word had left his lips in the bakery, he'd realized that this moment would come. He just hadn't expected it to hit him this fast and this hard.

When he could once more trust his voice, he said, "We're about an hour away from the cabin. I'll answer one question now, and the rest when we get there. Deal?"

She thought for a moment. "Deal. So what exactly is a Nash'terel?"

The tight feeling in his gut relaxed a little. This one he was prepared for. "In the culture I come from, the Nash'terel are a group of beings with tremendous powers. 'Kill at a touch' powers. They keep to themselves, associating with ordinary folk as little as possible, and for good reason. But they do come out into the world sometimes, just to remind people that the Nash'terel are real and that they still exist."

She threw him a skeptical look. "And grown adults actually believe this?"

"What's important is that the two men in the bakery did," he pointed out.

"Yes, and that leads me to another question—"

"Nope. Just one. That's the deal."

"You said you'd only *answer* one question. You didn't say I couldn't ask more than one."

He slumped his shoulders, pretending defeat. "All right," he conceded. "You've got me. Ask away."

She had a lot of questions, tough ones, posed between bites of a chocolate eclair. By the time it was gone and the Buick had passed the sign welcoming them to the cottage community on the shore of Georgian Bay, he still wasn't sure how to give her a safe answer to any one of them.

Chapter Eleven

———◆———

It had been nearly fifty years since the last time Bilyash had stayed at Maury's cabin. He remembered it as a small wooden structure with cedar half-round siding, sitting at the end of a long and narrow path that ran off the main road into the middle of a forest. The entrance to Maury's property was hardly noticeable unless you knew where it was and were specifically watching for it. Only Maury and Bilyash knew how to find it. That was the way Maury had liked it back then.

Evidently, things had changed since the 1960s. Now the entrance was marked by two slender posts, one bearing a six-digit street number, the other a standard metal mail box. And there was a gate across the path, a waist-high chain link barrier secured by a padlock and displaying a red hexagonal sign at its midpoint: TRESPASSERS WILL BE EATEN.

Bilyash pulled off the road in front of the gate and sat for a moment, thoughtfully fingering Maury's keys. They were the same ones he'd used to unlock the cabin all those years earlier, and the gate was a new addition. Maury would have given him an extra key if he'd needed it, so maybe this was an old lock.

Beside him, Angie and Poochie stirred and yawned in unison.

"Are we there?" she murmured sleepily.

"Almost," he replied. Keeping in mind Maury's penchant for setting traps, Bilyash stepped carefully over the spongy ground and inspected the keyhole in the base of the lock. He was pleased to discover that he'd been right: the hole was the same shape as one of the keys on Maury's chain. Bilyash wasted no more time. He opened the gate, swung it wide to admit the Buick, then closed and locked it again behind them.

The path was broader than he remembered, and a good deal less bumpy, but it was just as unpaved. And it was shorter. A scant fifty metres into the forest, it opened out into an illuminated clearing containing a large wooden structure that reminded Bilyash of a golf course clubhouse. This building was surrounded by smaller ones identical in shape and appearance to Maury's original cabin. Bilyash could see lights on inside the main house, and two people silhouetted against the curtains of a room on the first floor. As he brought the car to a halt, keeping the engine running just in case, the porch light came on as well.

Angie was now fully awake and upright in her seat. "What do you think?" she whispered tautly.

In truth, Bilyash wasn't sure what to think. Maury would never knowingly send him into danger. But Maury might not have set foot on this property for a decade or more, and a lot had clearly changed up here.

Poochie had caught the vibe in the car. He was standing on Angie's lap, his ears pointed forward, staring intently through the driver's side window.

Then the porch door opened and a rather large man came out,

smiling and waving at them as he strode toward the car. "Mr. and Mrs. Jones!" he called out heartily. "Doctor de Maur told us to expect you."

Bilyash shot a sideways glance at the Chihuahua. Poochie remained standing and silently attentive. Not quite ready to let his own guard down either, Bilyash cracked the window open just enough for a conversation.

"You know who we are?" he demanded.

"Yes, sir. Doctor de Maur said you would be in disguise, but he was quite specific about your dog. I'm Stan Dillinger, the general manager and head trainer. As instructed, we've made sure the cabin is fully stocked and the generator is topped up and running, and no one from the outside will be allowed past this point for the duration of your stay. To discourage unauthorized visitors, we have a staff of twelve, all brown belt or higher in a variety of martial arts. And may I say, it's an honour for us to be entrusted with the privacy of celebrities of your magnitude at our sports training camp."

Poochie sat back down, looking as smug as if he'd just won an Oscar and confirming what Bilyash suspected: this man was a human. Knowing Maury, however, at least some of his staff were probably Nash'terel. That was good reason for Angie, at least, to avoid contact with them.

"We were told that you already have a key to the cabin...?"

"That's correct," Bilyash replied.

Dillinger continued, "Then all you have to do is pick up the original trail behind this building and follow it to its end. If there's anything you need, anything at all, use the intercom to contact the main office and one of us will procure it for you and deliver it to your door."

Angie leaned over and piped up, "Are there any women on your staff, Mr. Dillinger? In case I run out of—well, you know."

"There's my wife and our two grown daughters. One of them is always on site."

Struck by a sudden thought, Bilyash added, "And when we're walking the dog?"

"This is old growth forest, standing thick pretty much all the way to the beach. Stay under the canopy and you can't be seen from the air or the water," Dillinger assured him.

And that explained the box of security devices in the trunk of the car, reflected Bilyash. Maury knew there was nothing in place to block an attack from the direction of the bay, so he'd given them an early warning system, with some assembly required. (Of *course* there was. Whatever condition the cabin might be in, Bilyash clearly had the rest of the night's work ahead of him to finish making it safe.)

"I think we're all set, then," he said. He closed the window and waited for Dillinger to step away, then put the car in gear and steered it around the side of the main building.

The rest of the trail was exactly as Bilyash remembered it, and so was the cabin—a dark and silent box tightly wrapped in forest. Many years earlier, he had stolen a car, not realizing that it belonged to one of the First. The outraged Yeng had vowed bloody vengeance, prompting Maury to spirit his wayward apprentice out of the city and deposit him here for safekeeping until a settlement could be negotiated.

This hideaway had been more than a safe-house back then—it had been a safe, invisible from all directions, its very existence a guarded secret. Now it was part of a sports training complex. The cabin was still a private place, protected by an elite corps of fighters who discouraged "unauthorized visitors", but no longer really secure.

Had it ever been? And could anywhere above ground be considered completely secure in this age of infrared satellite imaging? Maury was a realist. Perhaps that was why he'd traded secrecy for muscle.

Never underestimate the ability of a trained assassin to find you... and be prepared to move the moment he does, Bilyash added grimly.

He backed the Buick up beside the cabin and killed the engine. Immediately, the blackness of night dropped over them like a blanket.

"Well," said Angie with forced brightness as Poochie muttered and fidgeted in her arms, "it's certainly secluded."

Wordlessly, Bilyash stepped out of the car and shifted to his Nash'terel eyes. The sooner he got everything inside and shut the rest of the world out, the better they would all feel. Moving purposefully in the darkness, he found and opened the lock on the front door, then set about unloading the car, keeping Angie and Poochie for last. Still holding the dog, she let him lead her into the cabin. She felt her way blindly to a chair and sank onto it with an exhalation of relief, as Bilyash closed and locked the door and then toggled the light switch beside it.

Three lamps came on simultaneously, revealing a sitting area that was small and tidy and furnished in a style that would have been considered country chic half a century earlier. For Bilyash, it was like stepping through a time portal, fifty years into the past. Nothing had changed. Nothing appeared even to have been moved. Tartan cushions in autumn colours covered the seats of a wicker sofa and its two matching armchairs. A braided rug in those same warm tones hugged the hardwood floor in front of the fieldstone fireplace. A nest of walnut side tables seemed to cower in one corner. And a finely sculpted black wrought iron screen stood on the hearth, flanked by a set of andirons and a woven-wire kindling basket.

Turning in her seat to gaze admiringly around the room, Angie declared, "It's beautiful, Billy. Cozy and warm, just what a cottage should be. I'll bet you loved coming up here with your uncle when you were younger."

"I—couldn't really appreciate it back then," he managed to reply.

To his relief, she dropped the subject.

Maury had given them one hell of a cover story, and the Dillingers had apparently gone all out to make their celebrity guests feel welcome and comfortable. Not only was the cabin immaculate, a feat Bilyash would normally have considered nothing short of a miracle, but vases of fragrant lilac had been placed in every room. The fridge and freezer were packed, and there was enough dry and tinned dog food in the cabinets to open up a store.

"No beef *bourguignon*, Poochie. Sorry," said Bilyash.

The Chihuahua gave him a discontented grumble.

When they got to the bedroom, Angie gushed over the antique headboard and dresser. Then she yawned. This was what Bilyash had been waiting for. "Why don't you take the bed?" he suggested.

"But where will you sleep?"

"The sofa is plenty comfortable. And I'm not really tired yet."

"You're unbelievable," she declared. "It's past midnight, you've been driving for hours, and after the day we've had—!"

"I'm wired," he told her. "It'll be a while before I'm able to doze off. But you need your rest, so take it."

"But Poochie—"

"Give me the dog. I'll walk him while you remove your makeup. Carefully. When I come back, I'll tuck you in."

Her eyes widened momentarily. Then her lips curved in a smile that kindled a delicious warmth in his groin. "You'll tuck me in?" she teased.

"Or wear you out. Whichever works best," he replied with an answering grin.

"And who will you be? Billy Ash? Or dirty old Bill?"

He leaned in and whispered, "Maybe neither one."

Fairly shimmying with excitement, she dropped Poochie into his arms. "Out of here, both of you! I need to make myself young again."

The leash was flimsy and already showing wear, but it didn't really matter. Poochie was apparently scared of the dark. The Chihuahua kept close, nearly tripping Bilyash up a couple of times as he hiked through the woods, wearing his Nash'terel eyes. In about fifteen minutes, they were standing where forest met beach, looking out at a full moon suspended over a luminescent expanse of water.

Bilyash remembered an old story, told to him centuries earlier by a mother whose face he could barely recall:

Long ago, when the world was new, the moon fell in love with the sea. He wanted to reach out and touch her, but the distance between them was too great. So he turned his love into pale silver light and poured it over her, hoping that she would notice it and love him back. Unfortunately, he had a rival who was much closer to the sea—the wind. Each time the moon painted the sea silver, the wind would swoop in and kiss her, making her tremble with passion, and that would shatter the moon's light into a million pieces. Brokenhearted, the moon couldn't bear to watch the happy couple beneath him, so he turned his back. After a while, he wondered whether the sea had tired of the fickle wind, and the moon turned back around to woo her once more. But again the wind claimed the sea's love for himself, and the moon hid his face and wept. Over and over the moon returned, and each time the jealous wind saw to it that the moon's love was spurned. To this day, the moon keeps turning his face away and then back, hopelessly in love, as he tries and fails to win the sea's affection.

The first time he'd heard this tale, Bilyash had scoffed at the idea of any being falling in love with someone so distant and so different from himself. Now, however, he was beginning to think that he might have been wrong, that such a feeling might not be impossible after all.

Bilyash sat down on a fallen log. When Poochie growled an inquiry and pressed, shivering, against his leg, he reached down a hand and began massaging the sweet spot behind the dog's ears. But the Nash'terel's thoughts were elsewhere.

Somehow, he'd crossed the line between needing Angelina Fiore's essence and simply wanting her company. When he looked at her, it was no longer thirst he felt—it was happiness. Nothing in his upbringing had prepared him to experience such emotions, and why would it? To the Nash'terel, humans were a source of nourishment, just like the cattle they bred and slaughtered for their own consumption. Even Maury, who deplored the brutal murders committed by Yeng hunters on innocent human prey, still considered their essence to be food. So did Bilyash, come to that. He was relying on Angie's essence to keep him strong. As long as she continued to believe that his kisses and lovemaking sprang from a human desire for physical intimacy with her, she would share that essence willingly. And if she ever discovered what he truly was, what he'd actually been taking from her and why...?

She'd said it herself: she'd had nightmares about encountering creatures that looked like him.

Bilyash let out a long breath and got to his feet. Halfway to the cabin, he grasped a low-hanging branch with both hands, consciously relaxed his mind, and reshaped his face into the one belonging to Billy Ash. The Chihuahua stood by, head tilted curiously, not uttering so much as a squeak the whole time.

Angie had evidently been much more tired than she thought. By the time Bilyash returned and stood peering into the bedroom, she lay sound asleep atop the sheets. Her face was scrubbed of makeup, and she was wearing only her bra and a pair of neon green panties that clashed with the red and purple splashes on her ribs and upper thighs.

Rolling a car and hanging upside-down from a seat belt tended to have that effect, he reflected. She'd been right earlier—it had been quite a day, for both of them.

"No magical mojo for *you* tonight," he murmured, pulling the bedspread up to cover her and feeling strangely as though he'd just dodged a bullet.

Bilyash closed the bedroom door and turned his attention to the large cardboard box sitting in the middle of the living room floor. As quietly as he could, he removed everything that wasn't a phone or a gun and laid the pieces out on the kitchen table. These were the components of the alarm system and the parabolic microphone. They were grey market at best, stolen goods at worst. In any case, they came without instructions for assembling or testing them. It would probably take him the rest of the night to figure them out. And then what?

When Maury had purchased all this security gear, he had to have known that most of it would be useless. The parabolic microphone wouldn't work as an early warning device, not until the assassin was in a direct line of sight, and that wouldn't happen until he was already close enough to the cabin to see them if they tried to leave it. And the alarm system was meant to give them time to call for help. How? There weren't any cell towers in this area. But even if there were, who would they contact? The police? Fat chance.

They could use the intercom to summon Dillinger's Dozen, Bilyash supposed, except that cutting the land lines was the first thing any competent assassin would do.

What had Maldemaur been thinking? Without a phone signal, there was no way to call him and find out. And since Maury was effectively "in the wind" now that Shred had burned down his house after killing the assassin...

The thought struck him like a physical blow.

Shred burned down the house, and Maury posed as the neighbour and made the 9-1-1 call!

Bilyash wanted to head-smack himself. He'd been thinking like a human when he should have been thinking like a Nash'terel. To a Nash'terel, the world was made up of traps, offering three choices: you could avoid the trap, fall into the trap, or reset the trap to catch someone else. So, Maury might have sent him into a trap, but he had also equipped Bilyash to turn it to his own advantage.

With a growing sense of excitement, Bilyash spilled the remaining contents of the cardboard carton out onto the table and took a quick inventory: two tasers, the untraceable phone, a pistol, and a box of ammunition. The parabolic microphone, he now realized, would come in handy after all. In addition, he had half a dozen pressure-sensitive pads and all that wiring from the alarm system, and the generator with its tank nearly full of highly explosive propane, sitting in the crawl space directly beneath the cabin. Crude but effective, as Maury would say. Yes, this would work.

Bilyash checked his watch. It was half past one. By now the third assassin had probably picked up their trail. If so, he would attack them at night, possibly even within the next few hours. That didn't give them much time to prepare.

He hated to do it, but Bilyash went to the bedroom to wake Angie up.

She turned at his touch and arched her back, apparently still in the middle of a very pleasant dream. "Mmm... Are we there yet?" she sighed sleepily.

His heart clenched. "No, Angie, we're not. Wake up, please. I need your help."

Her eyes snapped open then and searched his face. "Billy? What's wrong?"

"There's no time to explain. We're leaving. I have to booby-trap the cabin and you have to pack. Now."

He half-expected her to pepper him with questions, but she simply dragged herself up to a sitting position on the bed. Of course. She'd gone through this exercise at least once before, with her parents.

"Hand me my clothes," she said.

One hour later, the cardboard box was full of food and was sitting at the door, waiting to be carried out to the car, along with the makeup kit, Angie's suitcase, and Bilyash's travel bag. Angie's bloodied clothing had been removed from its hiding place in the lid of the kit and now lay crackling and curling in the blaze he'd set in the fireplace. And Bilyash was putting the finishing touches to a propane-fuelled bomb and hoping he remembered correctly what he'd seen Macy's pyrotechnics coordinator do on the set of *Zombies Take Graceland*.

He'd converted the burner phone into a detonator. With luck, this explosion would be triggered when Bilyash punched the 'send' button on his own device. Traps were a Nash'terel specialty, one that Maury had turned into an art form. Bombs, not so much. Not on purpose, anyway.

Then again, Bilyash reasoned, car theft was something that *he* had turned into an art form. The kid knew cars, as Armin liked to say, and what was a car but a bomb on wheels?

This would work, he told himself. Give the cabin four tires and a tranny and he could drive it straight into the Dillingers' back yard.

"Ready when you are, C.B.," quipped Angie's voice just behind him.

He took a final look around, reassuring himself that pressure pads, trip wires, and tasers were all in place. "Kill the lights," he instructed her.

Poochie was already in the Buick, acting as their lookout, as Bilyash escorted her from the cabin to the driver's side door and ushered her into the front seat. "If he starts barking before I've finished loading up the car, you drive straight to the sports camp and raise the alarm," he told her, handing her the keys. "Then you go. No heroics, you hear me? Get as far away from here as you can, as fast as you can."

"I don't want to lose you, Billy!" There were tears in her voice.

"You won't," he assured her. "Just do as I say and we'll get out of this. If we're separated, I'll find you."

No longer caring whether she saw his Nash'terel eyes, Bilyash hastened to fill the trunk, moving purposefully between the whispering light of the fireplace and the still and utter blackness outside. When he was done, he closed the trunk lid quietly, then knocked twice on the rear window, signalling to Angie to move the Buick a safe distance away down the trail.

Bilyash hoped she would obey his instruction to remain inside the vehicle, and not only because she was his getaway driver. He didn't want her to see the monster that he might be forced to become, both literally and figuratively, in order to eliminate this particular threat to their safety.

Pressing a hand to his jacket pocket containing the loaded pistol, Bilyash ducked into the trees and made his way to the spot where he'd earlier set up the parabolic microphone. It was trained on the cabin. The trap had been set and both he and the bomb were armed. There was nothing to do now but wait.

Chapter Twelve

———— ♦ ————

A window was sliding open. Yes, there it was, picked up by the mic, the scraping sound of a sash being raised. Bilyash tensed, willing the intruder to keep going, to climb through the window, to trip the concealed wire...

He turned his Nash'terel eyes on the flickering yellow rectangle to the right of the cabin door. The living room window was the only one on this side of the building. Even as the fire in the hearth burned down, it still gave off a glow, bright enough to silhouette anyone moving around inside. That was assuming he'd managed to sidestep the trap Bilyash had set just beneath the bay-side window. Unlikely, he told himself. The assassin might be clever, but Bilyash had learned about traps from Maury, and Maury was a genius.

A syllable of surprise was cut off by the hard sizzle of a taser. Good! The intruder had tripped a wire. But was it the one in the bedroom, or the one in the living room? And what if the taser hadn't completely stunned him? Human technology wasn't infallible. One of the leads might have missed its mark. Or the assassin might be resistant to the electric shock. If he wasn't fully incapacitated when the bomb went off, he could very well escape to continue the hunt, and that was something Bilyash simply refused to allow.

In an instant, he was on his feet and racing toward the front door of the cabin, his jaw clenched, pulling the gun out of his pocket as he ran.

He paused on the threshold, just long enough to confirm with a sweeping glance that the living room was empty. In three strides he was in the bedroom, standing over a man who lay gasping on his back on the floor, his limbs feebly twitching. The two wires of the taser were embedded in his chest. Bilyash stuffed the gun back into his pocket, then knelt beside his prey, surveying him with Nash'terel eyes. The man's face contorted with fear. In fact, he stank with it, but this wasn't the smell of a Yeng with altered essence. It reminded him more of the toilet odour that had filled Cora's bedroom when she'd died.

For the first time, Bilyash felt a twinge of doubt. He leaned over, covered the prey's lips with his own, and drew out a mouthful of essence to taste.

His instincts were correct. What he'd caught was not a Yeng. It was a decoy. Disgusted, Bilyash spat out the essence, then demanded softly, "Who hired you, human?"

Nothing. The man was speechless with terror, still trembling even though the taser's charge had been exhausted.

"Say goodnight, Gracie," Bilyash muttered. He reached out a hand to cup the crown of his victim's head, pausing when he heard the stutter of the second taser going off in the other room.

The assassin had arrived. There was no time now for finesse. Bilyash stood up, took out his gun, and shot the human once in the heart. Then he eased himself past the bedroom door and into the living room, crouched low and prepared to fire.

One step into the room, he felt a mortal chill envelop his body. The taser was silent. The space in front of the window was empty. And there was a faint, familiar aroma drifting on the air. Belatedly, Bilyash recalled what had happened when Angie had shot the Yeng under the bridge, and he cursed himself for thinking like a human again. It had been a mistake to stay inside the cabin. The moment he heard the second taser discharge, he should have jumped out the bedroom window, raced to pick up the phone he'd left beside the parabolic mic, and detonated the bomb.

"*Esstateh'mesh ma Nash'terel!*" hissed a voice somewhere to his left. A split second later, something came down hard on both his wrists, deadening his hands and sending the weapon skittering across the floor. Bilyash dived after it, finding cover behind one of the chairs. The pain in his wrists was deepening by the second, but he'd managed to scoop up the pistol. Once he'd regained some feeling in his hands, he might even be able to shoot it.

Bilyash peered carefully around the side of the chair. The assassin was nowhere in sight. He was most probably hiding behind the breakfast counter in the kitchen. Not very assassin-like of him, Bilyash mused. So perhaps he hadn't just tripped the taser trap to draw his target out of the bedroom. Perhaps he'd been caught, however briefly, and had suffered some effects from the electric shock after all.

"All we want is to be left alone," Bilyash called out. "Come on, think about this. I'm no threat to anyone on the other side. I don't even want to go there. I *like* it here."

"The Nash'terel are an abomination!" The Yeng's voice sounded strange, almost as though it were travelling through water. But its point of origin was definitely in the kitchen. "The emperor will not rest until you are wiped out of existence!"

Thinking furiously, Bilyash glanced at the cabin door, just a few feet to his left and behind him. He flexed his fingers. His wrists still hurt enough to make him wince, but he could once more make a fist. He could hold the gun and pull the trigger. If he fired a few discouraging rounds over the back of the chair first, he could probably escape out that door. Just one problem: the assassin would be right on his heels. Fighting for his life in the woods had never been part of Bilyash's plan. He'd counted on the taser trap to give him an advantage, but the Yeng had turned it to his own use, and now they were both caught.

Bilyash swallowed hard. Somehow he had to find a way to keep the assassin inside the cabin *and* detonate the bomb, but without losing his own life in the process. He was damned if he was going to do this killer's job for him.

"Come out, come out, Billy Ash," the assassin taunted him in a burbling singsong voice. "That is what you're calling yourself these days, isn't it? Not too imaginative, I must say, although it certainly saved us some work tracking you down. You and I both know that you're as good as dead, so you may as well show yourself and get it over with. Accept the inevitable and I can promise you a swift and painless end. But if you stretch things out, testing my patience—"

At that moment, a storm of canine hysteria exploded outside. The Chihuahua had never made such a racket, not even at Mom and Pop's Place. Poochie had evidently caught the scent of the monster that had ripped his master apart on the sound stage. He was barking and howling at the top of his lungs; and from the sound of it, he was also determinedly scratching his way right through the cabin door. The continuous noise was beyond irritating. If it was making Bilyash uncomfortable, he could only imagine the effect it was having on the assassin. After all, this was the sort of commotion that attracted witnesses.

You go, Poochie!

Smiling thinly, Bilyash brought the muzzle of the gun up and rested it on the arm of the chair, pointed in the direction of the kitchen. Ten seconds passed, then twenty, as the dog continued to rage fiercely outside the door.

Finally, the Yeng rushed out from behind the kitchen counter, giving Bilyash his first clear look at what had earlier knocked the gun out of his hands. It was one of a number of long sinewy tentacles. Some served as legs, but there were at least half a dozen with stingers on the ends that now cracked like whips in every direction as the assassin scuttled with surprising speed across the floor of the living room. The Yeng had shapeshifted into a creature roughly the height of a cow. Its body was a translucent orange sac that swayed and jiggled like freshly-set gelatin, occasionally revealing blurry hints of internal organs suspended inside. At the centre of this mass, Bilyash saw what appeared to be flashes of lightning.

No way could he allow this grotesque jellyfish to leave the cabin. And good luck getting a bullet far enough into it to do any real damage.

Then he noticed the eye.

Set atop the sac, a large orb swivelled at the end of a short ropy stalk. It fairly begged to be shot at. Knowing how quickly a Yeng could heal, however, Bilyash aimed carefully for the stalk, and the optic neural conduit that had to be running through it. If by some miracle his bullet eluded those flailing tentacles and actually managed to hit the target, one of two things would probably happen. Either the assassin would be forced to revert to his true

Yeng shape, a process that would preoccupy his brain for at least half a minute, or the blinded monster would begin wildly thrashing around the cabin, making Bilyash's situation ten times more dangerous.

Admittedly, it was far from an ideal way to buy himself some time, but it was the best thing that came to mind.

Bilyash fired once. The shot snipped the stinging end off one of the whip-tentacles, stopping the Yeng in its tracks. The bulbous body shuddered as the eye swung around to search for him. Not good. A wicker chair didn't offer much protection against something like this.

He aimed and fired again, this time at the eye. It swallowed his bullet, literally without blinking. As the monster turned to charge his position, Bilyash cursed and fired a third time, at the largest available target, and got his miracle. This shot found the base of the eyestalk, blowing a hole right through it.

The monster let out a screech that reminded Bilyash of the Volkswagen sliding on its roof down the embankment. Then the jellyfish attacked, its flailing tentacles pounding everything they could reach. Within seconds, the chair and the sofa had been reduced to kindling. Fortunately, Bilyash had already flung himself across the hearth and pressed himself into the corner with the nesting tables.

About to jump out the living room window to his right, he felt something drop into the pit of his stomach as he realized how little time he'd bought himself. The eyestalk was healing as he watched. In a moment the jellyfish would be able to see again. *Damn!*

Then he noticed the taser still taped to the wall beneath the windowsill. The device hadn't fully discharged. And he had a talent. The effect wouldn't be as strong as the one produced by the subway tracks. Luckily, it didn't have to be.

Bilyash released the magazine from his pistol into the palm of his hand and imbued both magazine and bullets with his essence. There were eight shots left. Eight small, powerful magnets that he would shoot into the monster's body. Somewhere in that quivering sac was a brain that operated on electrical impulses. He just needed to randomize them for thirty seconds—no, a minute. He wouldn't be able to retrieve his essence, and it would take him longer to get to the parabolic mic if he was running on weakened legs.

Bilyash shoved the magazine back into the pistol, took a step into the room, and shot the monster rapidly eight times in what appeared to be its rear end. It emitted another roar and began to turn around, its tentacles snapping viciously.

His heart nearly stopped. Perhaps it had been a mistake to use up all his bullets. Then, abruptly, the jellyfish halted in place. Its legs were shaking and it seemed to be having a problem controlling its whips.

Bilyash pulled the taser off the wall, reset the gun, and fired it into the monster's unprotected side. Both leads found their marks, igniting an electrical storm inside the gelatinous body. As the Yeng twitched and writhed, Bilyash dived head first out the living room window, remembering to tuck and roll before he hit the ground. He got to his feet as quickly as he could and hurried around the side of the cabin. Poochie was still scratching at the front door, barking hoarsely. Bilyash bent and scooped him up, then made for the spot in the trees where the mic and the phone were waiting.

Angie was waiting as well, with an expression of horror stamped on her features. It sent something sharp and cold right through him. But there was no time for that. Thrusting the dog into her arms, he snatched up the phone and pressed the button.

"Run to the car!" he shouted, pushing her ahead of him.

One second later something hit him hard in the back, slamming him face down onto the dirt path. He heard a scream, felt a searing pain in his shoulder, and had just enough time to hope he wasn't on fire before everything went black.

He heard the voices first. Some louder, some soft, they faded in and out, like snatches of a dream.

"...He's a tough guy, all right, and damned lucky. You both were..."

"...heard that he did all his own stunts, but I didn't believe it until now..."

"...I swear that propane tank was inspected by the county only last week..."

"...grateful there won't be a lawsuit over this. Dr. de Maur won't be pleased..."

"...still burning? Well, at least it's under control and we won't have to involve..."

"...Are you sure? 'Cause I can have an ambulance here in twenty minutes..."

"...don't think any of us want to be at the hub of a media frenzy, least of all you, Mr. Dillinger..."

That was Angie, being firm and rational. So she was all right. Good.

Gradually, Bilyash became aware that he was lying on his stomach, surrounded by the smell and feel of crisp, clean sheets. He was tired. Very tired. His left shoulder held a deep, throbbing ache. And his belly was burning. Healing took energy, and he'd invested a lot of his essence in those bullets. If he didn't feed soon...

"Welcome back," said a male voice behind him. "And I do

damned good work, if I say so myself."

"Are you the one who fixed me up?" Bilyash asked. "How bad is it? And how long have I been out?"

"It's been about eight hours. You were caught in the open when the blast wave hit. The back of your body was chopped up pretty badly by flying debris. Luckily for you, it was red hot debris. It cauterized a lot of your wounds, kept you from losing too much blood. I got to you first and made it look like minor stuff, knowing that a few hours later, that was all it would actually be. But that's not the work I was talking about."

Intrigued, Bilyash turned his upper body, grunting against the pain in his shoulder, and saw a familiar figure standing at the foot of his bed.

"Roy Rogers?" he said incredulously.

The man grinned. "It's Pyotren. I'm Armin's cousin. And I'm impressed that you recognize this face. Not many remember the old western movies these days." Pyotren sat down in the chair beside the bed and continued in an undertone, "Your car is in good shape. It took some shrapnel, but that was mainly in the trunk lid and rear bumper. Nothing inside the car was damaged as far as I can tell. If you're worried about your phone, there's no need. I found it on the ground beside you and slipped it into one of your suitcases, since the clothes you were wearing were pretty much destroyed.

"Like Armin, I can shape-shift things and other beings at a distance. So, as long as you're here, I'll keep you and your companion looking like the big shots Dillinger believes you are. When you're ready to leave, I'll escort you to the gate and reset you both back to normal. And I'll put a permanent fix on the car to keep it looking like new and change your licence plate number, just in case."

Dealing with Armin had made Bilyash cautious. Mentally counting the cash in his wallet, he asked, "What's the fee?"

Pyotren gave him a wounded look. "We share blood and a *hainbek*, Armin and I, but we have totally different values. I'm already being paid for this, so there's no charge to you." After a beat, he continued, "You look hungry, my friend. What can I get you?"

"For now, all I need is Angie."

Nodding sagely, Pyotren rose from the chair. "I thought as much. She's standing just outside. I'll make sure you aren't disturbed."

Struck by a sudden thought, Bilyash said, "Wait. About Angie—you must have noticed. Are any of the other staff—?"

"—Nash'terel? A few. But none of them have come into contact with her, and none of them will. You're in Dillinger's residence now, and I'm the only staff member who's allowed inside, on Maldemaur's express orders." He resumed moving toward the door.

"What about the cabin? Do any of them go in there?"

Pyotren paused in mid-step and turned to face him. "We're going to find a body, aren't we?" he said with dread in his voice.

"Two of them," Bilyash replied. "One human, one Yeng." *The assassin and his decoy,* he wanted to add, but stopped himself, not knowing how much Maury had shared with this "employee".

"Well, all of our staff are accounted for, and the celebrity couple you're impersonating can't have died in the explosion since they're still alive and well and travelling all over the world." Pyotren's expression hardened. "Dillinger mustn't become suspicious—Maldemaur was very specific about that. Leave it with me. I'll think of something before the fire burns itself out. Meanwhile, I believe your... *friend* is impatient to join you."

He opened the door and called into the hallway, "He's awake."

A woman rushed into the room, wearing a huge, much-photographed smile. One look at Bilyash's face, however, and the smile wilted as her joy dissolved into confusion. She halted near the foot of the bed, staring at him with eyes wide as traffic lights. He knew exactly how she felt. Clearly, she hadn't seen herself in a mirror lately.

"Billy?" she whispered. "What did you—? When—?"

Behind her, Pyotren was struggling to keep a straight face. He left the room, closing the door behind him.

Bilyash sighed. "It's me, Angie."

"But you look exactly like—"

"I know. And you look like his wife."

Her not-Angie face fell. "I do? But that's impossible!"

"Trust me," he told her wearily. "Right now, you're her identical twin."

Angie's gaze darted around the room, apparently seeking a looking glass. When she couldn't find one, she carefully groped her face.

"It's not a makeup job," she declared, her voice rising in pitch. "Oh. My. God. How can this be happening?"

Meanwhile, Bilyash's chest was heating up. If he and Angie didn't lock lips within the next few minutes, Pyotren would have more to clean up than just a couple of burnt bodies pulled from the ashes of a secluded cabin. Gritting his teeth against the pain in his shoulder, Bilyash rolled himself onto his side and up onto his good elbow.

"It's not a trick, I swear. We're safe here. I'll explain everything to you later. For now, come over here and let me kiss you."

Why was she staring at him like that? Wasn't it every human female's dream to be kissed by this particular male?

"Angie, please! I need to hold you."

"Not until you tell me what the hell is going on," she shot back.

His chest felt as though it was on fire. "There's no time! I—!"

He closed his eyes and went limp, pretending to lose consciousness, then began counting the seconds.

One.

"Billy? Oh, no...!"

Two.

Her voice was growing nearer. "Billy, I'm so sorry! I didn't realize—"

Three.

She was beside him, leaning over him. He could feel her breath misting his cheek. "Don't you die on me, Billy Ash! I *need* you!"

Not as much as I need you right now, he thought.

Quickly snaking his right arm around her waist, he pulled her down on top of him. Then he twined his fingers in her hair, planted his lips over hers, and drank until her struggles ceased and the ice of her essence had quenched the flames of his thirst.

Chapter Thirteen

———— ◆ ————

"I owe you an explanation."

Nada. The wall of silence in the car was impenetrable. A glance in the rear-view mirror showed him Poochie, curled up on the back seat with his paws protecting his head. Animals could sense when a bad storm was coming.

Bilyash returned his attention to the darkened road ahead of them. He'd known from the moment Angie woke up that she was royally pissed. She'd been gracious and pleasant at the dinner table to the Dillingers and to "Pete", the name Pyotren had given her while introducing himself. For Bilyash she'd had nothing all evening but dagger looks, even as she made a point of lavishing affection on the bewildered Chihuahua.

When it was time to leave, Billy hadn't been certain at first that she would even let him get behind the wheel. It was her car, after all. Then Pyotren had made a point of handing him the car keys, and she'd evidently decided it wasn't worth arguing over. (Fuming over was a different matter. Angie had been a sullen presence in the front seat of the Buick since they'd left the sports camp some thirty minutes earlier.)

True to his promise, Pyotren had ridden with them to the gate and had undone all his modifications to their human appearances before letting them drive off into the night. Being returned to his Billy Ash shape by another Nash'terel hadn't felt comfortable—it was akin to being swarmed by a mob of crazed acupuncturists—but at least the residual itching had been mild and short-lived.

Angie had felt the same thing. When she'd asked Pyotren what the hell he was doing to her, he'd grinned and replied, "I'm a sorcerer, and I'm freeing you from a spell." Then he'd winked at Bilyash.

Unfortunately, his joke had only deepened her scowl.

Bilyash tried again. "Angie, we need to talk about what happened back there."

"Stat ay mesh maw Nash'terel," she muttered. Just hearing those Yeng words spoken by a human seemed to drop the air temperature in the car by several degrees. Angie turned in her seat and demanded, "What language is that, and what does it mean, Billy?"

So, she'd overheard the scene inside the cabin, and the moment of truth had arrived, on a wave of something strangely like relief. He'd been hoping to have this discussion with her in a warm, intimate moment when she was feeling a lot more mellow and, hopefully, forgiving. On the other hand, travelling at ninety kilometres per hour along a deserted country road at night wasn't a bad second option. It meant she would think twice before trying to jump out of the car—which was a distinct possibility given what he now had to tell her. At this point, he decided, he would take whatever small advantage the universe permitted him.

Bilyash swallowed hard. "It's my parents' first language, and it means 'ignoble death to all Nash'terel'."

Angie sat back slowly, digesting his words. "He said the emperor wouldn't rest until the Nash'terel were wiped out. Is that why you're here? To escape a genocide?"

"I'm afraid so," he replied. "And if there are assassins hunting Maury and me, it means the war on our kind has followed us here."

"Why didn't you tell me this before, instead of cooking up a story about beings with godlike powers, able to kill at a touch?"

It would be so easy to slide a lie into the conversation right now, to plead reticence due to fear or shame, or the simple fact that they'd only known each other for a couple of days. She'd practically invited him to do it. But there had been that incident in the pastry shop earlier, and Bilyash knew from experience that loose ends always came back with sharp teeth for biting. And besides, there was a part of him that *wanted* her to know the truth about him, to know it and to like him in spite of it. After less than seventy-two hours. It made no sense, but there it was, tying him in knots and turning his life in unexpected directions. And the only way to face it was head-on.

So, he mentally crossed his fingers and said quietly, "Because it wasn't just a story. Where my parents were born, the word *nash'terel* means 'secluded ones', and what I told you about them—about *us*, and having special powers... It was the truth. I'm Nash'terel."

A moment of silence, then, "So, can you?" When he didn't reply immediately, she went on, "Kill at a touch, I mean. Or was that just a figure of speech?"

"Yes."

She frowned. "Yes to what?" she demanded, a tremor trickling into her voice. "Yes, you can kill at a touch? Or yes, it's just a figure of speech?"

She was asking for truth but looking for reassurance. He decided to give her both. "Angie, anyone—even you—can kill at a touch, given the proper training and equipment. Are my Nash'terel abilities potentially lethal? Of course. But that's not the way I was taught to use them. "

"And that's why I pass out every time you kiss me? Because it involves touching and that activates your special powers?"

He stole a sideways glance, wondering whether she was teasing him, and was surprised to meet her steady, sombre gaze.

"Or is it because you're consciously using them on me?" she wondered aloud, putting an edge on each word that made him feel as though the ground had suddenly shifted under his feet.

"Well, yes, sort of," he mumbled reluctantly.

Perhaps full disclosure wasn't such a great idea right now.

"Your magical mojo." She crooned it as though it were a mantra.

Angie passed out when he kissed her because it wasn't really a kiss—it was a feeding. But what would happen, he wondered, if he did simply kiss her? Could he restrain himself from taking her essence? Was a Nash'terel even capable of such a thing?

There was only one way to find out, and no better time to try.

Bilyash pulled over to the side of the road and turned off the Buick's engine.

"What are you doing?" she asked warily.

He turned in his seat to face her. "It's an experiment. When I kiss you, you pass out. Let's see what happens when you kiss me."

She stared at him for several seconds, then giggled. "Seriously?"

"Seriously," he said, leaning toward her. "I'm ready for my close-up, C.B. And... action."

She leaned in, tilted her face, and lightly touched her lips to his, once, then again. Now her hands came up, cupping the curve of his jaw, her thumbs tracing the outline of his ears as he felt his lips being urged apart and her small pink tongue coming inside to play with his own…

…and a slow heat in his groin that had nothing to do with feeding, but everything to do with appetite. Its warmth flowed into his legs and rose like a tide in his belly. It danced all over his skin, making him want to laugh and cry at the same time. In his entire life, Bilyash could not remember ever feeling this way.

When Angie pulled back, her eyes searching his face held a glow, and he realized two things: first, she must have unconsciously transferred some of her essence—it was the only possible reason for her kiss to affect him like this; and second, he wanted more.

"So, what inferences are you prepared to draw from this experiment, Mr. Ash?" she murmured suggestively.

He licked his lips, not wanting to waste even a molecule of her, and replied, "I believe you've got some magical mojo of your own, Ms. Fiore."

She sat back and squared her shoulders. "Just some?" she challenged him.

"Well, we'll need more than one sample in order to validate our results and arrive at a meaningful conclusion."

Angie slid a little closer to him. "What you're saying is that the experiment isn't over yet."

He leaned in, lips at the ready. "What I mean," he told her, "is that it's barely begun."

An inquiring mutter froze them both in place.

Bilyash turned his head and saw Poochie sitting on his haunches in the middle of the back seat, wearing a huge doggy grin. The Chihuahua was enjoying the show. All he needed now was popcorn.

Nash'terel and human looked at each other and said in unison, "We need to get a room."

On the outskirts of Stayner they found what they were looking for, a small, unprepossessing motel with a rear parking area. This time, Bilyash grew a beard before checking them in. It was a change he could make and reverse quickly while walking between the car and the motel office.

Once Poochie was safely settled in the washroom of their unit, the experiment could continue. Working quickly, Angie pulled out the bowls and filled one with dry dog food, then handed them both off to Bilyash while she unmade the bed. He filled the second bowl with water from the washroom tap, splashing some of it onto the floor in his haste. Annoyed with himself, he mopped up the puddle with the only fluffy towel large enough to be Poochie's bed as the Chihuahua looked on reproachfully. This was ridiculous, Bilyash scolded himself. He was behaving as though he were about to experience sex for the very first time.

Then he thought about it and realized that in a way, he was. He'd had physical relations with many human females over the centuries, but always as a predator, a taker of essence. Tonight, he was going to abandon that role and lie with a woman capable of giving her essence to him freely, as a partner, not a prey. And if the kiss in the car was any indication, the final result was going to be nothing less than spectacular.

Bilyash stepped out of the washroom and found Angie standing in her underwear on the other side of the bed. The sight of her gave him pause. Humans didn't heal as quickly as his kind did, not even an essence factory like Angie; and after the car crash and then the explosion, her body was dappled with bruises in a whole rainbow of colours. If they gave her any discomfort, she had evidently decided not to let it stop her. One eyebrow raised, she scanned Bilyash up and down and remarked, "A little overdressed, aren't you?"

Wordlessly, he proceeded to shrug off, pull off, and step out of his clothing, watching for her reaction as each piece in turn dropped to the floor. With every approving nod of her head, every impressed widening of her eyes, he could feel his confidence grow—among other things. Bilyash knew he was well-endowed, and with good reason: Billy Ash's body had been modelled on that of a porn star. Where else would a shape-shifting film student look for that kind of inspiration?

When there was nothing left to take off, he cleared his throat loudly to bring her gaze back up to his face. "Now who's overdressed?" he chided gently.

Angie's cheeks flushed. "You know, I always have a problem with these last two items. Maybe you'd like to help me with them...?"

He liked it very much. Angelina Fiore's body—bruises, scratches and all—was delightfully curved, soft and firm in all the right places, and suggestively warm to the touch.

Like a filled essence receptacle, Maury's voice inside his head reminded him.

No, Bilyash rebutted it, *Angie is much, much more than that.*

It took every bit of self-control he possessed, but he had decided to let Angie have her way with him, and that was what he did. She didn't make it easy for him. Her kisses in bed were even more arousing than the one in the car. And kisses led to embraces, and caresses, and a whole catalogue of delightful explorations, culminating in a series of climaxes, each more powerful than the one before, and one final, heart-pausing, moon-circling incandescence of pleasure that left them both gasping for breath. At last, Nash'terel and human lay awake side by side on the bedsheets. Angie looked tired but satisfied; Bilyash felt fortified and utterly invincible.

"So, what do you think of my magical mojo now, Mr. Ash?" she inquired softly.

"I think we're very well matched, Ms. Fiore. In fact, I would call this experiment an unqualified success," he replied, adding as he became aware of a persistent scratching sound coming from the washroom, "And I think we'd better let the dog out of there before he destroys the door."

The next morning, while Angie was showering and as Poochie watched with interest from his improvised bed near the motel room door, Bilyash dug through their suitcases and located his personal phone. Pyotren had sealed it inside a plastic freezer bag, more for the sake of the clothing around it than to protect the phone itself, Bilyash guessed. Found on the ground beside his unconscious body? Not likely. Judging from the amount of gouging and dirt on the casing, it had probably ended up half buried beneath him. At least it was still in one piece. With luck, it might even be usable.

Bilyash punched up Maury's number and was pleasantly surprised when the call actually went through.

Voicemail cut in after the third ring. "You've got a hell of a nerve bothering me at this hour," it snarled. "If it's important, leave a message. If it's not, go fuck yourself."

Bilyash waited patiently for the beep, then said, "It's me, with good news. Two down, one to go. But the cabin is demolished and we're on the road. Call me back and tell me where we can meet."

Less than a minute after he'd broken the connection, the phone buzzed.

"Billy, listen carefully." It was Shred, speaking in a low, taut voice, as though to avoid being overheard. It set off alarms in Bilyash's brain. "A meeting is out of the question. There is no safe place for you, kid, not anymore."

"What are you talking about? There's just one assassin left. If we act together we can—"

"You really think it stops there?" he hissed. "You think three is all the assassins we're allowed, and once they're dealt with we can relax? I guarantee you, there are more, sniffing us out as we speak."

Casting a furtive glance at the washroom door, Bilyash lowered his voice. "That's all the more reason for us to combine forces. You split us up to divide the assassins as well, and it worked. Now that I've disposed of the one that was after me, I can help you protect Maury. And you're pushing me away? Why?"

"Because the best way for you to protect Maury right now is to stay away from him. Don't you get it? Those assassins were after you, kid. The ones who came to Maury's place even asked for you by name. And the moment we realized what they were and what they intended to do, we attacked them."

"You attacked *them*?" he echoed faintly.

"Yes, to protect you. And when we offered to go on protecting you, you blew us off. But, hey, that was your decision and we respected it. After all, you are nearly an adult now."

Ignoring the dig, Bilyash continued, "I still don't understand how they could have known about me."

"It's not just about you, Billy. They're targeting all the

Earthborn. The Yeng may be blood-sucking shapeshifters, but they don't have our Nash'terel talents. Elders like Maury and me are a lot harder for them to kill than young ones just beginning their training. Another one was murdered early this morning, along with her parents. They were taken by surprise while on a camping trip. The park rangers are blaming a bear, but every Nash'terel knows different."

Bilyash sank slowly onto the edge of the bed, feeling a sudden chill as pieces of earlier conversations replayed in his memory: Assassins always researched their targets. They evidently knew who all the Earthborn were and exactly where to find them. The ambush on the movie set was ample proof of that. Maury had talked the Council of the First into protecting both of them, but Bilyash had refused to give up his independence in exchange for safety... and Gershred couldn't be in two places at the same time.

So, if Bilyash was the assassins' primary target and Maury could take care of himself, why was this bodyguard protecting Maldemaur and cutting Billy loose?

The answer came to him almost immediately.

"You work for the Council of the First, and they're only interested in Maldemaur," he said dully.

"You said it yourself, kid. He's the one who can turn a toaster into an essence receptacle, so even though you're the primary target, he has to be my main concern. Those are my orders. It's nothing personal."

"For you, maybe. Can I talk to him, at least?"

"Not now, I'm afraid. He's busy. Maybe later."

"So, I'm completely on my own," he said, the flat finality of the words feeling like a smack of cold water on his face.

Unexpectedly, Gershred chuckled. "Not exactly."

"What's that supposed to mean?"

"Maldemaur has a plan."

"Really? What kind of plan?" he said warily.

A pause, then, "I guess it's safe to tell you. We're going to British Columbia to find Vincaspera and put an end to her genetic experiment."

For several seconds, Bilyash was at a loss for words. When he found them again, they came out sounding half an octave higher than normal. "He's going to hunt down Vincaspera? And do what?"

"Whatever it takes. Discredit her, blackmail her, buy her out, or maybe all of the above. In any case, her little cult is going to be history."

Bilyash could see how that would ruin any scheme the First might have hatched to capitalize on the Nash'terel's work. It would also remove a major irritant from Maury's life. But... "How does destroying Middlevale help *me*, exactly?"

"That's where it is? Good to know. And to answer your question, assuming you can keep yourself and the female human alive long enough, it leaves you with a powerful bargaining chip. You can use it to negotiate your own deal with the Council."

Still hearing the pattering of the shower behind the closed bathroom door, Bilyash hissed angrily into the phone, "Trade Angie to the First in exchange for my own safety? Not a chance!"

There was an audible sigh from the other end of the call. "Then think of *her* safety. There are a lot of Yeng in this world, and a fair number of Nash'terel. They thirst for the kind of essence that practically pours out of her, and you can't be constantly at her side to hold them off. The First will understand how unique she is. They won't let anyone get close enough to her to fall into a feeding lust."

"No, they'll just imprison her and milk her for her essence until she's old and all used up. Then they'll butcher and eat her as if she were an ordinary food animal."

"Isn't that what she is? And isn't that what *you're* doing?" Gershred pointed out.

It was a good thing they weren't in the same room. Bilyash flexed the fingers of his free hand. They were aching to reach right through the phone and give Maury's bodyguard a cerebral hemorrhage.

"Think about this, Billy. Maldemaur knows that he can eventually negotiate a truce with the First because of how highly they value his knowledge and his *hainbek*, so he's willing to risk their wrath by taking out the purest and richest source of essence on the planet. That leaves the way clear for you to strike your own deal with the Council. They get the last remaining essence factory in return for an iron-clad guarantee to protect you from any future assassination attempts. It's a win-win."

"Except for Angie."

"She's a human," said Shred, with an infuriating shrug in his voice.

"She's *my* human," Bilyash bristled, "and I decide what happens to her, not you, and not Maury. This may be too radical a concept for you to grasp, but her life is important to me."

There was a moment of leaden silence at the other end of the call.

"So he was right," Shred finally said. "You're in love with her. How long do these creatures live, Billy? A century? And that's if they're lucky, which most of them aren't. If we lived only a century, they'd be dead in less than two years. It's no time at all—a blink!"

"Exactly. And that's all the more reason for the two of you to stay out of this. How I spend the next blink of my life is my business."

"Not if it leaves you angry and grieving for a thousand years afterward. Believe it or not, kid, it's your feelings that we're concerned about. Tell me, does she know what you are? What you *really* are? Have you shown her your Nash'terel shape? Your skull ridges? Your scales? Because, trust me, it doesn't take much to send a human screaming into the night."

"Wait a minute. You met me only a couple of days ago. How do you know I've got scales? And don't tell me it was a lucky guess."

"It wasn't," Shred snapped. "I was at your birthing, *ristim*. Maury and I go back a lot longer than anyone suspects, including the Council of the First. Now, listen to the voice of experience. Once a human female has seen our true form, it doesn't matter what we do or say after that, or even how she might have felt about us before. All she sees when she looks at us from that point onward is a monster. Whatever relationship you may think you've got with this girl, it's not real."

Bilyash felt the casing of the phone give under the pressure of his fingers. Forcing his lungs to accept a calming breath, he consciously relaxed his grip. "Angie's not like other human females."

"Okay," Shred conceded, "I guess you need to learn some things the hard way. Good luck, kid. You're going to need it."

With that, the line went dead, and Bilyash abruptly realized that he was slouching, his shoulders bowing as the phone had done, under the weight of the decision he now had to make. He hated to admit it, but Shred was right about one thing: a relationship—if that was what they had—needed to be based on trust. That meant sharing confidences. Angie had already told him the truth about her past. Now it was his turn to do the same.

"You look like someone who's just received bad news."

At the sound of Angie's voice behind him, Bilyash squared his shoulders and got to his feet, pinning on a neutral expression as he turned to face her. She was standing in the doorway to the washroom, wrapped in a pale green terrycloth robe and rubbing her hair dry with one of the motel's hand towels. Freshly scrubbed and exuding essence, her skin fairly glowed. For just a moment, his resolve faltered. Then he reminded himself: a lie of omission was still a lie.

"Not bad, exactly," he told her. "I just spoke to Gershred. He and Maury are travelling. They may already have left the province. We'll have to deal with the third assassin on our own."

She shot him a pained look. "And you don't think that's bad? Taking out the second one nearly got us both killed."

"I have a plan," he assured her. "But first…" He swallowed hard, mentally crossing his fingers. "I've been trying to think of the best way to tell you…"

She tilted her head. "…that you're an alien?"

Bilyash felt gut-punched. "How long have you—?"

"'Who hired you, human?'" she recited. "When you raced into the cabin, I ran over to the microphone and put on the headset. I couldn't bear the thought of simply sitting outside and wondering what was happening to you in there. When I heard you say that, I put it together with all the bizarre events of the past few days, and everything just fell into place. Macy's murder, Aunt Minerva, the incident in the pastry shop—it finally made sense." Tossing the towel into the bathroom, Angie plopped herself down on the chair by the foot of the bed, locked eyes with Bilyash, and informed him in a no-nonsense voice, "After all we've been through so far, I think I've earned the right to know. Are you ready to tell me the whole truth, Billy?"

Yes, he was. And it occurred to him, as he sat down opposite her, that what he had feared most about showing her his true self was not that she would "run screaming into the night" as Shred had put it, but rather the very real possibility that Bilyash might have to break the promise he'd made himself earlier and use force or even violence to prevent her from leaving him, not just for his own sake, but for her safety as well.

Simply contemplating that was enough to put knots in his stomach. They tightened painfully when he realized that having to guard a prisoner would also hinder his chances of eluding the next assassination attempt. That would put them both at increased risk. And if they were still on their own, he might have no choice but to implement Maury's odious plan. Another promise would be broken.

No, he decided. There was enough trouble on his plate without borrowing more. Staring deeply into Angie's large brown eyes, he told her, "My people are shapeshifters."

She gazed thoughtfully back at him. "That explains all your quick changes. And what I saw under the bridge after the car crash...? That wasn't instant hypnosis, was it?"

Reluctantly, he replied, "No. The shock of his injuries made it impossible for him to maintain his human shape. What you saw was his true form."

She went quiet for a moment, digesting what must have been a stunning revelation. Then she asked, in a hard, dull voice that twisted the knots of dread already planted in his midsection, "Is it your true form too, when you're not pretending to be Billy Ash?"

He reached out and took her hands, half-expecting her to pull away, immensely relieved when she didn't. "My people come in a variety of colours and sizes, just as yours do. So, to answer your question, no, my true form is quite different from what you saw earlier. And although my outward appearance might change from time to time and I have pretended to be various other humans in the past, Billy Ash is not an act. It's who I am."

Visibly gathering her courage, she said, "It's who you are on the inside. Now I want to see what you are on the outside. Show me what you really look like, Billy. Please."

Bilyash could think of any number of reasons not to grant her request, but all he could say was, "Why?"

"Because I have a gun, and if you are injured and forced to resume your alien shape, and I don't recognize that shape, never having seen it before, I will shoot you." She leaned back in her chair with a *Don't be so dense!* look on her face.

"I believe you would," he remarked.

"Damn straight, I would!"

"All right, then. One Nash'terel, coming up."

He stepped into the washroom and carefully closed the door. To a Nash'terel, full body transformation was the most private of bodily functions, primarily because it was a time of greatest vulnerability to attack. Even just the knowledge that someone was waiting impatiently in the next room had been known to interfere with the process. The humans had a name for this: performance anxiety. Bilyash had no idea whether he would be successful. All he could do was try and, if he failed, hope that Angie would understand.

Rapidly, he undressed. Then, standing in front of the basin, he gripped its sides with both hands, closed his eyes, and gave his body permission to resume its true form. As expected, his mind resisted the change, sensing the presence of another. An other. A human.

A beloved, he thought, in that instant realizing that just forming the word was a surrender to something more powerful than all the *hainbeka* of all the Nash'terel still living. As if in confirmation, the barriers in his mind came down. Skin, flesh and bones flowed together, reshaping themselves effortlessly into a broad-shouldered, narrow-hipped being with finger-like skull ridges, long, muscled legs, and iridescent scales shielding his face and armouring his shoulders.

For several minutes, he stood staring at his image in the mirror, caught between hopeful anticipation and sheer icy terror. How would Angie see him? He was afraid to find out. What had he been thinking, to imagine for one second that showing her a monster from her nightmares could end well for either of them? She was probably sitting there with her pistol trained on the doorway, just in case.

"Are you all right in there?" she called through the door.

He willed his stomach to stop churning. As long as she didn't scream and faint, or try to shoot him full of holes, then maybe this relationship had a chance. Maybe. There was only one way to find out.

Tentatively, he stepped out of the bathroom, stark naked.

Angie was standing at the foot of the bed, her eyes wider than he'd ever seen them before. She opened and closed her mouth several times without saying a word.

For a long moment they just stared silently at each other, Bilyash strung tight, waiting for some kind of explosion from across the room, Angie frozen in apparent disbelief.

"Well?" he finally ventured. "What do you think?"

Taking this as his cue, Poochie trotted over to Bilyash and gave his feet and ankles a thorough sniffing. Then, his examination completed, the Chihuahua sat back on his haunches, looking from Bilyash's face to Angie's as if to say, *It's him. What are you waiting for?*

Angie walked up to him and stopped. Wordlessly, she scanned him up and down before reaching a tentative hand toward the scales on his shoulder. Her touch was gentle, as though she somehow sensed how fragile he was at that moment. Her fingers moved to his face, caressing his cheek as her gaze roved across his forehead, taking in his scales, his eyes, his ridges. Igniting a familiar warmth in his groin. Making him desperate to take her in his arms and at the same time paralyzing him with fear. When their eyes finally met, hers were shining with unshed tears.

"Oh, Billy," she murmured softly. "Why did you hide this from me?"

In a heartbeat, her robe was lying on the floor and she was leading him by the hand toward the bed. And for the next couple of hours, Bilyash and Angie's essences mingled freely as they both discovered what it was like to be loved by an alien.

Chapter Fourteen

———◆———

"Tell me about your world," Angie begged him.

Gazing at the ceiling, he replied thoughtfully, "I was born on Earth, but I've heard stories about an ancestral home world, with land masses, lakes and rivers, hills and valleys, flora and fauna. There were small towns and large cities, not so very different from the ones on this planet. That was a long time ago, though, long before my people migrated to RinYeng. For all we know, the original world of the Nash'terel might not even exist anymore."

She propped herself up on an elbow beside him in bed. "Was your Uncle Maury born here too?"

"No. He was born on RinYeng and came to Earth with the other Nash'terel when the genocide began."

"RinYeng." She said the name as though she were deciding whether she liked the taste of it. "So, that's where the assassins are from?" He nodded. "And where the Nash'terel escaped from?" He nodded again and she went on, "And those two men we ran into in the pastry shop—are they from RinYeng as well?"

"Ye-es."

"But they're not assassins, and they aren't Nash'terel. There's a third group?"

"They're just Yeng," he confirmed.

Her cheeks dimpled. "Yeng from RinYeng, obviously. The 'ordinary folk' that the kill-at-a-touch Nash'terel try to avoid?"

Involuntarily, he smiled back.

Her expression became suddenly speculative. "Ever since I can remember, I've dreamed about escaping from Earth and visiting other worlds. I think it would be fascinating to go back through whatever wormhole or portal or device your people used and see RinYeng with my own eyes."

He stared at her for a moment, his mind a blur. She'd handled the sight of his true shape unexpectedly well, but they were still building trust. Revealing that members of his species regarded hers as a lower life form—a food source, in fact—would not be a good idea right now. So, he told her instead, "It's a beautiful dream, Angie, but I'm afraid it will have to stay that way, at least as far as RinYeng is concerned. Neither one of us would last five minutes there. Trust me, we're both much safer on this side of the rift."

"Safer," she repeated incredulously. "Really? With trained assassins chasing us all over the province?"

"Actually, they're chasing me," he corrected her. "And that plan I was mentioning earlier...?"

She shot him a reproving look. "Don't even think of dropping me off somewhere while you go into danger alone," she warned. "We're a team, Billy. For the first time in years I feel protected by someone I care about, and who cares about me, and I'm damned if I'll let some alien assassin take that away."

"Actually, I was just going to ask how you feel about roughing it in the bush."

Her indignation evaporated, leaving a look of mild apprehension on her face. "Oh. How rough is roughing it? Just so I know what to expect. Is it outdoor everything?"

"Not that rough. There's a cabin, with a wood stove, and a stream nearby to provide drinking water. Maury and I built this place to be a hideout. Last time I was there, it was surrounded by Crown land and the nearest neighbours were at least fifty kilometres away."

"And how long ago was that?"

He paused to think. How long ago had he slipped that human skin as a prank into the bundle of furs Maury was delivering to the Hudson's Bay Company trading post? A hundred and fifty years? Furious, Maury had erected a wall of light around the cabin, imprisoning him inside it for nine years as punishment, letting him out only to bathe and expel waste. After that, Bilyash had sworn never to return to the spot, and until now, he'd kept his vow. However, he knew that Maury had continued to maintain the cabin, visiting it every decade or so, razing and rebuilding it whenever time and weather rendered it uninhabitable.

"I'm only asking because if it's been more than twenty or thirty years, the area around your property might have been developed. I think you should prepare yourself for that possibility, Billy."

Reluctantly, he had to agree. However, if she was right and the cabin was no longer isolated, they would have to push farther north, where it really would be outdoor everything. And something told him Angelina Fiore wasn't an outdoor everything kind of girl.

"How long do you think we'll be there?" she asked, breaking into his thoughts.

As long as it takes me to become as hard to kill as Maury is, he replied silently. Aloud, he told her, "Hard to say. At a minimum, we should probably plan for a month. The food in the car won't be enough. We'll have to make several stops for supplies. And there'll be predators in the woods, so we definitely need to get a better leash for Poochie."

The dog had been unusually quiet. Bilyash leaned over the side of the bed and saw him snoozing near the door. Then a low-pitched burring sound cut through the silence, startling the Chihuahua awake. It was Bilyash's phone, vibrating. He reached across Angie and plucked it off the night stand.

The number displayed on the screen was not one he recognized. With a quizzical glance at Angie, Bilyash answered the call.

"Billy, this is Pyotren," said the anxious-sounding voice at the other end. "Are you two on the road?"

"Never mind that. How did you get this number?"

"I cloned your phone yesterday while you were unconscious. Listen, two men arrived at the sports camp this morning, claiming to be cops and looking for you, by name: William R. Ash. They got really interested when Dillinger mentioned the propane explosion. They even poked around in the ruins for a while. Dillinger had a freaky fit when they found a gun and the remains of two bodies, and he instantly spilled his guts about the 'celebrity couple' and their dog who were staying in the cabin. I'm afraid your cover is blown, my friend. If you're not already a moving target, you need to become one, ay-sap."

Bilyash swung himself out of bed, cursing inwardly. In all the excitement of trapping and eliminating the second assassin, he'd forgotten about the police. There were a lot of them, too. It was a good thing Maury was halfway across the country, unaware of just how badly his apprentice had messed up.

For starters, the Toronto police were bound to want to question him and Angie regarding Cora's death. Then there were the York Township police, twice. They had taken his and Angie's statements at the scene of Macy's murder, specifically instructing them both not to leave town—good luck with *that*—and they would also have been called to the scene of a serious car crash involving a certain yellow Volkswagen Super Beetle, scant hours later. Finally, there was the matter of the two dead bodies at the sports camp. Whose jurisdiction was that? Simcoe Regional Police? The Provincial Police? Or, since an alien was involved, a federal force like the Mounties?

Not too bright, kid, said Shred's voice inside his head, and Bilyash wanted to kick himself.

The voice was right. Law enforcement agencies shared information electronically these days, thus amplifying the nastiness that always ensued when a Nash'terel came to the attention of the local constabulary. Worse, it made connecting the dots on a series of police blotters a relatively simple matter for a trained, shape-shifting assassin on the hunt.

Except... there had been two visitors. An assassin and his dupe? Or was another triad now on his trail? Whoever they were, they were getting dangerously close. Bilyash shuddered, feeling as though something with icy claws had just walked down his back.

It's not paranoia if somebody's actually trying to kill you, Maury's voice chimed in.

"You said they *claimed* to be cops," Bilyash pointed out. "What did they do that made you suspicious?"

"Little things. I mean, they showed us badges, and they questioned everyone and dropped samples of stuff into plastic baggies, just like the cops on television," said Pyotren, a note of urgency creeping into his voice. "But when they took bits of the corpses for testing instead of calling for the coroner's wagon, that just struck me as wrong. And you should have seen their reaction when the remains of a phone turned up inside the cabin. I figure it will take an hour at most for those fake cops to determine that you didn't die in the explosion, and another hour before they're back at Dillinger's to try to pick up your trail again. I've put on your face and am headed east, making myself as memorable as I can without getting arrested. With luck I can decoy them and buy you some extra time."

Bilyash shook his head in wonderment. "Maldemaur can't possibly be paying you to do all this for me."

"You'd be amazed what Maldemaur can do. One more thing: whether or not they take the bait, they found you once by using your phone and they can do it again. You need to dispose of it as soon as possible. Smash it with a rock and throw it into a dumpster, or toss it out the car window into a hedge. Just get rid of it."

"I will," he promised, and broke the connection, adding silently, *after I've done one last thing*.

Shred picked up on the first ring. "You okay, kid?"

"So far. Put Maury on the line."

"Can't. He drank some bad essence and is currently *harruffing* his guts out."

"Just give him a message for me, then. Tell him I'm going to Plan Omega. Then get rid of his personal phone. Throw it off the train, or the bus, or however you're travelling. Tell him someone used mine to track me down, so there may be a tracer on his as well."

Shred uttered a low whistle. "Will do, kid. Good luck."

Bilyash ended the call and turned toward Angie, who had heard every word and was now sitting up in bed, staring gravely at him. "Get dressed and pack everything up," he instructed her. "We're leaving."

Then he dropped the phone onto the floor, stomped the device under one of his big scaly feet, and kicked the broken pieces under the bed.

Half an hour later, Bilyash stepped out of the washroom wearing an identity he'd hoped never to have to assume again, not because it was shocking or ugly, but because it was so bland and generic as to be utterly forgettable. He'd perfected it during one of the humans' many wars, blurring his features and adopting an indeterminate colour for his hair and eyes to ensure that no one could be certain enough of his appearance to describe or identify him. Then, it had allowed him to pass easily through both friendly and enemy lines. Now, it was reserved for times when he needed to move around unnoticed, blending into crowds until he was able to find a safe place to go to ground.

Today was such a time, and this would be his default shape until they reached Maury's cabin near the old logging trail.

Bilyash surveyed the room, noting the two packed suitcases standing at the foot of the bed, as well as his makeup kit, still shoved beneath the broad ledge beside the dresser. There was no sign of Angie or Poochie, or the two food bowls. One of the motel's bath towels was missing as well, so she was probably outside, getting the dog settled in the back seat of the car.

A minute later, the door swung open and Angie entered the room. At the sight of Bilyash's new persona, she did a double-take and nearly tripped over a chair leg.

"Billy?" she ventured, keeping a wary distance.

"He's gone. I'm John Jones. You're Mary Jones."

Bilyash strode to the makeup kit, unlatched the case, and pulled out a blonde wig, styled in a short pageboy, that he'd thought to lift from one of the stations in the makeup trailer at Alpha Dog Studios.

"Wear this," he told her, thrusting the wig into her hand. "And sunglasses, the larger the better, and a headscarf if you have one. And make sure you go to the washroom before we leave. It's at least a ten-hour drive and you won't be getting out of the car."

Hearing that, she shot him a look of disbelief. Nonetheless, she hurried wordlessly into the washroom to don her disguise.

Shortly after leaving the motel, 'John Jones' was cruising along the main street of Collingwood, looking for an angled parking spot on a block containing a scattering of storefronts separated by the branches of three different banks. The building on the corner, a two-storey brick and stone edifice with concrete steps rising to an imposing pillared entrance, had once housed a bank as well, he recalled. There were many examples in this town of century-old architecture, many of them now wearing the colourful facades of various businesses, but Bilyash had a soft spot for that particular building. Like him, it had needed to inspire trust. And so it sat, an unabashed reminder of an earlier, more prosperous time, oozing permanence the way Angie oozed essence—although, during its construction, the other members of the work crew had thought it gave off a different sort of air.

After nosing the Buick into an available slot, Bilyash shut off the engine and turned toward his bewigged passenger.

"Stay here with Poochie," he instructed her. "If he starts barking and I'm nowhere in sight, lock the doors and hunker down. And keep the windows closed. This may take a while."

"Which bank are you going into?" she inquired.

He closed his eyes briefly. "All of them."

This wasn't going to be fun.

Step one of Plan Omega was to acquire a supply of cash by closing one or two of his accounts at each of the major banks before heading north. The smart part of doing it in Collingwood was that all six banks had branches here and all of them were located close together on the same street, thus saving him a considerable amount of travel. The unfortunate part was that each bank knew him as a different person, with a different name and wearing a different shape.

Everything was security-monitored these days. Whether he accessed his funds at an ATM or made an in-person withdrawal, Bilyash knew he would be appearing on-camera. So, since time was of the essence, he would have to shape-shift multiple times in relatively rapid succession, a process that he knew from experience would burn through much of his energy and leave him feeling as though he was wearing all his nerves on the outside of his skin.

Not too bright, kid.

Bilyash began with the bank farthest away from the car. Thankfully, his face was all he had to change to become Randy Pennington, Minerva's great-nephew and heir to her estate. At the second bank, he also had to grow several inches and add some shoulder width to transform himself into Kenneth Smart. After that, he needed to find and avail himself of lockable washrooms as the shape shifts became progressively more demanding. Erwin Schultz was shorter and heavier than Billy Ash. Muriel Nathanson was a ruddy-cheeked woman in her middle years. And so on.

Foreseeing all these disparate identities, Bilyash had made a point of dressing in layers of clothing that he could remove and rearrange to create a different look for each one. (Muriel's was especially problematic, straining credibility along with the seat of his trousers.) However, nothing was going to make the shape-shifting process itself any less painful.

By the time Bilyash returned to the car with nearly twenty-five thousand dollars in his various pockets, John Jones's face felt as though it was trying to peel itself off the front of his skull. As Angie watched, he dropped with a groan into the driver's seat.

"Are you all right?" she asked.

In response, he clapped a hand to the nape of her neck, pulled her toward him, and planted a kiss on her lips. The icy current of essence began to flow immediately. Bilyash drank as much as he dared, ignoring the doggy mutterings emanating from the back seat as Angie went gradually limp in his arms. Then he propped her back into a sitting position and tightened her seat belt, arranging her limbs to make it appear that she was simply dozing. After a final inspection of her wig and sunglasses—and an anxious moment as he checked her pulse—he turned the key in the ignition, mentally plotting his route to the supermarket at the extreme east end of town.

This was step two of Plan Omega: to purchase everything they would need for the next month, but without buying too much at any one place. Another of Collingwood's virtues was that it had four major supermarkets, spaced about two minutes apart by car along a single main thoroughfare. Bilyash intended to visit them all, moving from east to west across town and doing an ordinary week's worth of shopping at each one while Angie slept in the car in the parking lot.

It was going to be a challenge, he realized as he stood with his empty cart in the produce section of Sobey's, eyeing the baked goods and deli counters. Most of the foods he liked were perishable. The artisanal cheeses, the organically grown fruits and vegetables, the mushrooms with multi-syllabic names... and the steak tartare, raw liver and juicy steaks. They all required refrigeration, a luxury he was pretty sure the cabin didn't have. For the next month, it appeared, he would have to content himself with sharing an ordinary, nonperishable human diet with Angie—and other than what he had already seen her eat, he had no idea what her preferences would be.

He also had only a limited time in which to make his purchases.

So, he cruised up and down the aisles, bravely filling his shopping cart with a selection of interesting-looking tins and boxes, things that became food when added to water (or when water was added to them, although he really couldn't see the difference), powdered stuff in pouches, and jars and bottles of clear liquid containing a variety of supposedly edible items, most of which didn't interest him at all, but that he figured there was a fifty-fifty chance Angie might like.

Drawn to the meat counter, he longingly surveyed the various cuts of beef before deciding to splurge on a couple of "BBQ Thick" steaks. After all, he reasoned, the training he now had to do would be intensive. Working his talent up from apprentice level to adept was going to take most of his energy each day, and Angie's essence, though delicious, couldn't supply all his dietary needs.

He wasn't sure what he would do if she insisted on ruining this meat by actually exposing it to fire. He had, however, thought of a way to keep things cold.

At the checkout desk, he was pleasantly surprised to discover that the total charge for his cartful of supplies was no more than three hundred dollars.

His next stop was the Loblaw store, and after that the Metro. At each supermarket, he tried to select no more than one or two of each item so as not to attract attention. Except at the meat counter. Bilyash needed animal protein. Luckily, so did the humans. They even ate organ meats like liver and kidneys, packaging them for sale before displaying them behind the glass doors of refrigerated cabinets.

By the time he'd checked out of the Metro and returned to the car, Poochie was raring to go for a walk and Bilyash had purchased enough raw meat to fill a large picnic cooler. He stopped at the Canadian Tire store to pick one up, along with a case of four dozen chemically activated cold packs and a strong leash that could be extended and retracted with the push of a button. Fortunately, he was able to squeeze everything into the trunk of the Buick before taking the dog on a brisk circuit of the huge parking lot. By the end of his walk, Poochie was yawning, glad to curl up on his towel in the back seat.

As Bilyash pulled into a parking spot in front of the fourth supermarket—Freshco—he glanced at the digital clock on the dashboard and made a face. Step two was taking much longer than he'd anticipated, and the gas gauge was registering less than an eighth of a tank. This would have to be a very quick visit.

Hurriedly, Bilyash got out of the car, pulling a coin out of his pocket to unlock one of the shopping carts lined up just inside the store entrance. Whipping past the produce section, he threw a couple of bags of hamburger buns into the cart (loaded with preservatives, they were sure to last a good long while), then headed past the refrigerated aisle, planning to zigzag his way to the far wall.

At the end of an aisle he found pasta. *Perfect.*

However, just as he was reaching for a bag of fusilli, "*There* you are!" carolled Angie's voice behind him.

Bilyash nearly leaped out of his skin. He'd forgotten how quickly she could recover from being fed upon. At least she hadn't brought the dog inside with her. That would have made them the centre of some very negative attention.

"Let's see how you're doing so far," she said, pawing through the items he'd already picked out. When done, she looked up at him with reproach in her eyes. "Well, the bread is a good choice. But, really, John. Artichoke hearts and pickled herring?"

A woman shopper passing by them smiled knowingly without turning her head.

"We're attracting attention, Mary," he pointed out in a stage whisper.

Angie leaned in and replied in the same low tones, "Better a little attention now than a whole lot later on. Leave the bread, put the rest of this stuff back, and I'll show you how a human shops in these places."

"I happen to *like* artichoke hearts and pickled herring," he informed her.

She scowled at him. "Fine! But you're the one who's going to eat them, not me."

With that, she wrenched the cart around and pushed it stubbornly all the way back to the produce department, not even glancing behind her to see whether he was following.

Half an hour later they were checking out with items Bilyash had overlooked in the three other stores, such as dried fruit, fancy crackers, olive oil, honey, and two identical, manually operated can openers.

"Because if we only get one, it will break within the first couple of days," she'd told him by way of explanation.

"And you know this because...?"

"It's Murphy's Law. If anything can possibly go wrong, it will, at the worst possible time and in the worst possible way. Like what happened to Cora."

Then she gave him a look that brought his neck hairs to attention as the suspicion tiptoed through his mind that Angelina Fiore might already have figured out a good deal more about Cora's death than any human could safely be allowed to know.

Chapter Fifteen

———◆———

By three o'clock, the Buick's tank and Angie's stomach were both full, human and Chihuahua had made final pit stops, and Bilyash was ready for step three of Plan Omega: going to ground in a place where nobody on Earth, whether human or Yeng, would think to look for him—or so he hoped.

Maury was the exception to that, and possibly Shred, because the cabin buried deep in the bush just south of Timmins was Maury's Plan Omega as well.

Bilyash doubled back through Collingwood, headed for Highway 11 northbound. There were clouds rolling in from the west, with rain expected overnight. With luck, it would hold off until the Buick arrived and was unpacked at the cabin.

Displaced by cases of bottled drinks and packages of paper products, Poochie had been moved to the front seat, where he now lay dozing on Angie's lap, stirring restlessly to get her hand moving again each time she stopped stroking his back.

She sat silently gazing out the window for a while. Then, "Why did you put me to sleep just before starting the grocery shopping?"

she asked. "We both know you can kiss me without knocking me out, so that means you did it on purpose. Why?"

He set his jaw, sensing a different kind of storm on the horizon. "It wasn't my choice, Angie. It was necessary."

"Necessary?" A tremor crept into her voice. "What aren't you telling me, Billy? Was there something you didn't want me to see? Something terrible?"

"You've got it wrong. I wasn't trying to protect you from the truth again."

She paused, then resumed speaking in a quiet, resigned voice. "You did it at the sports camp, when you were injured. And when you came back to the car after visiting all those banks, I could tell you weren't feeling well. Cora passed out every time you made love and it took her days to get her strength back. I think I know what you are, Billy. I've probably known all along. I just didn't want to believe it."

"And what could that be? You already know that I'm an alien," he pointed out.

"You're more than that. You're a vampire."

"I'm not a vampire," he protested, then thought about it a moment. "Well, maybe just a little."

She shot him a look. "Being a vampire is like being pregnant, Billy. You either are or you're not. There's no 'just a little'."

"I don't drink human blood." *Although I could, in a pinch.*

"Do I hear the sound of a hair splitting?" she remarked dryly. "It's obvious that you're taking *some*thing from me."

Clearly she had no intention of dropping the subject. In a way, he was glad. It was one of the few lies of omission that still stood between them. "I drink essence."

"Essence?" she echoed, frowning.

"Essence, life force, whatever you want to call it. In addition to eating food, I can draw strength and sustenance directly from other beings. Shape-shifting uses a lot of energy. When I'd concluded my business at the banks, I was exhausted and needed to—"

"Feed," she supplied sharply. "Let's call it what it is. You're an alien parasite, sucking the life out of people."

She'd probably had nightmares about this as well.

Bilyash could feel panic rising in his throat. "No, Angie, I—"

"Don't!" She raised her hand between them as though to push him away. "Don't say another word to me!" And she turned on the radio, raising the volume to a level that effectively discouraged any further attempts at conversation.

For the next hour they drove without speaking, the blaring radio building a wall of noise between them as the air in the car seemed to grow thicker with each kilometre they travelled. Bilyash wondered what was going through her mind, certain that he needed to know but dreading what he might find out. Several times he decided to simply pull off the road and demand that she talk to him. Each time, a glance at her stony expression was enough to make him reconsider.

Then, just when he felt ready to explode from the tension, "And now for the news," said the announcer after a string of ads for everything from milk to mattresses. "An autopsy performed on the body of Cora Dolson, the movie makeup legend who was found dead by her cleaning service in her apartment two days ago, has revealed evidence of a previously unsuspected medical condition. According to a report filed by the Toronto Medical Examiner's office, the cause of death was a burst aortic aneurysm, a weak spot in the wall of a major blood vessel near the heart that eventually gave way, leading to massive internal hemorrhaging. Her death has therefore been ruled 'due to natural causes'."

Angie leaned forward and turned off the radio, then settled back into her seat with a loud sigh... of relief? All at once, Bilyash believed he understood.

"You were afraid it might have been me," he said quietly.

"Wouldn't you have been, if you'd just learned what I did about our relationship?"

He shifted uncomfortably in his seat. "I suppose. And what are you thinking now?"

"I've been going over everything in my mind, all the strange things that have happened over the past couple of days. The pastry shop. The way your uncle and his friend looked at me when they said goodbye. I'm remembering what you said earlier about your powers being potentially lethal, and..."

"And?"

"...and it occurs to me that if you wanted me dead, I'd already be dead."

She was staring at the side of his head again, speaking in a tight, tremulous voice.

"Now I can't help thinking that the only reason you're keeping me alive is so that you can—"

"Stop right there!" he commanded her, swerving the Buick onto the shoulder of the road and slamming on the brakes. Bilyash turned in his seat and showed her his Nash'terel eyes. "I'm not just 'keeping you alive', Angie, I'm protecting you," he said fiercely. "And I'll go on protecting you no matter what, because I care about you, because your life is important to me, and not just as a source of nourishment. The moment we first met, I felt a connection with you, one that I'd never experienced with any human before. It confused me. I didn't even know what to call it. I only knew that I wanted to spend time with you, get to know you better. Did you mean what you said earlier today, when you thought I was going to leave you behind?"

"Every word," she told him, gazing earnestly into his John Jones face.

"Well, I feel the same way about you. I *like* you, Angie. A lot. Now, can we get back on the road, please? I want to arrive at the cabin as soon as possible."

"All right, fine," she replied. "Just don't try to kiss me for a while, okay? I don't think I could handle it."

As if *he* could!

Ten hours and three pit stops later, including a bathroom break for the dog, Bilyash found the entrance to Maury's private road and steered the Buick carefully between the trees, grateful for his Nash'terel night vision. Branches scraped along the roof and windows of the car as it ran a gauntlet of dense overgrowth, following a narrow, curving path a good four hundred metres into the forest. Feral eyes shone in the underbrush—the only disadvantage of arriving so late at night with a trunkload of food and a Chihuahua, Bilyash reflected. They would have to be careful about closing doors behind them as they carried everything inside.

He tried to imagine what the latest incarnation of Maury's hideout might look like. The one he remembered had been a single room about six metres square, strewn with fur pelts, and with a pot-bellied wood-burning stove in the middle of it and a trap door leading to a root cellar in one corner. Beyond that, the picture in his mind grew hazy.

As Angie and Poochie sat quietly staring out the windshield, listening to the *croosh* of tires rolling over the forest floor, Bilyash negotiated the trail, hoping that it wouldn't dead-end before they'd reached the cabin. He didn't relish the thought of having to hand-carry all that food through the bush, on foot.

After what seemed a very long time, the Buick's headlights captured the outline of an apparently windowless building directly ahead. Bilyash pulled up beside it and turned off the engine, noticing that Poochie now stood growling on Angie's lap, his ears pointed forward.

The dog's instincts had been spot on so far.

"Wait here," Bilyash said. "I want to scout a bit before we unload the car."

All his senses alert, he stepped out, closed the driver's side door as quietly as he could, and crept around the corner of the cabin. It was a board and batting structure, roughly the same size as he remembered... and it was occupied. Bilyash halted, staring warily at two faintly glowing windows, one to either side of the front door. His first impulse was to get back in the car and leave without being detected. Then he realized that the only way to turn the vehicle around was to circle the cabin, in the process driving right past those windows.

So much for that idea. Option B wasn't any more practical. Bilyash seriously doubted whether a squatter this far in the bush would leave peacefully in the middle of the night at anyone's polite request.

Of course, there was another way for a Nash'terel to get rid of an unwanted guest. Angie was in the car and wouldn't have to see...

Bilyash's fangs began to itch.

Then a familiar, booming voice nearly sent him scrambling up a tree. "Well! It's about time you two showed up!"

A lanky human shape stood silhouetted in the open doorway,

with his legs braced and his hands resting on his hips. "I hope you brought plenty to eat, young apprentice, because you're going to need it."

Bilyash stepped warily closer. "And who are you supposed to be, now?" he called out.

"I'm Mel Demarest, the Nash'terel trainer who's going to whip you into shape for your next encounter with an assassin. But as long as we're out here in the wilderness, you can continue to call me Maury if you like."

"Uncle Maury got here ahead of us," Bilyash told Angie when he returned to the car. "I need to warn you, though—he's shape-shifted, and he's calling himself Mel Demarest."

"Of *course*, he is," she said. "Honestly, I don't know how you people ever recognize one another."

With Maury's assistance, Bilyash was able to empty the car in short order. Understandably, he saw relief on Angie's face as she entered the cabin, which was lit as well as warmed by the glow of a modern-style fireplace. The hearth sat in the middle of the room and was open on both sides, creating two distinct spaces.

On one side was the kitchen, equipped with a propane camping stove and a sink next to a hand pump, presumably for drawing water from a well. Poochie had already been fed and walked, so Angie turned her attention to the rough-hewn wooden table covered with bags and boxes of groceries, and the tall cupboard with empty shelves waiting to receive them. Setting the Chihuahua down on the floor, she got to work unpacking the food and putting it away while he trotted off to explore the new accommodations.

Maury drew Bilyash away to the other side of the cabin, where a sofa-bed and an easy chair waited, mismatched in style and colour but both facing the flickering light of the fireplace.

"So!" said Maury once they were settled side by side on the sofa. "Are you ready to resume your training?"

"Under the circumstances, I don't seem to have a choice. I'll do whatever is necessary to ensure my safety, and hers."

"Focused on survival, like a true Nash'terel. It may comfort you to know that despite the potentially destructive capabilities of your talent, there isn't enough time right now to turn you into an offensive weapon," Maury told him. "However, I can teach you a couple of useful defensive skills that will set you on the path to becoming an adept. You know, I was worried that you'd assimilated too deeply into human society, that you'd permanently abandoned your studies and would never be anything more than an apprentice. But Shred was right. He bet me that if you felt truly endangered, you would get back on track."

Bilyash's jaw dropped. "If I *felt* truly endangered? Are you telling me this assassin thing was just a ploy to make me want to be more Nash'terel?"

"Not at all. The threat to all our lives is very real, Billy. And I would certainly never lie to you about something like that, any more than I would burn my own house down as a prank."

"But you would pull back and leave me to deal with the danger on my own, to make a point?" he said, putting a hard edge on every word.

"You haven't been on your own. We've been nearby the whole time."

It took Bilyash a couple of heartbeats to realize what he was talking about. "The tracer on my phone. You're the one who's been tracking me."

Maury bobbed his head in confirmation.

"But what about the two fake cops who came to the sports camp? Pyotren told me—"

"—exactly what I instructed him to say. There were never any cops at the sports camp. We just had to increase the pressure a bit, to push you into Plan Omega. After you made that final phone call to Shred, he let me know that you were on your way here."

"Where is Gershred, anyway?"

"He didn't tell you?"

"He said the two of you were on your way west, to eliminate Vincaspera's operation."

"Well, that was half true."

"Really? You've sent your Council-appointed bodyguard across the country without you? And he defied his employers and went?"

"Not really. Shred and I began watching each other's back while we were still apprentices on RinYeng. Once I'd convinced the First that only a Nash'terel master could protect another Nash'terel master, they let me choose my own bodyguard. Naturally, I picked my old friend. The Council may think he's working for them, but he isn't."

"He's working for you?"

"No, of course not. We're partners. We work together."

"So, whenever he told me he was following the Council's orders, he was lying to me," Bilyash said accusingly.

"Not every time. Like I told you, we took the trap the First had set for us and turned it to our own advantage. Sometimes their orders coincided with our main purpose—helping you to stay safe in spite of yourself. Those were the ones he followed. The rest he ignored."

Something clicked into place then in Bilyash's mind. "The First never agreed to treat us as a unit, did they?"

"No. I never even raised the subject with them," Maury confessed after a beat. "I've been observing the Yeng on this world since long before you were born, and it's brought me to an important conclusion: the less they notice us, the safer we are. It's best if the Council remains unaware of you, Billy, until you're an adept, at least. When you're ready, Shred and I will teach you how to handle the First and its minions. But for now, fighting off Yeng assassins is going to take everything you've got."

A growling sound in the vicinity of his ankles was Bilyash's cue to look down. Poochie stood stiffly, his ears pointed forward, his fangs bared, giving Maury the canine version of an evil eye.

"He doesn't trust you," said Bilyash.

"He's a very intelligent little animal," Maury remarked. "I can see why you keep him around. He knows that I'm wearing a disguise and is instinctively suspicious."

"Poochie?" called Angie. "Where are you?"

The dog didn't budge. A moment later, she came to fetch him. "Come on, Pooch, let's get your bed set up." She scooped him into her arms and headed back to the kitchen. Halfway there, she turned and said to Maury, "Will you be sleeping over, Mr. Detweiler?"

"Demarest," he corrected her pleasantly, "and no. I'm staying in another cabin a hundred metres or so downriver."

"In any case, we don't sleep much," said Bilyash.

"I've noticed," Angie remarked. "You don't sleep, you hardly eat..." She gazed around the cabin with a look of consternation on her face. "Do you ever pee?"

Maury's shoulders were shaking with laughter. "You couldn't see it in the dark," he told her, "but there's a washroom beside the cabin. Outdoor access only, I'm afraid. One of these decades I'll get around to installing a connecting doorway in here."

"Not to worry," she said evenly. "I don't mind roughing it."

Turning to address Bilyash, Maury said, "We'll begin your training at dawn. Have protein for breakfast. And you," he added, pointing at Angie. "I hope you've brought plenty of reading material with you, because he's going to be too busy to pay you much attention for the next few weeks."

"I've got fifty novels on my e-reader," she replied, "and an adapter that lets me recharge it using the car battery. Will that be enough?"

"Clever girl," he said. "I like this one, Billy. She's a keeper. See you in about five hours."

"He likes you," Bilyash repeated after Maury had left.

"Should I be worried?"

"Your essence is safe. Maury's cabin will be well stocked. And if he ever gets the urge to snack between meals, there's always the artichoke hearts and pickled herring. He likes them as much as I do."

As the first light of the new day trickled shyly through the treetops, dappling the ground around the cabin, Bilyash resumed the shape of Billy Ash. Then, wearing no clothing, he opened the picnic cooler and selected a nice lean rib steak to be his breakfast. Poochie lay sound asleep on his towel near the doorway. He didn't even stir as Bilyash devoured the raw meat over the kitchen sink, tearing into it with fangs that had been itching for nearly an hour. Finally, his face and torso streaked with blood, he walked down to the river bank and waded into the water to clean himself up.

When he came out again, retracing his steps back to the cabin,

Maury, or rather, Mel Demarest, was waiting for him. Demarest had brought over a couple of folding lawn chairs for himself and Angie. They both sat, watching with interest as Billy strode naked through the woods toward them.

"Very nice," said Demarest. "Now get dressed in something you would wear every day at your workplace so we can start your training."

"Will I need a cup?" Bilyash wanted to know.

"If you ask an assassin that question, do you think he'll answer it?" demanded Demarest. "Or will he correctly assume that you're unprotected in a delicate part of your anatomy and just aim everything he's got at your *dashniholla*?"

Bilyash already knew the answer to that. What he didn't know was, "For training purposes, should I wear some protection?"

Demarest's patience was clearly being tried. "Only if you intend to wear that same protection 24/7 for the rest of your days. Time is short, so we have to train you in real life conditions."

In other words, no. Bilyash swallowed his next words. This was going to be painful enough. Pissing off the instructor would only make it worse.

Angie, meanwhile, got to her feet, not bothering to conceal her amusement. "I'll leave you boys to play," she said, and went inside the cabin.

Fifteen minutes later, Bilyash had put on a worn pair of jeans and his "Space—The Cerebral Frontier" T-shirt, and he and Demarest were standing alone in a clearing near the river bank.

"All right. I'm an assassin and I've just surprised you in the woods. Show me what your talent can do," Demarest ordered.

At a loss, Bilyash glanced around him for something that might spark an idea and came up empty. Even if he could think of a way to use magnetism, there was nothing containing metal in the immediate vicinity. Finally, he said, "I can run like hell. Or I can climb a tree, or jump in the river and swim."

"In other words, you can die," said the older Nash'terel, snapping each word at him like a whip. "The only reason you managed to survive the attack at the sports camp was that the assassin overestimated what you were capable of. You laid a crude human trap where he was expecting something complex and sophisticated. Your next attacker will have learned from that, so we need to make sure he'll *under*estimate you when you finally meet up again."

"And how do you propose we do that?"

"Let me demonstrate," said Demarest. "I want you to pick up something and throw it at me, as hard as you can."

Gladly, thought Bilyash, frustration tightening his neck muscles. He walked over to the river and found a baseball-sized stone lying in the shallows near the bank. Then, without warning, he whirled and pitched a strike straight at Demarest's chest. To his amazement, the rock froze in place about fifteen centimetres from its target, dropped to the ground, and bounced harmlessly away.

"I created a shield out of the ambient light," Demarest explained. "And you can do something similar with magnetism. To borrow an analogy, you already know how to control the outward and inward flow of your magnetizing essence. Now we're going to work on all the other directions."

"I thought it was too dangerous for an apprentice to project an untrained talent."

"You won't be projecting. You'll be turning your entire body into a magnet with the poles at the ends of your arms. After practising for a decade or two, you should be able to do it at the speed of thought. For now, I'll settle for the speed of your fingers on your skin."

Bilyash spent the rest of that day learning to create larger and larger magnetic fields around his body, beginning with his hands and working on including his arms, upper torso, and head. It was harder to do than he'd expected. By the time Demarest ended their session, Billy was depleted and ready to feed.

Angie was waiting for him inside the cabin. She gazed a question at him as she stood wiping her hands on a sheet of paper towelling.

"He did fine for his first day," Demarest called through the doorway. "See you tomorrow, kid." Then he wheeled and walked back into the woods.

"He's not coming in?" she asked.

Bilyash sank with a groan onto the bench at the kitchen table. "He just wanted to make sure I got home safely."

She scanned him up and down, an expression of concern on her face. "You look exhausted, Billy. Would you like some dinner?"

For a moment he debated with himself. Her essence was pure enough to qualify as food, but it no longer felt right for him to simply take it. So he replied, "A nice bloody chunk of the liver in the cooler would hit the spot."

"You eat it bloody?" A note of dismay had crept into her voice.

"We prefer our meat raw."

Now the note was a melody. "Oh."

He turned and stared at her, suddenly realizing what he had been smelling. "Please, tell me you're not cooking the liver."

She reached over and gave the knob on the stove a decisive twist. "It's still raw inside. All I've done so far is sear it to keep the juices in," she told him stiffly. "It's a large piece, so I kind of assumed we'd be sharing it."

"Angie, I—"

"No, it's all right," she assured him, now wearing a martyred expression. "You need to keep your strength up. I can always wade into the river and kill a fish if I need protein, since you clearly bought all the beef parts for yourself. Or maybe I'll open a tin of Poochie's gourmet dog food. It seems I was right earlier—you *do* like him better than you do me."

He shook his head wearily. "Are you going to be like this all month?"

"You betcha. Seriously? A whole cooler for steaks and liver and not even a crummy chicken leg for me?"

"What about all those tins of flaked meat that I picked up at the other three stores?"

Angie drew herself up and declared, "I am not a cat!"

"Maybe not in *this* life," he muttered.

Then they locked eyes and both burst out laughing.

In the end, they compromised. Angie sliced off some of the liver to finish cooking for herself and served the rest to Bilyash, mostly raw, with a side of onions sautéed in olive oil, a fresh green salad with balsamic vinaigrette, and a promise never to cook his meat again.

When they were done eating, Angie carried their plates to the sink, then returned with a sparkle in her eyes and the top three buttons of her shirt unfastened. "Ready for some dessert?" she invited him.

A familiar warmth was spreading upwards from his groin.

"Sure," he told her. "There's always room for dessert."

Chapter Sixteen

———— ♦ ————

Over the next couple of weeks, Bilyash's life fell into a daily pattern: a pre-dawn breakfast over the sink, followed by a gruelling day of practice, an evening meal eaten human-style with Angie, a walk in the woods with Poochie, and a gratifying portion of essence served to him in bed.

"Why do you keep referring to your Uncle Maury as Dempster?" she asked him one night after they'd made love. "He's still the same person, just inside a different body."

"That's Demarest," he corrected her patiently. "And I do it to remind myself how important his teachings are right now. When Uncle Maury was training me earlier, I didn't really take things seriously."

"You need to see him as a different person so you don't fall into old habits."

"I guess so."

"Are you still working on turning yourself into a magnet?" she inquired.

"We're past that. Now I'm working on doing it faster. Practising my quick draw." Quoting Demarest, he deepened his voice and recited, "A shield is only as good as the speed with which you can raise it."

Angie looked skeptical. "But don't magnets usually *attract* metal objects?"

"At their poles, yes," he explained. "But a magnetic field will actually repel charged particles, and according to Maury—sorry, that's Demarest—the vast majority of the assassin's arsenal is ion-based."

"And when he realizes that his ray gun isn't working...?"

"Then he'll switch to shooting bullets and throwing knives. And that will be my cue to switch defensive strategies as well."

"To what?"

He shrugged. "I don't know yet. It's the next thing Demarest has promised to teach me."

Angie fell silent then, with a worried expression on her face.

"It'll be all right," he told her.

"I know it will. It's just—"

He waited patiently for her to find her words.

"We've been having unprotected sex for a while now, and I can't help wondering what the chances are..."

"...of your becoming pregnant?" She nodded. "They're zero."

"That was quick. Is it because our genomes are too different from each other?"

"I'm not a scientist, so I wouldn't know about that. Nash'terel don't reproduce often, but we do it in pretty much the same way as humans do."

"Then how can you be certain I won't get pregnant?"

"I've been taking precautions." Noticing the befuddled expression on her face, he explained, "I'm a shapeshifter, Angie.

That means I have conscious control over every cell of my body, including the ones in my reproductive system. When conditions are right for me to become a parent, I'll activate them. Until then, they remain dormant. So there's no need for you to be concerned. You're safe."

"Oh. I guess that's good, then."

Bilyash was confused. He didn't know what he was hearing in her voice and seeing in her eyes at that moment, but he was pretty sure it wasn't relief.

At the beginning of the fourth week, Gershred showed up in the clearing. He positioned himself near the edge of the woods and watched with apparent amusement as Demarest threw a knife at Bilyash's head, and Bilyash stuck a fry pan in front of his face to deflect the weapon.

Demarest was not happy. "No, no, *no!*" he railed. "You were supposed to magnetize the pan and draw the metal blade off target, not just throw it up as a shield."

"You can't argue with the kid's speed, though," Shred remarked.

"I can argue with anything I damn well please. Is everything taken care of?"

"Everything that was on your list. I even picked up a fresh supply of food for both cabins. Billy's pet human was very grateful for the delivery."

"Her name is Angie," Bilyash corrected him through gritted teeth.

The big Nash'terel flashed him a broad grin. "Take it easy, kid. I'm just teasing you." Turning to Demarest, he said, "Pyotren has seen to it that no bodies will be found at the sports camp, and Dillinger doesn't want to jeopardize a cushy job by raising questions, so we're okay there. And Armin was able to doctor the scene before anyone else came across the car crash at the bridge. He removed the Volkswagen and fixed the abutment on the east side, so as far as the cops are aware, it was a single-car accident and the driver fled on foot."

Bilyash's surprise must have shown on his face. Demarest gave a snort of laughter and said, "You thought I was exaggerating earlier when I said there were eyes on you the whole time?" Addressing Shred, he added, "What about the situation at Alpha Dog Studios?"

"I whispered a few questions in the right people's ears. The insurance money has been held up, pending investigation of certain irregularities in the claim, and the movie has been mothballed until everything can be sorted out. They're estimating another three weeks. Will that be long enough?"

Demarest grimaced in Bilyash's direction. "Hard to say."

"Wait. You're sending me back to my old job?"

"Of course," Shred scolded him. "Who do you think you are—Bonnie and Clyde? You've been missing for weeks. Billy Ash on location with another film company in an area without cell towers is a story that will make sense. Alpha Dog will believe it and so will the police."

"And my landlord?" Bilyash reminded him.

"He received an email and a couple of checks from the producer of your current movie, *Wendigo*, as soon as we knew you were following Plan Omega," Shred replied. "I'm very detail oriented."

"So you lied to me. Neither one of you was ever actually headed to British Columbia," said Bilyash.

"I didn't lie," Demarest said with a shrug. "I told you it was a half-truth and you chose the wrong half to believe. At some point, we are going out there to put a stop to Vincaspera's operation."

Shred's lips quirked briefly, as though he'd been about to say something but changed his mind.

"Listen up, apprentice! When we're done here, which will only be when I'm satisfied that you've got a better than even chance of surviving the next assassination attempt, you return to your life as if nothing has happened," Demarest instructed. "You work on that zombie movie and you stay on your guard. Keep practising your shield-raising. Remember that anyone you meet could be a Yeng in disguise, whether you can smell it on them or not, and the attack can come at any time, from anywhere."

All at once, Shred's arm was moving, his hand cupped and the air around it seeming to shimmer. Reflexively, Bilyash brought the fry pan up between them to deflect the flow of essence from the heat lord, and not a moment too soon. A heartbeat later the pan was almost too hot to hold.

"See?" said Shred archly. "I *told* you he was fast."

Among the provisions Shred had dropped off at the cabin were a variety of raw vegetables, a dozen eggs, a couple of packages of sliced bacon, a selection of cheeses, and five kilograms of extra lean ground beef. Angie was delighted to have some variety of proteins in their diet again, Bilyash even more so when she immediately turned half a kilo of the hamburger meat into his favourite dish, steak tartare.

For the next couple of weeks, Bilyash ate well and trained hard, in daylight and in the dark, knowing that he had Angie's smiling face to come home to. However, her smile wilted one day when he reported a conversation he'd had earlier with the other two Nash'terel.

"So, they're using you as bait to draw the assassin out? They're purposely putting you in mortal danger, Billy. Surely you can see that!"

Yes, he'd seen it. At his current skill level, he'd also seen no way around it. However, the forecast wasn't all doom and disaster. Setting traps was what the Nash'terel did best, and two elemental masters, a light lord and a heat lord, had promised to be monitoring this one at all times. Once it was sprung, all he had to do was use his newly acquired defensive skills to stay in one piece until they arrived. It didn't seem too tall an order.

"Listen, you'll be safe up here," he told her. "No one can track you to this cabin, and Maury and Shred will make sure you have everything you need."

"That's not the point! Honestly, Billy Ash, for someone with a magical mojo, you can be awfully thick-headed at times."

"Thick-headed for a human or for a Nash'terel?"

She uttered an exasperated syllable and pitched her balled-up serviette across the table at him. "You idiot! Haven't you figured out yet that I—?" Angie paused, visibly recomposed herself, then demanded, "Are we a team or aren't we?"

"Of course, we are."

"Then we stick together. I don't care how safe this cabin is, I'm not staying up here without you. And if you're determined to go along with this scheme of theirs, then you have to make me a promise. I care about you, and I don't ever want to lose you."

"Don't worry, I'll be very careful," he assured her.

"Careful might not be enough."

"Then what is it you want me to do?"

She inhaled deeply and said, "I want you to impregnate me. It may not work. Conception for humans is never a sure thing. But I want to try. It's Murphy's Law, Billy. If you're prepared for something, the odds are it won't happen. I want you to come through this unharmed. So I need a way to keep your memory alive in case you don't make it. I need to have your child."

"Are you out of your mind?" demanded Shred.

Demarest just stared at Bilyash, at a loss for words.

"How can you even think of reproduction at a time like this?" Shred went on.

"See, that's the difference between us," Bilyash retorted. "To you, she's just another animal to exploit. Animals reproduce. People have children. Angie is a person, one whom I care about deeply, and she wants—no, strike that—*we* want to have a child together."

"Half human, half Nash'terel, neither one nor the other," Shred pointed out sharply. "If you think humans can be cruel to us in our true shape, just wait until you see how they treat one of their own kind that's different."

Demarest found his voice then. "Billy, why does she want this?"

"Because she's certain I'm going to die when we return to the city and she wants to hang onto some part of me."

Shred was stunned. "You told her the plan?"

"We're partners," Bilyash snapped. "We're staying together, and she has a right to know what's going on."

"I don't believe this," Shred declared.

"Unfortunately, I do," said Demarest.

"Listen, I don't need your blessing or your permission," Bilyash reminded them. "The only reason I told you *our* plan was that, if it works, Angie will need help when it's her time to give birth, and there can't be any humans around to witness it. Will you do it?"

Gershred and Demarest exchanged a meaningful look.

"If any human female has the constitution to carry off a Nash'terel pregnancy, it's this one," Demarest conceded.

"Only if she isn't drained of all her essence by the first thirsty Yeng she encounters once Bilyash is—" Shred stopped himself barely in time. "Sorry!"

"Then we'll just have to give her some protection before she leaves for Toronto," Demarest decided. "We'll do it tonight. I'll need to prepare, so let's meet at the cabin at midnight."

Shortly before the witching hour, Demarest and Shred arrived at the cabin. The flickering golden light of the fireplace lent a clandestine air to their visit, as though the four of them were spies, risking their lives by coming together in one place, or sorcerers participating in some sort of occult ritual. Poochie, meanwhile, had been dozing peacefully for the past twenty minutes on a blanket placed underneath the kitchen table.

"Angie," said Demarest, sitting down beside her on the sofa, "has Billy told you why we're here?"

"He says you're going to protect me from being bothered by Yeng when he's not around."

"Bothered!" Shred snorted. "That's one way of putting it."

Ignoring the outburst, Demarest pulled a pale leather pouch from the inside pocket of his jacket and loosened the drawstring.

"This is a piece of jewellery that you have to keep visible at all times," Demarest told her. "I've put it on a chain so you can wear it as a necklace. In cold weather, you can pin it to the outside of your coat." He upended the pouch and spilled its contents into the palm of his hand.

Angie took an audible breath. "It's beautiful," she whispered.

"We call this mineral *dashkra*. It's been found in only one place: in the mountains bordering Nash'terel land on RinYeng," Demarest explained.

Actually, Bilyash thought, that wasn't quite accurate. Raw *dashkra* had been found in only one place, but jewellery made from the cut and polished stone was given to every Nash'terel as part of the rite of adulthood. No one knew for certain how many pendants and brooches were currently being worn, because, unlike human jewellery, the bloodstone was not a fashion accessory or decoration. It was a symbol of belonging that (on this planet, at least) needed to be concealed from view. Pendants were kept next to the skin, and brooches were pinned to the inside of the clothing, to be shown only if necessary as proof of one's Nash'terel identity.

Nash'terel adulthood was not defined the human way by having reached a particular age in years, but rather by having achieved a certain level of mastery over one's *hainbek*. It was a safe bet, therefore, that both Maldemaur and Gershred wore pendants. Bilyash's hand went to the centre of his chest, where by now his own bloodstone would be hanging if he hadn't neglected his studies in order to experience the human way of life... and then abandoned them altogether to pursue a career in the movie business, which in turn had led him to find Angie.

Maybe the universe was on his side after all.

Now she was about to receive something that it was forbidden even to *show* to a human, let alone give to one. And breaking this taboo would somehow protect her from the thirst of other Nash'terel? What was Maury up to now?

Leaning in curiously, Bilyash saw a large oval-shaped stone suspended in the middle of a spherical cage made of fine golden filigree. The stone was flat and milky white, laced with veins and whorls of a slightly brighter white, and divided in half diagonally by a narrow band of metal.

"This piece of jewellery has been specially prepared," Demarest was telling her. "It's what we use for the blood ceremony."

"Blood ceremony?" Angie echoed faintly.

"Don't be nervous, my dear," he said. "That's just what it's called. Among the Nash'terel, we use these stones for various rituals, including to signify that two individuals are mated."

Her face lit up with comprehension. "It's like a wedding ring."

"Only better," said Demarest. "Watch what happens when I place a drop of blood on one half of the stone. Billy, your finger, please!"

Bilyash hesitated, frowning. "What's with the cage?" he demanded. "I've never seen that before."

"It's a warning. Human females who are pregnant advertise the fact by what they choose to wear—such as T-shirts that say things like 'bun in the oven'. Ours do the same, by caging their mating symbol and keeping it visible," Demarest replied with growing asperity. "The cage stands for the mother's body, the bisected stone for the child within. Essence production increases during gestation, which is why our pregnant females need to signal their condition to other Nash'terel to avoid being mistaken for... food sources. Now, stop being difficult and give me your damned finger."

Bilyash stepped forward and extended his index finger for pricking. If Demarest was telling the truth, he reasoned, then this bloodstone was quite possibly the only way to protect Angie and their future unborn child from being attacked. Unless, of course, she crossed paths with an assassin, for whom a gravid Nash'terel female might appear to be an easy target...

No. Bilyash forced his attention back to the ceremony, and the wonder on Angie's face as she stared at the stone in Demarest's hand. This was what he wanted filling his thoughts right now. This was how he wanted to remember her when her too-brief human lifespan had reached its end. And it occurred to him then in a flash of insight that their having a child together would also be a perfect way for him to keep *her* memory alive.

The milky stone absorbed his blood, channelling it along the veins and whorls on one side of the diagonal band, turning them a deep velvety red and infusing the surrounding mineral with overlapping splashes of indigo, burnt orange, and olive green.

"What you are looking at is Bilyash's bloodline," Demarest explained. "Each of the founding families is represented by a different colour. The dominant strain occupies the veins of the stone, while the lesser ones tint its substance. Now it's Shred's turn."

"Wait. What about my turn? I'm the one who's going to be wearing this pendant and I'm the one who's going to be having the baby," Angie pointed out. "So shouldn't it be *my* blood that gets dropped on the other half of the stone?"

"Human blood has no effect on *dashkra*. In order to protect you, this pendant has to convince others from our world that you are one of us," Demarest replied, the expression on his face making its own unspoken statement: *...and you are not one of us and never will be.*

Angie drew herself up in her seat and said quietly, "Since there are eight distinct types of human blood, how can you be so certain that mine won't change this stone, even a little?"

Bilyash willed him not to reply. In the five hundred years that they had known each other, Maury had spilled immeasurable quantities of human blood in the interests of his research. It was something Angie was better off not knowing.

"Humour me," she persisted. "Please! If this is supposed to be a kind of wedding band, then I'm the one Billy should be marrying. Maybe you're right and my blood won't work. But you can at least let me try."

From his place beside the hearth, Shred let out a gravelly chuckle. "That sounds an awful lot like a proposal, kid. What's your answer?"

"Stop right there!" Demarest commanded, exasperation sharpening his voice. "This is not a wedding band because this is not a wedding. It's a ruse. It's protective camouflage. That's all it *can* be, because Nash'terel do not mate with other species!"

A few choice words leaped onto Bilyash's tongue then, but before he could deliver them, Poochie rounded the corner of the fireplace. Growling and doggy-muttering, he trotted past Shred on stiff little legs, the canine version of a grumpy old man who didn't appreciate being rousted awake from his nap. With all eyes upon him, the Chihuahua stopped just out of arm's reach, stared around at the entire group, then singled out Demarest and barked loudly at him for several seconds, as if to say, *You've got it backwards, chum. The other species are the ones refusing to mate. So shut your pie-hole and quit disturbing the neighbourhood!*

Then, having spoken his piece, the dog sneezed and sat back on his haunches, glaring a challenge at the unpleasant-looking man on the sofa.

Demarest's face darkened. Before he could say anything, however, Shred dropped down beside him and cut in, "Maldemaur, do you remember how our parents reacted when we broke the news to them about us?"

Startled, Demarest turned and locked eyes with him, then

snapped, "This isn't the same."

"I never said it was. I'm only asking: Do you remember?"

"Vividly," Demarest replied, adding, "It still hurts every time I think about it."

"Me too. Let these kids pretend to have their wedding. What's the harm? And who are we to judge? If her blood doesn't change the colour of the stone, we can simply add a drop of mine on top of it."

Bilyash and Angie exchanged a wordless look of surprise, then watched tautly as Demarest seemed to debate with himself for a moment. "All right. Give me your finger, Angie," he said at last. "This *dashkra* will probably reject your human blood but, as you suggested, we can try, and the spirit of the attempt ought to count for something."

Once again they all observed closely. As Demarest had predicted, some of the blood drop slid across the surface of the stone and off its edge, falling through the cage into the palm of his hand. And yet...

"Some of it is being absorbed," noted Shred.

Demarest glanced sharply at Angie. "It's one thing to be absorbed. It's another to be recognized and accepted by the stone."

Resisting the urge to remind them once again that Angie was unique among human females, Bilyash trained his gaze on the milky half of the *dashkra*. For a long moment, it seemed that Demarest was right and nothing would change. Then one of the veins turned pale turquoise. The colour began slowly to expand, spreading like a stain into the other veins, then trickling into the whorls in the mineral. The entire process took about a minute. No other colour appeared.

"That's impossible," murmured Shred.

"No, it's not," Demarest said with barely controlled excitement. "I recognize that shade of blue and so should you. It's Vincaspera's dominant strain. Now we know how she got her results. She took a shortcut and fudged the experiment, just as she did back on RinYeng. Only this time I can show proof."

Chapter Seventeen

———◆———

"What are you talking about?" demanded Angie. "Are you saying I'm part of an experiment?"

Demarest stared a question at Bilyash, who shook his head in response.

The older being paused, visibly choosing his next words. "You appear to be related to a Nash'terel bloodline, my dear. It's a very distant connection, and how and when it might have been made is a mystery, but the stone doesn't lie. That's why it changed colour the way that it did. And I would venture to guess that it's also the reason for your abundance of essence, and why you'll probably sail easily through any pregnancy." *Just like one of us.* This retraction of Demarest's earlier message hung in the air, unspoken.

"Don't we still have something to finish?" Bilyash prodded. "The other half of the stone. It can't show only a partial bloodline or it won't work as camouflage."

For several heartbeats, Demarest stared longingly at the delicate turquoise pattern. Then he reached for Gershred's hand. "All right," he said. "It's a reproducible phenomenon, and in any case, the others will most likely insist on witnessing the effect themselves—"

Bilyash reacted swiftly. He leaned over, grabbed Demarest by the wrist, and said in a menacing undertone, "You're not showing her to anyone from the Science Guild. They'll declare her an abomination."

"Relax. Your... *mate* is safe. I'm sure there are others just like her out in B.C. who will serve my purpose just as well. Now, if you don't mind...?"

Still unconvinced, Bilyash released his grip so the ceremony could proceed. Angie needed that pendant for protection. Once she had it, he decided, he and Maldemaur were going to have to get a few things straight.

It was almost three o'clock in the morning. After their two visitors had left, Poochie had managed to get back to sleep right away. For the human and the Nash'terel, however, this was proving to be a very long and difficult night.

Angie was still sitting on the sofa, fingering the pendant that now hung around her neck and showing no signs of being ready for anything to do with bed. With his Nash'terel eyes, he would have had no problem letting the fire die out. Angie, however, needed light to see by, so he'd stirred the embers back to life and laid some kindling and another log on the hearth.

The fireplace had been crackling for more than an hour. During that time, Angie had remained statue-like, lost in thought. Processing what had just happened, he guessed. Meanwhile, Bilyash had tried to do what he usually did while she slept—prowl the cabin in his true form, review and practise the day's lessons, snack on something from the pantry—but he'd found it impossible to concentrate with so many unspoken questions hanging in the air. And so much unexpressed fear!

Some of it was his own. With his stomach slowly curling into a knot, he'd planted himself in the easy chair, resting his scaly hands on its arms as he watched a whole parade of expressions cross her face and a storm slowly build in her eyes. When she did finally speak, the matter-of-factness of her tone was so at odds with what he expected to hear that it jarred his senses.

"So, Maury and Shred are a couple?"

His jaw nearly dropped. *This* was what she'd been mulling over so darkly for the past sixty-plus minutes?

"What? You thought only humans could form that kind of bond?"

"No. It's just—" Her shoulders sagged as she continued, "When I was little, I used to daydream that beings who came here from another world would be somehow better than us. That they would have risen above such things as racism and intolerance. But between the genocide on Maury's home planet and what I overheard tonight..."

"We've burst your bubble."

"Totally demolished it," she agreed with a pained half-smile.

She'd seen nothing yet, Bilyash thought grimly. There were even more devastating truths waiting to take centre stage, and they wouldn't stay in the wings for long.

"What did he mean, there are others like me in B.C. who would suit his purpose?" she demanded abruptly.

"Brace yourself, Angie. You're not going to like what I have to tell you."

"I *am* part of an experiment, aren't I? A genetics experiment, run by Victoria Spears?"

He should have expected that she would put some of the pieces together on her own. There was a tremor in her voice, caused by anger, he reckoned. It certainly wasn't put there by fear. The Angie Fiore he knew was about as courageous as a human could be.

"Unfortunately, you're right," he confirmed. "That's why the town had to be so isolated, and why you couldn't be allowed to choose your own mates. You were being selectively bred."

"Bred? Like animals? Why?"

"To purify your human essence, just as the cult leaders promised. At first, Spears probably just wanted to prove that it could be done. Now that your generation has achieved her goal, we think she's set a new one: getting rich by harvesting the essence and selling it for consumption by others like Maury and me."

"Like some sort of alien dairy farmer," Angie said, spitting the words out as though they burned the inside of her mouth. "And the purpose that Demarest mentioned?"

"I gather he intends to discredit Victoria Spears by revealing that the results of her experiment are tainted by Nash'terel DNA—specifically, Spears' own blood injected into her test subjects."

"And that will end the experiment! That's good!" Angie said.

He fell silent, trying to think of the least painful way to explain things to her.

The pause made her visibly uneasy. "It's not good?" He heard her gasp as a couple more pieces clicked into place in her mind. "No, it's terrible! You said—You said they would declare me an abomination. And then what? Would they kill me?"

She would have to find out eventually, he told himself.

"Not just kill you, Angie. First they would drink all your essence, draining the life right out of you. Then they would rip your dead body apart and consume your raw flesh."

"They would eat me?" she whispered. In the dim light cast by the fireplace, Bilyash watched her face go deathly pale. "Oh, no! Oh, my God! 'It isn't banishment.' That's what my father said. That must be what he saw that scared the daylights out of him. Oh, God! Poor Brendan! What a horrible way to—" She gasped again. "And poor Terrence Macy! That's what the assassin must have been doing to him when the guard raised the alarm." She lifted eyes wide with horror to Bilyash's face, making him wish she were seeing Billy Ash, or dirty old Bill, or anybody else but himself at that moment. "And what those men, those *monsters* in the pastry shop would have done to *me* if you hadn't—!"

He flinched. An instant later, Angie was trembling all over. She was taking in air in huge, sobbing gulps while tears streamed down her face. Bilyash's first impulse was to gather her to his chest and assure her that she was safe, that everything would be all right. Then he looked at his arms, with their green skin and their oddly fashioned joints, and reluctantly quashed it. A monster was the last person she would want touching her right now.

So, he stiffened his resolve and told her, "Yes, they would have fed on you! And that's what will happen to the entire human population of Middlevale if the other Nash'terel find out what Vincaspera did. Angie, focus!" Bilyash ordered her, bracketing her shoulders with his large, scaly hands. "How many people were in the cult when you and your parents escaped? Look at me!" He willed her to raise her head and meet his Nash'terel eyes with her own. "How many lives are at risk?"

Panting as though she'd just run five klicks at full speed, she finally stared bleakly into his face.

He felt a momentary pang, then shoved the emotion to the back of his mind.

"Think, Angie! How many?" he repeated.

She blinked hard. "I—I'm not sure. I was a kid then. Several thousand maybe," she stammered.

"And how many of those were children?"

She was finally beginning to calm down. "When I was a student, our school had an enrolment of fifteen hundred."

Fifteen hundred sources of pure essence? Tainted or not, Vincaspera's experiment had been a roaring success. The First would jump at the opportunity to capitalize on it the moment Middlevale was brought to their attention. That was assuming they hadn't already found out about it when they summoned Maury to meet with them.

Angie took a deep breath, let it out slowly, and went still. Satisfied that she was once more in control of herself, Bilyash dropped his hands from her shoulders.

"Are you okay?"

"What kind of dumb question is that?" she demanded. "Of course, I'm not okay. Billy, we have to do something. We can't let Demarest go ahead with his plan and condemn all those people to the worst of all possible deaths."

"I agree. But Maury is a Nash'terel master, Angie. It's going to be nearly impossible to stop him."

"Then we need to approach the problem from a different angle. What if we beat him to Middlevale and got everyone out of there before he arrived?"

"All several thousand of them at once? That would be an enormous undertaking, even if you were able to convince them that they are, in fact, prisoners. That's the problem with cults. Having the illusion of free will blinds them to the chains they're wearing."

"Then we need to show them what my father saw," she decided. "Monsters feeding on human flesh."

Bilyash winced at the reference. "And once they'd left Middlevale, where would they go? Where could they hide? Do you remember what you told me earlier, about your parents living in fear?"

Her chin wobbled, and for just a second he regretted the harshness of his tone.

"We'll do something, Angie, I promise. But we can't just rush in there on the spur of the moment. We'll need to think things through. We'll need to plan."

"Fine. You let me know when you've worked out every single little detail," she told him stiffly. "Meanwhile, I'm going to bed."

Bilyash the hunter went out to prowl the woods. The sun wouldn't be up for at least a couple of hours, but the air in the cabin had become oppressive. In the forest, it was cool and still as he slipped easily through the trees, a shadow among shadows, following the sound of rushing water that always seemed much louder in the dark. Eventually he found himself at the edge of the river, staring at a pair of baleful yellow eyes on the opposite bank and wondering what the blood of another predator would taste like.

"Lovers' quarrel?" came a familiar-sounding voice from behind him.

Or maybe the blood of another Nash'terel, Bilyash amended as Shred stepped up to join him. In his true form, Gershred was a being of slender build and impressive height, with a thick mat of fur hugging most of his body.

"I could ask you the same question," Bilyash remarked evenly.

"That was quite a bombshell you dropped earlier."

"Yeah, Maury had a few choice things to say about my timing after we got home. He'll be fine once he calms down. Are you all right with what we are?"

"I suppose I am. Mainly, I'm wondering why Maury never told me about you. I was his ward for five hundred years and he never even mentioned your name to me, let alone that you were in a relationship together."

"Your parents disapproved of us. No, that's an understatement," he corrected himself. "Maury's parents disapproved of us. Yours believed, as so many others did at that time, that same birth-gender couples like us were an aberration, a mistake in the Nash'terel genetic code that needed to be eradicated in the name of racial purity. So, we pretended to be 'normal'.

"When the villagers killed your family and Maury took you into his home, we knew how you'd been raised. We both felt it would be safer and simpler for everyone if we kept up the pretense. After all, we'd been doing it for centuries at that point. It had become a habit. Then I saw the expression on your face when Maury made that comment about interspecies mating and I decided that you needed to know the truth, and he needed to be reminded of it."

"So, all those close female friends that I've seen Maury with over the past five hundred years—they were just you in different shapes?"

Shred chuckled. "They do say variety is the spice of life. Oh, we've been buddies, too. Worked together as colleagues from time to time. And we've taken occasional vacations from each other. That's important for a healthy long-term relationship. Not for yours, of course. Once you leave for The Big Smoke, you and Angie will need to be inseparable if you want to stay healthy, period." A pause, then, "What happened to spark your little tiff, if you don't mind my asking?"

"She wanted to know what would happen to a human that the Science Guild decided was an abomination, and I told her the truth. The whole truth."

Shred pursed his lips. "Uh-huh. Not what I would have done. However... I gather she didn't react well."

"You could say that. She used the word 'monsters'."

"Have you shown her your true form yet?"

Bilyash paused, remembering the look of wonder he'd seen on her face when he stepped out of the washroom at the motel.

"You're smiling, so I'll take that as a yes," said Shred dryly. "So, clearly, she doesn't see *you* as a monster. It's the rest of us she has a problem with. Meanwhile, I've known some humans who would consider *her* to be a monster. In fact, that's probably what drew you together. You're a couple of misfits, perfectly matched."

"Is this your idea of comforting me?"

"If we were humans, then you'd have just married a cow, so yes, this is the best you can expect right now."

Despite himself, Bilyash burst out laughing.

"Listen, kid. We know you're young—a lot younger than Angie thinks you are, for sure—but Maury and I are both aware that you have to live your own life. He knows it deeper down than I do, so it's taking him a little longer to recognize it. Meanwhile, the rift has closed for another hundred years. Once all the assassins who came through it from RinYeng have been identified and eliminated, the threat level will drop back down to what it was before. Problem is, it will never be even close to zero, not as long as there are Yeng exiles on this world who blame us for spreading the blood sickness on their home planet and would love to make us pay for it."

Bilyash swallowed hard, but the lump in his throat refused to budge. "So, the humans fear us and the Yeng hate us and they both want us dead. You're telling me my life will always be in peril," he said soberly.

"Unfortunately, yes. And by association, your mate will be in the crosshairs as well. This is what Maury was afraid would happen. It's why he's been so desperate to protect you for all these years. And now that it's come to pass..."

"There's no going back and undoing it, is there?"

"No. But there are ways to minimize the danger."

"Please, don't you start lecturing me about security. I get enough of it from Uncle Maury."

"I wouldn't dream of it," Shred assured him with a smile in his voice. "Once we've disposed of your third assassin, Maury and I will be setting in motion a plan to provide a safe alternative to your life so far among the humans. If you're smart, you'll accept the offer. Either way, though, we'll respect your decision."

"And will this invitation to safety include Angie and our child?"

Shred looked both startled and offended by the question. "Of course! You're the closest thing we have to a son, Billy. When push comes to shove, we'll always be on your side, and theirs. You're going to have some difficult choices ahead of you. But know that you can count on us to ensure that your own offspring comes safely into this world."

With that, Gershred melted back into the forest. A moment later, Bilyash turned and walked back to the cabin. Angie had pulled out the sofa bed and was lying on top of the covers. He knelt on the floor beside her and softly spoke her name, and the large brown eyes blinked open.

"Billy?" she murmured. "What time is it?"

"It's time we made a baby," he replied. "Yes?"

Her arms slid around his neck. "Very yes, Billy Ash. Very, *very* yes!"

Two and a half weeks later, Bilyash had mastered the fry pan trick... sort of. The bullet aimed at his heart grazed his shoulder instead, and Demarest declared him ready to return to work at Alpha Dog Studios. The following morning, Billy and Angie set to work packing everything into their car for the long drive back down to the city.

Shred had been in the Greater Toronto Area for several days, laying the foundation for the trap in which, with luck, they would catch the third assassin. Bilyash hoped it wouldn't involve his apartment. He'd finally gotten it furnished and decorated to his liking and was looking forward to spending time surrounded once again by his favourite things. He was looking forward even more to sharing them with Angie.

As if reading his mind, Poochie barked a reminder from his improvised bed in the back seat of the Buick, and Bilyash paused to amend his thought: he would be sharing his home with Angie and their dog. Shred could joke all he liked, but there was no denying where the Chihuahua felt he now belonged.

"Remember the rules," Demarest told him when they were all packed and ready to roll. "You're Billy Ash day and night until the trap is sprung. Assume that the assassins know where you live and will be surveilling you. Stay on high alert, keep practising your skills, check in with us regularly, and don't agree to meet privately with anyone without letting us know."

"Where will you be?"

"A lot closer than you think. You'll understand when you get there. Now, off you go!"

Under Demarest's stern gaze, Bilyash started the engine, steered the car in a slow circle around the cabin, and headed back to the main road. They had a whole day's journey in front of them, including pit stops and meal breaks, and an assassin could pick up their trail at any time.

Bilyash's jaw clenched. This was not going to be a relaxing drive.

"Are you going to get that?"

Angie's voice pulled Bilyash back to the moment. He wasn't in a good mood right now. They were still two hours away from Toronto, following a swarm of red taillights down the black ribbon of road bordered by fields and forests that was Highway 11 at dusk. A light rain had begun to fall. Lulled by the rhythmic *thud-thump* of the windshield wipers, Bilyash had let his thoughts roam, and where they'd chosen to wander was through a jungle of unpleasant future possibilities.

He tossed a puzzled frown across the front seat at her. "Get what?"

"I don't think that's a bumblebee trapped in the pocket of your jacket," she remarked. When he didn't respond right away, she added impatiently, "Your phone is buzzing, Billy."

"I don't have a phone anymore, remember? I turned the burner phone into a detonator and destroyed my personal phone after we got that call from Pyotren."

"Well, *some*one in this car is being paged," she informed him. "My phone is turned off, and I very much doubt whether Poochie has one."

Without taking his Nash'terel eyes off the heavy traffic ahead, Bilyash checked his pocket, found the vibrating cell phone, and passed it over to Angie. "Read me the call display."

She did. It was a number they both recognized.

"Terrence Macy's office," mused Bilyash. "They're probably rounding up the crew to resume filming."

"Shall I take a message?" Angie said.

He put out his hand for the phone. "Turn it off. I'll call them back."

A half-hour later, Bilyash steered the Buick off the highway and up to a gas station pump. While Angie was visiting the convenience store and making use of the facilities, he filled the car's fuel tank, paid the kiosk attendant in cash, then pulled into a parking spot near the store entrance to wait for her.

Involuntarily, his hand went to his jacket pocket. Trust no one, Maury had told him.

A call from Macy's office number wasn't necessarily from Macy's film company. After all, an assassin had gotten inside the sound stage undetected once before. This could easily be the same killer, trying to confirm his target's possession of the phone being used to track his location. And yet...

If Bilyash had acquired this device just before leaving the cabin, only two people besides Angie could have put it into his pocket, and he had no reason to distrust either of them. If he'd carried the phone up there with him unknowingly and the assassin was using it to track him down, there should have been an attempt on his life sometime during the past few weeks, and there hadn't been.

Bilyash decided to gamble. He pulled out the phone and turned it on.

It was his. Everything was there. His apps, his photo gallery, his contacts, his texts and saved voicemail, all were there, along with a couple of new messages. He checked the GPS setting. To his relief, it was disabled.

Then he remembered: Pyotren had cloned his phone, and Shred had later paid a visit to the sports camp. He could easily have picked up the clone while he was there and slipped it into Billy's jacket while delivering groceries to Angie.

Bilyash checked the new messages. They were both from Macy's number and both asking him to call back. Again, he decided to gamble. He waited, every nerve taut, as the phone rang at the other end, four times, five times...

"Hello!" said a male voice that immediately set off alarms at the back of Bilyash's brain. He'd heard this person speak before. But where?

With effort, he kept his own voice casual. "This is Billy Ash. You were trying to reach me?"

"Yes! Thank you for calling back. I'm Corin Ellsworth, the new producer of *Zombies Take Graceland*. I'm trying to reassemble the film crew for a one month shoot so we can wrap up production. The length and suddenness of the hiatus threw a wrench into everyone's plans, so it hasn't been easy getting the key personnel back together, as you can imagine. Like you, many of them signed on with other companies. I've been in touch with Golden Bough Films, and they tell me principal shooting of *Wendigo* is completed. Congratulations, by the way, on your first official gig as Key Special Effects Makeup Artist."

Bilyash smiled. Shred hadn't just given him a cover story, he'd given him a promotion as well. "Thank you, Mr. Ellsworth."

"If you would be willing to come back and help us finish up Terrence's movie for the original credit as Makeup Artist, I can guarantee you the money will match what Golden Bough is paying you for *Wendigo*."

"When are you planning to resume shooting?" Bilyash asked.

"If you're on board, in three days' time. But we're having a memorial service on the sound stage first."

He paused, pretending to consider the offer, then replied, "Okay. I'm on board. Please notify security that I'll be coming by to pick up my keys first thing in the morning." Then, noticing Angie standing at his elbow with an urgent expression on her face, he added, "Oh, by the way, Mr. Macy had an unpaid intern from Ryerson on the set, Angelina Fiore."

"Yes, I've been reading Macy's notes. She was supposed to turn his dog into a zombie. Great idea, but the mutt has run off somewhere, and—"

"I have Poochie," Bilyash cut in, "and Angie's with me as well. She was invaluable on location for *Wendigo*, and if you don't mind, I'd like to bring her along to work on this movie too."

"We still won't be paying her," Ellsworth warned.

"That's not a problem."

"Then I'll see you both in my office tomorrow morning to dot a few 'I's and cross some 'T's. Have a good evening, Billy."

The line went dead.

"Well?" Angie prompted.

"You're in, and zombie Chihuahua is a go."

Chapter Eighteen

Poochie was obviously glad to return to the comforts of civilization. He did a little dance when Angie put him down on the chocolate-coloured broadloom in Bilyash's apartment. Then he rolled onto his back with a doggy grin on his face and squirmed energetically, as though trying to wrap himself in the feel of the carpet.

"I think that's his version of kissing the ground after a bumpy plane ride," Bilyash remarked, on his way to the bedroom with their overnight bags. These were the last two pieces to come up from the car. Pausing to survey the home he'd half-expected never to see again, he added a heartfelt, "Me too, Poochie. Me too."

Angie leaned into the living room from the kitchen, where she'd been putting away the perishable food. "I wonder how happy he'll be when we take him back to the sound stage tomorrow," she said. She glanced longingly at the tan leather recliner, then returned to her task, raising her voice to be heard over the sound of cartons scraping, wrappers crumpling, and cupboard doors being opened and closed. "There was an awful lot of blood spilled on that set. I doubt whether any amount of scrubbing would have gotten rid of all of it."

Bilyash dropped onto the chair she'd been eyeing. He watched as the Chihuahua trotted from room to room with his head tilted and his nose twitching inquisitively. "If they've done it right, that set's been completely struck and rebuilt from the ground up, on a brand new floor," he told her. "I don't think he'll have a problem with it." Then, raising his voice, he added, "But I will have a problem with *him* if he pees on any of my stuff. You hear me, Poochie? You keep all four paws on the ground!"

The dog emerged from the bedroom, the portrait of wounded innocence, and marched past him to the kitchen. As he entered, Angie appeared in the doorway. "He needs to mark his territory."

"I know," Bilyash growled. "I just don't want him marking any of *mine*."

"Then take him for a walk outside," she advised. "Do it now, Billy, before he starts making a mess."

Bilyash blew out a disgusted breath. He'd purposely insisted on feeding and walking Poochie before they arrived home so he wouldn't have to go out again, alone, tempting a watchful assassin to make his move before the bait was even in the trap.

He pulled out his phone and punched up Maury's number, hoping the answering machine hadn't been set up yet. Bilyash was in no mood to be sworn at right now.

Shred picked up on the second ring. "What's up, kid?"

"We're home, but I have to go out again. I have to walk the dog."

"And what? You want my permission?"

Bilyash could feel his patience giving way, one strand at a time. "No, I want to know whether it's safe for me to escort this pee factory around the block while he marks his territory," he snapped.

Shred chuckled. "*His* territory?"

"It's either that or he ruins my furniture. And I'm not even sure pets are allowed in this building." He paused, remembering the night he'd killed Cora, and suddenly realized: "You've got the place staked out again, haven't you?"

More chuckling.

"I'll meet you on the street," Bilyash decided, then pressed the 'end call' button.

Gershred was waiting at the corner of the block, a tall, angular figure framed by the light of an overhead street lamp. Very dramatic, Bilyash thought. Very graphic novel noir.

Shred fell into step with them as Poochie passed by. The Chihuahua paused and gave him a cursory sniff before continuing his doggy quest for trees and fire hydrants to anoint. Meanwhile, the extendable leash paid out and retracted with a hissing sound that reminded Bilyash of fishing line, which in turn reminded him of bait, which was what he and Angie were until Maldemaur said otherwise.

"You wouldn't happen to know where Maury is right now?" Bilyash asked. "And please don't tell me he's on a train bound for British Columbia."

"He's close by, and that's all I can tell you. The good news is that we've detected no one else surveilling your building yet, and there's no way an assassin could have foreseen your needing to take this particular walk, so you could probably have done it alone in safety. Nonetheless, calling us first was the right thing to do."

"The bad news?"

"Dog walking is a routine activity, and assassins love it when a target's movements can be predicted. Keep changing up the times and places of these walks, or get someone else to do them for you."

"Noted. By the way, I've heard from Macy's replacement. Corin Ellsworth. Not a name I'm familiar with, although his voice certainly rings a bell. I just wish I could place it. He wants to meet with me and Angie tomorrow morning in Macy's old office at the sound stage."

"Before filming resumes, I take it?"

"Two days before. There may or may not be construction crew on the site, but there's bound to be security."

"People in uniform, for camouflage. Good to know. All right, kid. Go to the meeting with Angie, but leave the dog in the car. If Ellsworth is a Yeng, he may or may not be giving off a smell, so watch how he reacts when he sees the *dashkra* around her neck. If he recognizes the stone for what it is, you'll notice it in his eyes. Either way, it's important not to let him know that you know. Just quietly throw up your shield and back out of the meeting if you can."

"And if we can't? What's to stop him from trying to kill two Nash'terel instead of one?"

"Then I guess you'll just have to improvise. Yell for help and we'll come running."

The person sitting behind the desk in Macy's former office looked far too young to be the producer of a feature-length horror movie. Standing just outside the door, Bilyash peered around the jamb, saw a mop of curly blond hair and a round, peach-fuzz face, and guessed Ellsworth's age to be no more than eighteen.

The voice on the phone yesterday had sounded a lot older than that.

Then Bilyash remembered Maury's warning, and the mental alarms that had shrilled when Ellsworth had begun speaking. If an assassin wanted to lull or disarm a target, assuming the shape of a youngster would be a good way to accomplish it. Bilyash took a moment to redirect his magnetizing essence, readying it to form a shield. After nearly two months of practice, he knew his "quick draw" was pretty damned fast. However, as Maury had repeatedly pointed out to him, a trained assassin would probably be faster.

"Ah! You're here! Please, come in," the kid called out, getting to his feet and showing them a row of shirt buttons being strained by what was undoubtedly a soft, round belly. The image of a baby seal popped into Bilyash's mind.

Billy turned and glanced a question at Angie: *Ready?* She nodded briefly in response, her hand rising to touch the pendant.

As they stepped into the office, Ellsworth's face lit up with a welcoming expression. He waved them toward the two guest chairs in front of his desk, then dropped back onto his own seat with a brief sigh of satisfaction.

"I'm really glad you could both come back for this," he told them. "My uncle spoke highly of your talents. And you said you have his dog...?"

Bilyash felt knocked sideways. This was not the voice he'd heard on the phone. It wasn't even close.

"Poochie's in the car for now," he finally managed to reply. "I thought our meeting was with Corin Ellsworth."

"It is." The baby face frowned briefly, then lit up with comprehension. "Oh! I see. You thought that *I* was—! Forgive me. They haven't put my name on the door yet. I should have introduced myself right away. I'm Arnold Macy, acting as Mr. Ellsworth's executive assistant for the next month. He's waiting for you in his office trailer. I'll take you there now."

"He's in a trailer and you're in here?" Angie wondered aloud.

Arnold shrugged. "He's here for one month and I'm here for the next six after that, making music videos. I guess he was trying to minimize the amount of moving around we'd have to do."

That, and the fact that a trailer was self-contained and mobile, Bilyash reflected, making it the perfect disposable murder scene. Clearly, this assassin had a learning curve.

It's not paranoia if someone is actually plotting to kill you, Maury's voice reminded him.

Macy's nephew led them to the north side of the sound stage, through the busy workspace of about a dozen tradespeople, some in beige jumpsuits, others wearing blue denim coveralls and steel-toed boots. Interestingly, none of the workers seemed to notice the *dashkra* hanging around Angie's neck, although several of them were openly admiring of her figure. Bilyash couldn't blame them for that. She had a very attractive shape, especially when seen from behind.

He glanced around and saw a pair of plant wranglers unloading potted shrubs from a dolly, while the rest of the construction crew wielded saws, screwdrivers, and paint brushes, putting the finishing touches on a couple of new sets. One of them Bilyash recognized from pre-production sketches. The other he hadn't a clue about. In any case, "We're not going back to the burnt-out chapel?" he asked.

Arnold swivelled and walked backwards several steps. "Between the mess from the murder and the police taking pieces of the set for forensic analysis, the chapel was beyond saving. It wouldn't have been cost effective to completely rebuild it for just the one remaining scene, so Mr. Ellsworth decided to revise the script instead. Come see me before you leave and I'll give you copies of the final pages and the new production schedule."

"Thanks. That'll be helpful," Bilyash replied.

Ellsworth's trailer was actually a rather large motor home, parked just a few metres away from the sound stage and connected to it by a covered walkway. Bilyash could understand why a producer would prefer this to setting up temporary shop in Macy's old office. In addition to its broader dimensions, the RV presented a sleek and modern exterior, bright white walls with blue and green window awnings. It made a statement, loud and clear: *I am not Terrence Macy's understudy.*

Arnold approached the door of the trailer with deference, knocked twice, then disappeared inside, presumably to announce their arrival. Bilyash felt the light touch of Angie's hand on his arm.

"What do you think?" she stage-whispered.

"If Ellsworth is on the level, I think the bus driver is doomed, with or without his survival clause, and zombie Chihuahua will be the one that kills him."

Just then, Arnold leaned back out the trailer door and told them, "Mr. Ellsworth is ready to see you now."

The RV was even more impressive on the inside. It had been customized into an office on wheels, the sort of office that would have perfectly complemented a multi-million dollar mansion. Bilyash saw a full-sized wet bar, a wall of mahogany bookshelves, and a desk that looked as though nothing less than a crane could move it.

On top of that desk sat two pieces of paper, one before each of the French Provincial guest armchairs facing it. And behind it, his bulky build and chiselled expression giving the impression that he would be even harder to move than his furniture, was the man purporting to be Corin Ellsworth.

As they watched, he heaved himself to his feet and extended his hand across the desktop for shaking. "Billy Ash and Angelina Fiore!" he declared heartily. "I've heard good things about you both from Golden Bough Films. Please, sit down!"

This sounded more like the voice Bilyash had heard on the phone. He didn't have to sniff the air to detect the scent of cologne. It was strong enough to mask the fishy odour of altered Yeng essence, but that didn't mean anything. As Maury had often pointed out, the Yeng had no idea they gave off that smell, and not all Yeng were chemical users. Nonetheless, it was better to be safe than sorry. Once more preparing to throw up his magnetic shield, Billy glanced significantly at Angie before they took the offered seats.

"Now then," Ellsworth was saying. "I just need you both to sign these letters of agreement so we can go ahead and finish Terrence Macy's movie. That's a beautiful stone, by the way, Ms. Fiore, quite unusual. I've been looking for a birthday present for my wife, and I think she would love something like that. Can you tell me where I might find one?"

When her hand went to the pendant, Ellsworth gave her a look that curdled something in Bilyash's midsection. That toothy grin might have been meant as a friendly gesture, but it felt far too predatory for his liking.

"Sorry, I can't," she replied. "It was a gift."

"Oh, well." Ellsworth switched off his smile, a transition even more disturbing than the smile itself. All business now, he pulled two expensive-looking pens out of a drawer and slid them across the desk. "These documents are addenda to the contracts you signed earlier with Macy and will be attached to them in my production files. Ms. Fiore, your letter simply confirms that you are returning to continue your internship under the same terms as before. Mr. Ash, yours confirms your return as well, with two changes to the original contract, as we discussed on the phone."

Bilyash read it through. Everything looked on the up and up so far. Maybe this large man with the unnerving grin was just that, and not a Yeng assassin. Maybe Bilyash had simply absorbed some of Maury's paranoia during their close association of the last few weeks and was seeing threats where none existed.

Once the documents had been signed and countersigned, Ellsworth gave Billy and Angie their copies. Then he cleared his throat and said, "Before you leave, we need to talk about the dog."

"What about him?" Bilyash wanted to know.

"He's not just a pet. He's a professional actor and a paid-up member of the Canine Performers' Guild. He was also the property of Terrence Macy, who is now deceased. Since you say you currently have Poochie, does that mean you've legally adopted him?"

Angie's eyes narrowed briefly. "Well, no, but—"

"How is this relevant, Mr. Ellsworth?" Bilyash demanded, cutting her off before she could give away any more information.

"Under the law, minor children and animal actors cannot be on a film set unless accompanied by a responsible adult. For a child, that's a parent or guardian. In the case of this Chihuahua, it would be either his owner or his registered trainer." He scowled at them for a moment. "I'm assuming that describes neither one of you."

"We've been his guardians for the past two months," Angie protested. "We've fed him and walked him and cared for him, and we're prepared to keep on doing it. So, you can say that we've adopted him."

Something hardened in Ellsworth's eyes, making Bilyash abruptly restless. Perhaps it was too soon to be dropping his guard and this man was a threat after all.

"That's admirable, Ms. Fiore, but completely unofficial. Due to insurance issues, every aspect of this production is going to be under intense scrutiny. That means I need a valid, recognized document in my files to cover every individual involved, including the dog. Neither one of you is legally empowered to sign a contract on his behalf. Unless and until that changes, I'm afraid Poochie cannot be allowed inside the sound stage."

Angie stiffened in her chair. "But you can't let a technicality—"

"Fine, then," Bilyash told him, laying a silencing finger on her forearm. "We'll get you whatever papers you need. We'll make it official."

Ellsworth's chair groaned as he leaned away from them, the smug expression back on his face. He steepled his hands and rested them on the polished surface of his desk. "That's all I'm asking, Mr. Ash."

"The nerve of that man!" Angie fumed as they left the RV. "He knows it will take time for us to meet with Macy's lawyer and the executor of his will and who knows who else. By the time we've gone through the formalities of adopting Poochie, the shoot will be over."

"It wouldn't have done any good to argue," Bilyash told her. "I suspect Ellsworth had his mind made up before we even set foot in his office. He'd probably already written the bus driver's dog out of the script." Pausing with his hand on the sound stage door, he continued quietly, "Besides, I just needed to get us out of there as quickly as possible."

As he swung the door open and stepped back to let her enter, she mouthed an 'oh!' of belated understanding.

"You think he's—" she whispered.

"I'm not certain. I was just getting some really unpleasant vibes from him."

It was dark inside. Not pitch dark, but still much too dark for this time of day. Bilyash risked a sweeping glance with his Nash'terel eyes and saw only two men at work, one perched on a stepladder in the middle of one of the sets while the other stood below him, handing up tools.

Judging by the sureness of their movements, they both had excellent night vision. Superhuman, in fact. Bilyash sniffed the air and detected a faint, familiar aroma. Instantly, every instinct he possessed snapped to attention. Here, not in Ellsworth's office, was where the trap had been laid.

"Where is everybody?" Angie wondered aloud. "It's a little early for lunch, isn't it?"

"Sorry, folks," called the man on the ladder. "We had to pull the breakers so we could work on the set lighting. There are tarps on the floor. Just be careful where you step."

Uh-huh. Keep your gaze directed downward so you can be caught by surprise.

"Which way is safer, Billy?" Angie murmured. "Forward or back?"

Back through that door, moving from dimness to sudden blinding sunlight, possibly straight into the sights of a waiting assassin while turning their backs on two more? Not a chance, Bilyash decided.

"Thanks," he called out, giving a cheerful wave to the man on the ladder.

Then he took Angie's hand, murmuring, "Stay sharp and be prepared to duck behind me," as he began leading her across the tarp-strewn floor.

A shaft of light stabbed into the room then as the south-facing door flew open, admitting a burly security guard with a frantically squirming Chihuahua in his arms.

"Hey, look who I found outside!" he crowed.

Barking a doggy war cry, Poochie wrenched himself free and hit the ground running. He jetted across the sound stage like a furry brown missile, directly at the startled workman standing beside the ladder. The Chihuahua was small, but he was ferocious. Without a moment's hesitation, he sprang, sinking his teeth into the man's lower pant leg and refusing to be shaken off.

"What the—!" yelled the worker on the ladder.

"I've got this," his partner called up, pulling a hammer out of his toolbox and raising it to strike.

A second later he screamed and dropped his weapon, staring in horror at the blackened remains of his hand. A second after that he was lying very still on the floor.

Bilyash heard running footsteps to his right and poured more essence into his shield, just as a second guard appeared. "Sounds like your alarm system is working just fine, Billy," said the guard, stretching out his arm. The air around his hand was shimmering.

Of course. Shred had promised that they would be nearby.

The being on the ladder swung around, holding something that looked like a nail gun. His eyes weren't human. They flashed and widened as he chose a target and brought the gun to bear. But he'd taken half a second too long. Bilyash felt rather than saw the heat energy that flowed from Shred to the weapon. The Yeng grimaced and juggled it, but was finally forced to let it fall to the ground, where it landed with a sound like glass breaking.

"*Esstateh'mesh ma na—!*" This shout was interrupted by the beam of the first guard's flashlight as it swept across the ladder, knocking it over and tumbling the would-be assassin to the floor beside it.

Shred pinned him there by planting a large booted foot on his throat. Poochie seconded the motion, bounding up to stand squarely in the middle of the man's chest. The Chihuahua's legs were braced and his fangs were bared, and his menacing growl sounded as though it was coming from an animal five times his size.

"I'm a heat lord," Shred informed him pleasantly. "Try to shape-shift on me, and I will incinerate you from the inside out."

The first guard moved to stand over the prisoner as well. "You know, I'm really getting tired of hearing that *esstateh'mesh* bullshit," he grumped.

...and there was Maury.

Angie stepped around Bilyash and demanded, "Where's Poochie? Is he all right?"

"He's a lion in the shape of a dog," Shred told her. "He's fine. So," he added, indicating the Yeng under his boot, "it appears we've been decoyed. Because this slogan-spouting piece of trash doesn't know the first thing about being an assassin. Do you?" he added, addressing the prisoner. "You're no more than a henchman, and a poor one at that. So who's calling the shots in this triad? Tell us and we may let you live."

Before the Yeng could reply, an angry voice demanded, "What the hell is going on in here?" Once again, it teased the margins of Bilyash's memory. "And what's with the lights?"

Everyone turned toward the sound.

Corin Ellsworth's large frame was silhouetted by the daylight streaming through the north-facing door. As it finished closing behind him, he stepped forward, cursing loudly when he nearly tripped over something in the semi-darkness.

"George, get your ass out here!" he bellowed.

Bilyash exchanged bemused looks with Maury and Shred. All three were wearing their Nash'terel eyes.

"Who is George, again?" Maury inquired.

"My production assistant," said Ellsworth. "But not for long if this is his doing. He knows how tight our schedule is." Squinting in the dimness, Ellsworth went on impatiently, "You've met him. Curly blond hair, a little on the pudgy side, looks like he just graduated from grade school...?"

"That was George? He told us his name was Arnold Macy," Angie replied.

"And that he's Terrence Macy's nephew," Bilyash chimed in.

"What?! Well, now I *am* going to fire his ass," Ellsworth declared, "because that's a fucking lie."

Uttering a syllable of frustration, the producer backed up and wedged the sound stage door open, letting in a beam of bright sunlight. Then he turned and pounded his way across the covering of tarps on the floor.

Meanwhile, the three Nash'terel had reverted to their human eyes. They watched with interest as Ellsworth pulled up short, his gaze shifting from the ladder at his feet to the forms of the two fallen Yeng beyond it. He scanned the faces of the two security guards and two visitors standing around the scene. Finally, his eyes came to rest on the small, snarling animal that perched atop one of the bodies as though protecting its ownership of a kill. Ellsworth evidently got the message. Keeping one wary eye on the dog, the man came no closer.

This silent exchange did not go unnoticed. The Chihuahua did not like Yeng. Or Nash'terel. Not on first meeting one, anyway, and in Maury's case not even after that. So, which kind was the producer, Bilyash wondered—Yeng or Nash'terel?

"What the fuck—?!" Ellsworth exclaimed.

"There's been a fatal accident, sir," Shred informed him in a deadpan voice. "Two dead, apparently by electrocution, although we won't know for sure until the medical examiner has filed a final report."

Two dead? Bilyash glanced downward. Shred was standing flatfooted on the floor, beside the failed assassin's crushed trachea. It was a brutal, human way to kill, but it was highly effective.

Still playing his role, Gershred shone his flashlight on the faces of the two Yeng and asked Ellsworth, "Do you recognize either of these men?"

The other being stared for a moment, then shook his head. "I personally hired everyone on my work crew, and I've never seen these two before. Who are they?"

"Unknown intruders, sir," Maury put in. "We've called 9-1-1 and the police are on their way. Maybe they can identify them."

Ellsworth huffed out an exasperated breath. "Isn't *that* just what this production needs—another reason for a delay. All right. I need to make a few phone calls. When the authorities arrive, bring them to my trailer. And find that good-for-nothing George." With that, the producer wheeled and stomped back out the door.

Poochie barked after him, long and hard, as though to say, *So long, pal, and good riddance!*

Meanwhile, Maury and Shred traded speculative looks.

"Well?" Maury asked him. "What are your warrior instincts

telling you?"

"Right now, they're having trouble reaching consensus," Shred replied. "Either George or Ellsworth could be the third member of the triad. I think we need to find George and have a word with him."

Angie scooped Poochie into her arms and carried him away from the bodies (which even she could probably smell by now, Bilyash thought). Then, all at once, three things happened.

The Chihuahua planted both his front paws on Angie's left shoulder and began yapping wildly at something behind her.

An arrow of light briefly pierced the room as the south-facing door of the sound stage cracked open and then immediately closed.

And Bilyash suddenly remembered where he'd heard Ellsworth's voice before. It was at Mom and Pop's Place. The producer was the third assassin. He'd just talked his way out of a Nash'terel trap. He could see in the dark as well as any Nash'terel. And he was getting away.

"There goes George," said Maury.

"But Ellsworth—"

"Come on, Billy!" Maury interrupted him. "Let's not waste time. We have to head him off."

So saying, the older Nash'terel spun and led the way out the south door, moving faster than Bilyash had ever seen him go.

"Ellsworth is the third assassin," Bilyash called over his shoulder as he broke into a run. "From the diner. Tell him, Angie!"

They emerged from the sound stage in time to see a silver BMW leave the parking lot, picking up speed as it rolled toward the road.

Then Maldemaur gestured with both hands, and two things happened simultaneously. First, the fleeing car appeared to be enveloped by an inky black cloud. Second, a painfully bright beam of light materialized, linking the end of Maury's outstretched arm to the edge of the metal barrier at the entrance of the driveway.

Bilyash had seen the older Nash'terel in action many times before, but those had been parlour tricks compared to what Maury was doing right now.

With a flick of his wrist, the light lord directed the luminous rod to swing the gate closed. At least, Bilyash assumed that was what he'd done, based on the shriek of metal crashing into metal that tore from the bubble of darkness just before it stopped moving.

Another wave of Maury's hands and both the rod and the bubble dissolved, revealing the BMW angled across the driveway, its front end crimped by the mangled barrier. Suddenly blinded, the driver had evidently accelerated straight into the edge of the gate as it was closing. Now he slumped motionless, looking from a distance like a bean bag chair that someone had stuffed behind the steering wheel.

"The gate is metal. If you were an adept, you could have used your *hainbek* to close it yourself," Maury pointed out as they jogged over to the driver's side door.

Bilyash let the jibe go unanswered. Yanking the door open, he saw what appeared to be a blond wig sitting atop the deployed airbag on the driver's side. Billy grabbed a fistful of George's curly hair and hauled his head upright.

The baby face split in a grin. "Congrats, you got me," he said in a faint, mocking voice. "Think you've won?" A blurt of laughter ended in a painful-sounding cough that brought blood into his mouth, painting his lower lip red. "You have... no idea... who you're fighting. They'll crush you... you and all your kind..."

This wasn't right. The Yeng reverted to their true form when they were injured, but George's shape wasn't changing. Something cold and hard landed in the pit of Bilyash's stomach as he realized what the reason must be: George had no other form. He was a human, but not a dupe. An accomplice. He knew about the conflict between the Yeng and the Nash'terel and he'd clearly chosen a side. And if the Yeng were recruiting humans to their cause, the odds against the Nash'terel became staggering.

Even a rank apprentice had what it took to be a stone cold killer when the circumstances called for it. Bilyash needed no prompting. He moved closer, cupped the back of George's head in his hand, and pulled a flash flood of red corpuscles from the human's body up into his skull. "Say goodnight, Gracie," he muttered. Limbs twitched briefly, then went limp as blood vessels burst, creating a massive, fatal cerebral hemorrhage.

"Neatly done," Maury commented, nodding with approval. "Now put your shield back up and follow me." He turned and walked back toward the sound stage.

"Wait!" Bilyash called after him, gesturing toward the corpse in the car. "Don't we have to...?"

"Take care of unfinished business?" Maury tossed over his shoulder. "Yes. But that's not it." And without breaking stride, he reached a hand behind him and beckoned to Bilyash to hurry and catch up.

"Did you stop him?" Gershred asked as they entered the building.

"Yeah," Maury replied sourly. "But we've got a much bigger problem than we thought."

As he filled Shred in, Angie stood silently by, holding Poochie in a death grip. Her eyes were saucer-wide. Bilyash felt his heart somersault in his chest at the sight of her struggling once again to process the events of a very violent morning. He crossed the space between them, wrapped his arms around her, and held on tight.

"It's all right," he assured her.

"No, it's not," she told him in a voice rapidly filling with tears. "Ellsworth got away again."

"He had some sort of small four-wheeler concealed behind the RV," Shred confirmed. "Silent running, so it was most likely electric. As soon as he realized his ambush was spoiled, he bailed. He could be anywhere and look like anyone right now. I'm sorry, kid. This Yeng is smart, he's persistent, and he doesn't work alone. It's a safe bet that he'll come after you again, so it looks like you're stuck with us for a while longer."

Bilyash squared his shoulders and raised his chin. "What do you want us to do?"

"There's a wardrobe department downstairs," said Maury. "Right now, you and Angie need to go there, change your clothes, and do something about both your faces. Then lock yourselves in until one of us comes to fetch you. Gershred and I have a mess to clean up. When we're done, we'll escort you home, in two cars and by different routes, just in case."

"And what about Poochie?" Angie sniffled.

"We'll keep him safe," Shred replied. "And that will keep *you* safe."

Chapter Nineteen

———•———

Home, it turned out, was not Bilyash's apartment, but rather a smallish, older, one-and-a-half storey wooden frame building on a quiet residential street at the north end of Richmond Hill. Both cars pulled into the driveway at about the same time. The being who opened the door to Maldemaur's knock and hurried them all inside was shaped like someone Bilyash recognized.

"Hopalong Cassidy. This is your place?"

"It's Armin's," Pyotren replied with a grin, "but he keeps guest rooms for people who need to crash. Or hide out." He gazed a question at Gershred, who had turned himself into a stereotypical middle-aged academic, completing the scholarly look with a V-neck cardigan and a pair of wire-rimmed spectacles from the wardrobe department at Alpha Dog.

"Don't worry. We weren't followed," Shred replied. To Bilyash and Angie, he said, "Until we're certain you'll be safe elsewhere, this is where you'll be living. You're not to leave this house for any reason. I'll bring your go-bags in from the car. Anything else you need, Pyotren will arrange to be brought here for you."

"Wait! Where is Poochie?" Angie broke in sharply.

"Here," said Maury, holding out a gift bag with a printed pattern of blue and white flowers on it and a pair of familiar doggy ears sticking out the top. "He fell asleep during the ride and was so quiet that I almost forgot about him." Addressing Pyotren, he added, "Assume that an assassin will know to look for a small dog, that Billy's apartment is under constant Yeng surveillance, and that they will have researched every shape he has worn over the past hundred years. And don't trust anyone who can't or won't show you a bloodstone. The assassin on Bilyash's trail gives off only a very faint smell and is an extremely convincing actor."

Pyotren nodded grimly. "Understood. Do you have a plan?"

Shred replied, "Not one that we're prepared to share just yet. Still working out the details."

"Okay, then. The three of us will hang out here—"

He was interrupted by a bark from the gift bag.

"Sorry," he amended with a grin. "The *four* of us will hang out and await further developments."

Bilyash and Angie had the top half-floor to themselves. At some point, it had been added to the house in order to create a master bedroom suite, with a full bathroom and an extra-deep closet. Now, it was a defensible keep, complete with an armed guard (and guard dog) watching the deceptively ordinary looking door that concealed the bottom of the stairs.

Like the Tower of London, Bilyash thought, only furnished in Scandinavian modern, with a queen-sized bed covered by a black and white striped duvet and a generous allotment of fluffy pillows and olive- and pumpkin-coloured throw cushions.

Angie sagged down on the edge of the bed and said with a sigh, "I'm sorry."

"For what?" he asked, frowning.

Her shoulders slumped forlornly. "For being the reason you're stuck here. If you didn't have me and Poochie to worry about, you could just change your shape and walk away. I know I said earlier that we need to stick together, but—"

"Don't even think it, Angie!" he snapped, bringing startled brown eyes up to meet his own Nash'terel gaze. "The reason I'm in danger has everything to do with the Yeng and nothing to do with you or Poochie."

"And this is the safest place for all three of you," came Pyotren's voice from the doorway. "Maldemaur's set up alarms all around this building, there's a bunker in the basement that locks from the inside, and reinforcements are on the way. So, you can relax. Things are well in hand."

Struck by a sudden thought, Bilyash asked him, "Can you change her appearance, like you did before?"

"Nope. There's a reason our pregnant females can't shapeshift, especially early in the gestation period. She may be human, but she's carrying a Nash'terel child. If she miscarries on my watch, Maldemaur will have my *dashniholla* for lunch."

"How can you be certain she's pregnant?"

Pyotren let out a snort of laughter. "I've got eyes, kid. There wouldn't be a cage around that pendant if she weren't."

And, still chuckling to himself, the shape lord went back downstairs.

Later that day, Jacomin (Jake for short) arrived. Another of Pyotren's numerous cousins, Jake was overweight and sloppily dressed and desperately in need of a haircut. He looked more like a sleepy-eyed couch potato than a bodyguard.

"Don't be fooled by his outward appearance," Pyotren advised. "He's a fifth-level adept with a heat *hainbek*, and many Yeng have died over the years because they underestimated him."

Jake was there to spell off Pyotren on guard duty, freeing him up to walk Poochie and go out in various shapes to run whatever errands were necessary.

Since Billy's apartment was now ruled off-limits, pet supplies became a priority item on the list of things to get. Pyotren returned from his first shopping trip with three sacks full of doggy stuff, including a dozen tins of Poochie's favourite, *boeuf bourguignon*.

Two days later, the question of whether Angie was pregnant was settled when she strolled into the living room, munching on a chunk of raw liver as if it were the most natural thing in the world for a human to do. With beef blood dripping off her chin onto the plate in her left hand, she turned on the television and took over the most comfortable chair in the room, shooting territorial glances at the five Nash'terel who came in after her to watch the morning news.

The story had finally hit the media: an expensively customized RV reported missing from the Alpha Dog Studios lot had turned up, burned to a charred husk, in a ravine in Innisfil Township. Apparently, a studio employee who had witnessed the theft had attempted to give chase in his automobile but had suffered a massive stroke moments after leaving the parking lot and subsequently crashed the vehicle into the gate at the foot of the sound stage driveway. The deceased's name was being withheld pending notification of next of kin.

"The collision was witnessed by a security guard who ran to

offer assistance but found the young man dead behind the wheel," the on-screen reporter was saying. "This is the second tragic death in as many months to strike Terrence Macy's last film, *Zombies Take Graceland*. Although it's unlikely that the production is cursed by his angry spirit, as is claimed by noted psychic Alma Heffernan, executive producer Corin Ellsworth has removed himself from the project, citing legal and financial concerns. With no one else willing to step in and take it over, an indefinite hiatus has been announced, leading industry insiders to wonder whether *Zombies Take Graceland* will ever be completed."

Bilyash let out an unhappy sigh. "Well, that's it, then," he announced. "My career is over. Humans in show business are very superstitious. No one is going to hire me now, for fear of jinxing their own production."

"And that's a good thing, kid," Shred told him sternly, pressing the mute button on the remote control. "For now, anyway. It means Billy Ash can drop out of sight without raising any questions."

"Besides, it's not the first career you've ever had," Maury pointed out.

"You're wrong about that," Bilyash countered. "The others were just jobs that I took to see what they were like. I didn't train for any of them. This one I went to school to prepare for."

"Uh-huh. Well, never mind, young one. There'll be other careers, I'm sure. Now listen to *our* news report. Shred and I have been following up on what that human in the car told us the other day—George? Arnold?"

"George," Shred supplied.

"George. Anyway, we now have a plan. But in order to set it in motion, we need to go out to the west coast. We expect to be gone for about a week, week and a half at most."

"The west coast? That's where Vincaspera is," Bilyash reminded them.

To his right, Angie drew a sharp breath. He laid a supportive hand on her shoulder.

"Yes, which is why we're going there," Maury explained with exaggerated patience.

"So you meant what you said before?" Bilyash demanded. "And it's for real this time? You're going to expose Vincaspera and shut down her experiment?"

This was what Billy and Angie had been dreading for nearly a month now. Maury's earlier lies about being on a train to Vancouver had raised hopes that the threat might be empty. Now those hopes were dashed. And the thousands of people inhabiting Middlevale were probably going to die.

Angie shrugged off Billy's hand and blurted, "You can't!" Then she added after a pause, "I mean... it makes no sense to waste a resource like Middlevale."

Maury fixed her with a curious gaze. "Waste it? What makes you think we would do that?"

Stung to action by Angie's beseeching glance, Bilyash waded into the discussion.

"Because she's not stupid, Maldemaur. None of the humans are. We're just really good at keeping secrets from them. Angie knows what we are and how most of us view her kind, genetically enhanced or not. And we all know what would happen to Vincaspera's test subjects if she were taken out of the picture and they were released into the outside world."

"Released?" Maury said, frowning. "I don't recall saying anything about releasing them, young one. The humans of

Middlevale are going to stay right where they are, living in blissful ignorance of our true nature.

"Meanwhile, recent developments have convinced Shred and me that we need to weaponize the *hainbeka* of as many of our Earthborn as possible. For that purpose, we've decided to establish a private training centre in a remote, isolated location, and Middlevale is the perfect venue. That is why we are going to make Vincaspera an offer she can't refuse, to buy the town and all the land around it."

And the livestock inhabiting it. He didn't have to say the words aloud. Every Nash'terel in the room knew what he meant. By the look on her face, Angie understood as well.

Bilyash had to remind himself to close his mouth. So, this was the "safe alternative to life among the humans" that Shred had alluded to up at the cabin? Combat training at a top secret boot camp on the other side of the country?

"Sounds like you're planning to build a Nash'terel army," he remarked stiffly.

"A defensive force," Shred corrected him, "to ensure the survival of the Nash'terel on Earth the next time the rift opens. An army of assassins will come pouring through it from RinYeng, and our best chance will be to have an arsenal of *hainbeka* waiting to engage them."

"Including mine?"

"You'll have a mate and a child to protect," Maury replied with some asperity, "so yes, when the facility is ready to accept trainees, we expect you to resume your apprenticeship there, for their sakes if for no other reason."

After Maury and Shred said their goodbyes and departed, Angie went upstairs and closed the bedroom door, leaving Bilyash to stare at the silent television screen while Pyotren and Jake busied themselves elsewhere in the house. The rest of the day passed quietly. Too quietly, Bilyash thought, although he couldn't blame Angie for retreating inside herself after that morning's revelations.

By now, the two older Nash'terel were well on their way to Vancouver. Maury refused to fly, so they'd be travelling by train. The Trans-Canada took three and a half days to cross the country. Would Angie be talking to him again by then? Bilyash had no idea. He moved from the sofa to the easy chair and eased himself onto it, feeling the weight of impending fatherhood settle heavily on his shoulders.

Maury and Shred would not force him to enlist in the Nash'terel army, he was certain. However, they were clearly not above using manipulation to convince him that he should. They were right about one thing—Bilyash would be heading up a family soon. Perhaps it was time he began making some of those "difficult choices" that Shred had mentioned earlier…

…such as trying to put some distance between his new, growing family and his adoptive one…?

Billy sat motionless for hours, running progressively more depressing scenarios in his mind. Not one of them ended well for an Earthborn, a human, and a hybrid offspring on their own. Staying put and taking orders from his elders did not sit well with him, but it appeared to be the safest option.

The world that had opened up for Bilyash with his acceptance to TAFA five years earlier had been like a carnival of new and exciting experiences. Now all the colour was bleeding out of it. He could practically feel his life spiralling in on itself, shrinking to the size of this single, stale, darkened room.

"Those must be heavy thoughts you're having," Jake remarked as he dropped onto the adjacent sofa seat. "They've kept you stuck in that chair for most of the day."

Bilyash glanced sideways to acknowledge the other Nash'terel's presence, then returned his gaze frontward. The television screen was blank and silent, and with the blinds down and the drapes drawn, it felt as though no world existed beyond the living room's bay windows.

"I've been considering my situation," he said, annoyed to see the other being's lips quirk briefly in a smile.

"And have you reached any conclusions?"

"Other than the fact that I'm screwed? No."

Bilyash turned in his seat and found himself staring at Jake's profile.

"Pyotren says you're a fifth-level adept with a heat *hainbek*. What does that mean, exactly?"

Jake remained facing forward but replied, "It means I can throw heat bombs and start fires. It also means I don't have to be physically touching something in order to change its temperature. As long as it isn't too far away, I can project my essence at it instead. If I were a heat lord like Gershred, I would be able to pull heat out of the air and move it around, but I'm not there yet. Maybe in a couple hundred more years."

"Can you create a shield?"

"No. Heat is an offensive weapon. Magnetism is defensive, so shields are your department... although Pyotren tells me you made good use of your *hainbek* back at the sports camp. Took out an assassin and his bait, I heard."

Bilyash shrugged. "I magnetized some bullets and used them to confuse his senses so he couldn't follow me out of the cabin before the bomb I'd made blew it up. It was the explosion and the fire that killed him, not me."

"But you're the one who thought up the plan and built the device. That took skill, and quick thinking. Not too shabby, kid."

"Maldemaur didn't think so. He called it a crude human-style trap. He said the only reason it worked was that the assassin was expecting something more sophisticated. Something Nash'terel."

Jake pursed and unpursed his lips. "And you took that as a criticism."

"Wouldn't you?"

"Tell me, where did you get the parts for your trap?"

"He bought them for me, just before—" Bilyash paused, frowning as pieces began dropping into place in his mind.

"Just before you left for the sports camp, right? For the cabin with the freshly topped-up propane tank?" Jake's shoulders were shaking with repressed laughter. "He gave you that human-style trap, kid, in pieces, figuring you would be clever enough to put them together the right way, and you did. Human traps are quite effective. He knew the strategy would work. "

Bilyash swallowed hard, recalling how close he'd come to death that night. "It nearly didn't. I made a mistake."

"And then you recovered from it. You survived. The assassin didn't. I repeat—not too shabby." Half-turning in his seat, Jake met Bilyash's gaze. "No one expects an apprentice to be perfect, Billy, especially not one in their first thousand years of life. And you were paired with an instructor who doesn't share your *hainbek*. Couldn't Maldemaur place you with someone else?"

"He did, but... they could see I wasn't a very dedicated student."

"Uh-huh," said Jake. He didn't sound surprised. "Clearly, you're not a traditionalist. Neither are we."

Unfamiliar with that term, Bilyash stared a question at him.

"Back on RinYeng, living in a closed society where everyone knew everyone else, all the Nash'terel followed the same rules and held the same values, outwardly at least," Jake explained. "When we fled through the rift to Earth, most of the twenty-three families kept their traditional ways. They went immediately to ground and became isolationists. The rest of us decided that life outside the bunker was more interesting, and we engaged with the human population—very carefully."

Recalling his earlier conversation with Gershred in the woods, Bilyash remarked, "My parents were traditionalists too, when they died. And yet…"

"You were Earthborn, and this world was full of new things to try. So, you rebelled against Maldemaur's expectations, rejected the training regimen he offered, and turned yourself into an easy target for Yeng assassins, all within the space of…?"

Bilyash thought hard for a moment. "…the last hundred and twenty years or so."

"Yeah, you're closing on nine hundred, so that sounds about right. Don't beat yourself up over this, kid. Other Earthborn have been doing the same thing, all over the planet."

This was not reassuring. As Maury had made a point of telling him more than once, Earthborn had also been *dying* all over the planet.

"And how many of them have mates and children to protect?"

"Only one that I'm aware of, and that's you," said Jake. "By the way, does Angie know about the difference in your ages?"

Bilyash didn't reply. As the silence stretched out, a grin crept across Jake's face.

"She has no idea, does she, just how young you are," he said.

"I'm old enough to father a child," Bilyash told him stubbornly.

"You *look* old enough to raise offspring," Jake corrected him, "and you've had enough time to do a lot of different things in your life, but in terms of maturity... let's see now. I came through the rift in my mother's arms, so I've been observing humans for well over a thousand years. I would guess that Angie has lived a quarter of her lifespan—yes, Pyotren and I are both aware that she's human—and that would make her fifteen hundred years old if she were Nash'terel. You, on the other hand, haven't lived even a sixth of your lifespan, which in human terms puts you somewhere around your sixteenth birthday."

Bilyash's jaw set. "It's just a number. It doesn't mean I can't have adult feelings and live independently," he insisted.

"Right. That's what all you high school dropouts claim," said Jake. "Are you going to tell her?"

"Are you?"

Jake shook his head. "It's not my place, or my job. Besides, it's blindingly obvious how much you two care for each other. Soulmates are meant to be together, even if one of you isn't a grown-up yet."

That stung. Bilyash changed the subject.

"What if I went back into training and became an adept? How well could I defend her?"

Jake paused, visibly choosing his words. "Well, it would take a couple of decades for you to get there, but as an initiate adept, you would have much greater control over your *hainbek*. You should be able to expand and fortify your personal magnetic fields. And I'm only guessing here, having no idea how much protection this would afford either of you, but I imagine you would be able to project your essence with accuracy to magnetize or demagnetize nearby metal objects. Depending on the relative weights involved, they would then either attract or fly toward other metal objects, with speed and force."

Hmm. Speed and force. Bilyash could work with that.

As Shred had pointed out earlier, there was no such thing as safety for a Nash'terel on this world. After the current cohort of assassins from RinYeng had been eliminated, the infected Yeng who'd been exiled through the rift earlier would continue to hate, hunt, and kill the secluded ones, as they'd been doing for centuries. Taking out Ellsworth and his henchmen would not remove the target from Billy's back. It would just reset the game, putting him back at square one.

The best and only way to increase his chances of surviving to protect his family, therefore... was to change square one.

Chapter Twenty

———•———

Bilyash awoke to the smell of strong coffee and the sound of dishes clattering as the kitchen table was set for breakfast. Voices were drifting his way as well. One of them was Angie's. Evidently, the way was now clear for him to go upstairs and take a shower.

Sighing with relief as jets of water pummelled his back and loosened the crick in his neck, he resumed the internal debate he'd been having when he dozed off on the sofa.

Bilyash loved Angie. He never wanted to do anything that would harm her or their offspring. But he'd determined that the fastest and most direct way to change square one was to train his *hainbek* at Middlevale, and now he was facing a dilemma with no right answers: how, when, and whether to break the news to her.

He hadn't forgotten Angie's confession in the motel room, describing her family's escape from the cult and their feeling of constant danger ever since. The prospect of being found and forcibly returned "home" by someone from Middlevale had spurred her to buy a gun for protection. And now that she knew what sort of secrets Victoria Spears had been keeping from her followers, just the suggestion that Angie accompany him back there would probably set off fireworks. He didn't even want to guess how she would react if he floated the possibility of leaving her with Maury and Shred for the next twenty or thirty years while he went to Middlevale alone.

As Bilyash towelled off, two things became crystal clear in his mind: first, the safety of his family was of paramount importance; and second, if he didn't give Angie at least the feeling that she'd participated in making this decision, he would most likely regret it for the rest of his life.

From the bottom of the stairs, Bilyash could see Pyotren and Jake quietly chatting in the living room. Angie was alone in the kitchen, doing something at the stove. That was good. Pots and pans were made of metal. If she hurled one at him, he could use his *hainbek* to skew its trajectory.

Bilyash padded into the room, sat down at the table, and cleared his throat. Addressing her stiffening back, he said, "Angie, we need to talk."

She froze, her knuckles whitening around the handle of a large and dangerous-looking spatula.

Uncertainty began squirming in his midsection.

"You're leaving me, aren't you?" she returned, the quiet resignation in her voice more stinging than any angry outburst would have been. "To go out west and enlist in that Nash'terel army they were talking about yesterday."

"Why would you think that?"

"Because it's what Uncle Maury has decided you will do."

Angie finished moving pancakes from the fry pan onto a serving dish. Then she set down the spatula and turned around, wiping her hands on her apron, and Bilyash's heart constricted in his chest. Her eyes were rosy-rimmed and shining with tears. She'd probably been kept awake half the night worrying about having to face the future without him.

"It's what he says he expects me to do. But since I hardly ever do what he expects, it's actually more like hoping." In response to the question on her face, he added, "Here's what you need to know about Maldemaur—he's certifiably paranoid, and he's been trying to micromanage my life ever since we met."

"Well, it feels to me as if he's successfully taken charge of it."

"All he wants is to keep us both safe. That's why we're here instead of on the road, fending off Yeng by ourselves." He leaned forward for emphasis. "We can't defeat Ellsworth alone. As long as he's on the loose and Maury and Shred are willing to watch over us and help us take him down, I'm inclined to let them run the show."

Lips compressed and brow furrowed, she placed the serving dish on the table and took the seat across from him.

"Run the show? For how long, Billy? Until Ellsworth is dead? That could be a while," she said, biting off each word as she savagely speared a couple of the fluffy pancakes and dragged them onto her plate. "In case you haven't noticed, they don't seem to be paying him much attention. It's the Middlevale deal that's front of mind for them right now, and who knows when *that's* going to close?"

Angie flipped open the cap of a bottle of maple syrup and proceeded to drown her breakfast with it.

"They'll be back here in about a week—"

"You're not hearing me!" she cried, leaping to her feet and slamming the bottle down on the table. "They're rushing to set up their training camp so they'll have somewhere to tuck you away when you finally get tired of being cooped up in this house. Don't you understand?" Tears began percolating into her voice. "Getting rid of Ellsworth is not part of their plan! *Not* getting rid of him *is*! They know I can't go back to Middlevale, so their solution to the problem of keeping us safe will be to split us up. They'll keep me here and send you out west and I'll never see you again."

"No! That's not going to happen," he declared, rising from his chair as well. "I told you, Angie, we're a team. We stay together, whatever it takes and wherever we go."

"Wherever we go?" she echoed shrilly. "Like British Columbia?"

Jake chose that moment to stroll into the kitchen. "Maybe we should leave her alone for a while so she can calm down and think more clearly," he said.

He took Bilyash by the elbow. Then, like a nightclub bouncer escorting a rowdy patron to the exit, Jake ushered him out of the kitchen and onto the back porch, closing the door firmly behind them.

The yard was a mess. It resembled a patch of wilderness, brought back as a souvenir from a camping trip up north.

"Don't step off the deck," Jake warned, unfolding a couple of chairs and shoving Bilyash down onto one of them. "Maldemaur's set traps all over the place to catch intruders crossing the property. It's a little over the top, but..." He shrugged. "It's Maldemaur. What can I tell you?"

Bilyash cursed under his breath. "What the hell is going on with her? And what am I supposed to do about it?"

"Just what I said. Leave her alone and let her calm down." Chuckling, Jake added, "You've never had to deal with a pregnant female, have you?"

"Have *you*?"

"Twice. So let me share some hard-earned wisdom with you. Your mate was a powerhouse even before she was impregnated. Now, her nervous system is marinating in hormones, sending her moods up and down like a yo-yo. Be glad she's on your side, kid, because in her current condition, if she ever decided to take you out, I'm not sure any of us could stop her."

"She doesn't have a *hainbek*," Bilyash pointed out.

"No, but it wouldn't surprise me if she had a human weapon in her go-bag. It's not a good idea to test her tolerances right now."

Bilyash paused, then asked, "How much of our conversation did you overhear?"

"Enough to get the gist of it."

"Was she right about Maury and Gershred not being in a hurry to take care of Ellsworth?"

Jake blew out a breath, finally replying, "Yes, but not for the reason she thinks. There's no nefarious plot here, just the temporary absence of a plan... and going into battle without some sort of strategy pretty much ensures that it won't end well."

"What if I came up with one? Would you and Pyotren help me pull it off?"

"Behind Maldemaur's back? Not a chance. But we could vet it for you, maybe do a little preliminary legwork to measure its feasibility. It would alleviate some of the boredom while we wait for them to return from the west coast." A pause, then, "You realize Angie is not going to settle for sitting on the sidelines...?"

"I know," Bilyash said with a sigh.

"Okay, for future reference, keep this in mind. Like it or not, you're living in Hormone City. Her feelings may be in flux, but they're valid. Take them into account. Be willing to accept a compromise in order to keep the peace between you. And for *shattra*'s sake, whatever you do, don't split up the team! You're defence, she's offence. Defence without offence will fail every time."

For the next several days, life at the safe-house was very quiet and polite. Angie moved like a ghost from room to room, wearing a distant expression, while Bilyash tiptoed around her. Poochie was walked, meals were prepared and eaten, dishes and clothing were washed, and messes were tidied, but without anything that could be called conversation.

Then, just as Bilyash thought he might explode from the tension, Angie's eyes snapped into focus and she said, "I'm sorry."

"About what, Angie?" he said.

She sank down onto the sofa beside him and elaborated: "I've been thinking about everything that's happened since we met, and how safe and protected I feel when we're together... and how many times you've stood up for me when Maldemaur and Gershred were seeing me as just another source of nourishment, or as your 'pet human'. One of the reasons I love you is because you've never looked at me that way.

"When I said I wanted to have your baby, you never doubted my motives or tried to talk me out of it. You trusted me not to do anything that would harm you, and you gave me what I said I needed. I should have done the same for you. Instead, I let my fear get the better of me.

"I'd been living with it for so long that I thought I had it under control, that it couldn't surprise me. I was wrong. The thought of living my life without you triggered a flood of terrible memories. They knocked me sideways, and I panicked.

"I need to work through the memories, Billy. I need to put them back in the past where they belong, so I can live without fear in the present. And then we can talk about the future, I promise. I simply need more time."

Before he could reply, Jake leaned his head through the doorway and announced, "Pyotren just texted me. He's on his way back with supplies. And he's heard from Maldemaur. He and Gershred are flying back to Toronto today. Their flight will be landing around suppertime."

"More supplies?" said Angie, frowning. "How much longer does he expect us to be here?"

"Hard to say. According to Pyotren, there's an op they need to launch before you two will be safe to return home."

"An op," Bilyash repeated thoughtfully. "To neutralize Ellsworth?"

"Maybe," Jake allowed.

"Did he tell you whether they bought Middlevale?" she persisted.

"Nope. I guess you'll have to ask him when he gets here."

With that, Jake disappeared again.

Bilyash reached out and took Angie's hand. "Listen, if I thought for one second that going out to Vancouver would put you and the baby in danger—"

"I know," she assured him. "But now is not the time to talk about it. Just be patient, Billy, please."

Reluctantly, he nodded assent.

An hour later, a red sports car pulled up behind the Buick in the driveway, and Pyotren stepped out of it.

Jake went out to meet him. "That's a little flashy, isn't it?" he remarked.

"I was getting tired of driving junk cars," the shape lord replied, grinning as he swung two large bags of groceries into his cousin's arms.

He had brought a cooler full of perishable food as well. While Angie busied herself transferring it to the fridge, Pyotren joined Jake and Bilyash in the living room.

"Well, Maldemaur wasn't exaggerating about Billy's apartment being under surveillance," Pyotren reported. "They've even replaced the concierge at the front desk with a Yeng. His stink is all over the foyer. I pretended to be looking for a unit to rent and chatted him up while he told me about a couple that were available. Apparently, the entire fifth floor has been vacated while apartments are being fumigated."

"Sounds like a trap, all right," Jake confirmed. "They're expecting a fight and want to avoid disturbing the neighbours."

"But we'll be able to infiltrate?" said Bilyash.

"Getting in won't be the problem," Pyotren told him. "Entering a trap never is. The Yeng won't stop us from reaching the fifth floor. The unknowable part is what will be waiting for us there."

Replacing that disturbing thought with another, Bilyash asked, "Is there anything you can tell us about the op that Maury and Shred are planning? And the offer to buy Middlevale from Vincaspera?"

"Not much, actually. You know how tight-lipped Maldemaur can be. From what I'm able to gather, the Middlevale deal is on hold until after the op has been launched, and an old war buddy of Gershred's is coming back east with them to help with that. They'll be using this house as their base of operations. I've been instructed to beef up security and to expect a lot of traffic over the next few days. And it's a black op, so I'm guessing that you and Angie are going to be spending some time in the basement to prevent you from overhearing anything you shouldn't know."

"And Poochie?" said Angie.

"Him too," came the reply. "I'm not convinced he's really a dog."

Privately, Bilyash agreed. He'd had the same suspicion for some time now.

Shortly after 8:00 p.m., Maury and Shred arrived on the safehouse's doorstep, along with a tall, heavily-built man with a square jaw and piercing dark eyes.

This had to be the old war buddy. Bilyash watched from the living room as the three Nash'terel swept through the front door and along the hall to the kitchen. Gershred made the introductions in passing.

"Pyotren, Jacomin, Bilyash, meet Barron, a heat lord also known as Barney Ross. He'll be handling the personnel involved in the operation, since they're all his former students."

Those disturbing dark eyes grappled onto Billy's face. "Bilyash," Barron declared, as though calling his name on a roll. "Magnetism *hainbek*?"

His voice was deep and jagged, almost as unsettling as his gaze.

Warily, Bilyash nodded confirmation.

"Still an apprentice, and yet you've already taken out three assassins, I'm told."

That was one way to look at it, Bilyash thought, restlessness growing in his core like an itch he couldn't reach. Old buddy or not, this being was dangerous.

"He's weaponized the *dashkra* in his blood," Maury explained, frowning, "but there has to be physical contact, and a Yeng won't come that close."

"As long as he can throw up strong shields, he'll do all right," Barron said. "There are murders to avenge, and we all have our parts to play. But first things first. Bilyash, does your mate have anything dressy to wear?"

"A baby shower?" Angie exclaimed. "You've got to be kidding me! Since when do the Nash'terel throw parties for *any* occasion?"

"It's an excuse for having fifteen extra people in the house in the middle of the afternoon," Bilyash told her. "They're not actually bringing gifts, Angie, and you don't need to be a hostess to a bunch of strangers. All you have to do is look welcoming when you open the door and let them in."

"And then what? Why are they coming here, Billy?"

He hesitated, considering. "It's for an operations briefing. That's all they've told me."

"Uh-huh," she said tightly. "I overheard something about vengeance. What are they dragging you into now?"

He took both her hands. "Angie, I share your frustration. Really, I do. But this is not a situation we can control. Whatever they've got in mind, I trust Maury and Gershred to keep us both safe, just as they did on the sound stage, and I need you to trust them as well. Can you do that? Can you try, at least?"

"All right. Fine," she said, biting off each word. "I'll try."

Chapter Twenty-One

They arrived in twos and threes, fifteen well-dressed women of various apparent ages, chattering happily as they got out of their cars, with colourful gift bags and decoratively wrapped parcels in hand. Peering between the slats of a window blind in the living room, Bilyash and Angie watched these "party guests" greet one another on the sidewalk. Some of them exchanged hugs as though they were old friends who hadn't seen one another in a long while. And perhaps they were, he mused, since all of these Nash'terel had been trained by the same elemental master.

As what, though? Barron was a heat lord, and masters typically took apprentices who shared their talent. It was unusual for a master to have more than six students in a lifetime, and yet Barron had supposedly taught more than twice that number. They couldn't *all* have heat *hainbeka*... could they?

Playing her role to perfection, Angie opened the front door for them, her cheeks dimpling, and welcomed them inside. Once out of sight of the street, however, all those smiles turned off as though controlled by a switch. Gift bags and boxes were tossed into the front hall closet, and the operatives filed, sober-faced, into the kitchen where Barron and Gershred were waiting for them.

Maury walked past Bilyash and Angie and pointedly closed the kitchen door.

"I know you're curious as hell, but you really shouldn't be listening to this," he said.

"Then you tell us," Bilyash demanded. "What's going on, Uncle Maury?"

The older Nash'terel pursed his lips and raised his eyebrows, visibly debating with himself for a moment. Finally, he said, "Not here. Let's go to the basement."

The door off the main hall opened onto a landing, with steps going down as well as up to the second floor. Moving quickly, Maury led the way downstairs, to an area that was almost identical in layout and furnishings to the living room overhead. However, behind the cream and moss green sofa upstairs was a dining room. Here, there was a wall with a safe-like metal door in the middle of it—the bunker that Pyotren had mentioned earlier, lockable only from the inside.

"I'm supposed to be part of the briefing, so I can't stay down here for long," said Maury. "Ask your questions and I'll try to answer them, but for fuck's sake, be quick."

"What's the story on Barron?" Bilyash demanded. "Is he in charge now?"

"And who are those women *really*?" Angie chimed in.

"They're Nash'terel operatives, all highly skilled graduates of Barron's assassin training program on the west coast. Barron and Gershred are both seasoned warriors, brothers-in-arms. They met on a battlefield hundreds of years ago and have served together in many human wars since then. Next?"

Frowning, Bilyash said, "So the women are assassins. And they're here to kill multiple targets?"

"That's the intent of the operation, yes."

"Won't that many murders all at once make headlines?"

"No. It's a long term operation, completely undercover. Unless something goes terribly wrong, none of the Yeng will even know it has happened."

Bilyash inhaled sharply. Fifteen assassins. If that meant fifteen Yeng targets...

"There are fifteen Yeng on the Council of the First," he mused aloud.

"Indeed, there are," Maury replied with a crooked smile. "And your time is up. Now go to your bedroom, both of you. That's an order. When the briefing is over and the operatives have left, one of us will come and fetch you to talk about Ellsworth. And this conversation never happened."

They waited in silence for Maldemaur to close the hall door behind him. Then Bilyash led Angie upstairs to the second floor.

"The Council of the First? Who are they?" she wanted to know.

"A bunch of Yeng who arrived on this world shortly after my people did. They wield some clout among the humans and fancy themselves to be a sort of government in exile."

Her jaw dropped. "Oh. My. God," she whispered, sinking down onto the edge of their bed. "This is big, isn't it? A bunch of coordinated assassinations..."

He didn't reply. Maury's smile had been as good as a wink, and Bilyash was recalling what George had told them just before he died: "*You have no idea who you're fighting. They'll crush you.*"

Well, somebody had obviously had an idea, or they wouldn't be taking aim at the most powerful group of Yeng on the planet.

When it came, the realization struck Billy like a physical blow, knocking him breathless as he dropped down onto the bed beside her.

The Council of the First had known how to summon the Nash'terel masters to a meeting, and the emperor's assassins, fresh through the rift, had been able to find and target the Earthborn, of whose existence they shouldn't even have been aware. Clearly, the "secluded ones" weren't as secluded on Earth as they thought they were.

Only one explanation made sense of this: the Council wasn't just receiving information from their contacts on RinYeng—they were also giving it to them, either for profit or to save their own lives. Information that they had probably been gathering for centuries, about the Nash'terel families. About the Earthborn. Then, as the emperor's agents were hunted down and eliminated by warriors like Gershred and Barron, the First had evidently given that same information to their own triads of killers.

"There are murders to avenge."

If Barron had been training assassins out in B.C., then he'd probably known for some time about the Council's involvement in the attacks on Nash'terel. Today's briefing was for a counterstrike that must have taken years to plan. And its base of operations was Armin's kitchen downstairs.

All at once, this safe-house no longer felt safe to Bilyash. He and Angie were caught in the middle of an undeclared war. If anything went wrong with Barron's op, the Yeng would be on them like a film of soot.

Drawing a deep breath, Bilyash turned and met Angie's wide-eyed stare.

"We may need to sneak out of here tonight," he told her. "Pack your stuff and be ready to move."

But she was shaking her head. "I don't think that's a good idea, Billy. We're in a fortress here, guarded by Nash'terel lords and masters who can wreak destruction on any Yeng stupid enough to try to breach Maury's security perimeter. Unless you honestly believe we would be safer somewhere else?"

For several heartbeats they sat there, each gazing stubbornly into the other's eyes. Then Bilyash flopped backward with a sigh.

She was right. Nowhere else was safe right now. Besides, they needed help to deal with Ellsworth, and making a break for it would not exactly endear them to the Nash'terel who would be providing it.

Two hours later, the briefing was over. Billy and Angie watched from the bedroom window as the "shower guests" trickled down the driveway in twos and threes, got into their cars, and sped off, most likely to shapeshift into something more suitable for an assassination attempt.

Startled by a loud knock on the door, they heard Pyotren announce from the other side of it, "Barron's called a meeting in the kitchen. He wants both of you there."

"On our way," Bilyash replied, exchanging significant looks with Angie.

The kitchen table had been set for afternoon tea, with five chairs around it and a tray in the middle. It held a large round teapot with matching sugar bowl and milk pitcher. On the table at one end of the tray sat five gold-rimmed porcelain cups on saucers, each paired with an artfully wrought spoon. At the other end lay a glass plate of assorted baked sweets.

Pyotren and Jake stood guard, one posted at each of the exits from the kitchen. Their presence, combined with the utter civility of the occasion, reminded Bilyash of a scene from a James Bond movie, in which the villain invites the captured hero to join him for a cuppa so he can outline his evil plan for world domination.

Mentally casting himself as Bond and Barron as Blofeld, Bilyash settled onto one of the chairs.

Then Angie snaked a hand past him and stole one of the tarts, earning indulgent smiles from both Maury and Shred and spoiling the film allusion.

"What?" she demanded, licking pastry crumbs off her fingers. "Lemon is my favourite."

"It will be the child's favourite as well," said Barron. "Lilly always—"

A sudden shadow fell over his expression.

"Lilly was Barron and Vincaspera's daughter," Shred explained.

"Wait. You're talking about Victoria Spears, the cult leader?" said Angie. "She and Barron had a daughter together?"

Barron and Shred traded glances. Barron punctuated his with a curt nod.

"Nothing you hear at this table leaves the room. Is that understood?" Shred said, gazing sternly at Bilyash and then Angie.

"Understood," they replied in unison.

"Barron and Vicky *had* a daughter," he continued, "until a few days ago. Lilly was young, about seven years old in terms of human development. A Yeng assassin broke into their apartment above Vicky's office while the child was alone. Maury and I were with Vincaspera when she discovered her daughter's body. The murder was savage."

Angie stiffened in her chair. "Like what happened to Macy," she breathed.

"Exactly. Vincaspera was insane with grief. She wanted every Yeng to die just as horrible a death as her child's, and she would have gone on a merciless rampage if we hadn't promised to visit justice on the ones who were actually responsible for it. That's what this black op is all about."

"You're terminating the Council of the First because they provided the information that led the assassin to Lilly," Bilyash summed up.

"As well as to other Earthborn. But we prefer to think of it as a purge," said Barron.

Bilyash squared his shoulders. "And now that you've deployed your assassins to conduct this purge, we have an idea for what comes next."

"Really!" Barron crossed his arms and leaned back in his chair. "And what do you think should come next, young apprentice?"

Billy glanced around the room. Pyotren was struggling to keep a straight face and Jake's shoulders were shaking with repressed laughter. For the first time, the thought occurred to him: Had they been having fun with him all along? Keeping the kid amused until Maury and Shred returned from the west coast?

No matter. He was in with both feet now. Bracing himself, Bilyash barrelled ahead.

"Ellsworth. That's the name he used last time we met, anyway. Pyotren has confirmed that my apartment is being watched by the Yeng. Since Ellsworth is the third member of the triad that originally targeted me, I think it's a safe bet that he'll be showing up there to make the kill, if and when I return to the building. That gives us a way to bring him to us instead of having to hunt him down. All we need then is the firepower to take him out, along with any henchmen he might have brought with him."

"And are you volunteering to be the bait in this trap?" said Barron.

"We both are," Angie cut in. "We're a team, and we stay together."

Maury snapped erect in his chair. "No! We never knowingly put pregnant females in danger!" he informed her.

Angie reached into her pocket and placed her pistol on the table. "Even if they can defend themselves and are spoiling for a fight?" she demanded. She folded her arms on the tabletop and leaned forward, meeting and holding Barron's startled gaze.

"Well, *that* changes things," he remarked.

Meanwhile, Maury looked as though he'd just swallowed his tongue.

Clearing his throat, Shred finally weighed in. "This plan of yours needs refinement, Billy, but I think it's viable. Count me in."

"Me too," said Barron, adding with a smile at Gershred, "Great minds, eh, Gordie?"

Okay, *now* they were playing with him, Bilyash decided. They'd probably come up with the exact same plan during the flight from Vancouver. Was it important? No. All he cared about was neutralizing the immediate Yeng threat to his and Angie's safety.

"I still don't like the idea of their leaving this house," said Maury. "We're shapeshifters. We can impersonate them."

"I thought we'd settled this," Barron told him. "They're easier to protect if they're together, and keeping them with us avoids the need to split up *our* team."

"But Bilyash can't fight! And if we're all engaged, one little pistol won't be enough to protect them both," Maury argued.

"Maybe this will help," came Pyotren's voice over Billy's

shoulder. A moment later, a second, familiar gun was sitting on the table in front of him. "I rescued that from the cabin at the sports camp," Pyotren explained. "It's cleaned and loaded, and I've put a spare magazine into the glove box of the sports car for you."

"Wait. I'm driving the red sports car?" said Bilyash. "The one that stands out like a sore thumb and screams 'Shoot me, I'm a target'?"

"It's a trade-off. It also makes you easier to keep in sight while we're escorting you from here to your apartment," Shred pointed out. "We'll be in two cars, one in front of you and one behind, and we wouldn't want to lose you in traffic."

Exhaling gustily, Maldemaur subsided into grumpy silence.

"You've already thought out the details, haven't you?" Bilyash demanded.

"Yeah," Barron replied with a broad grin. "We're pretty much a go."

The following day, everyone put on a disguise for the drive into the city. Bilyash had traded Billy Ash's face for one that resembled a young Jimmy Stewart and was now headed south on Bathurst Street, with a bewigged and sunglassed Angie-as-Mary Jones riding shotgun while a discontentedly muttering miniature poodle sat on her lap.

Pyotren and Jake had transformed themselves into Billy and Angie lookalikes and were following in the Buick, as a decoy. Pyotren's instructions to Bilyash had been clear: the shape lord and the heat adept could take care of themselves, and Maury, Shred, and Barron were nearby to take care of the apprentice and the pregnant lady. So, regardless of what appeared in the rear-view mirror, the red car was to keep going.

It was nearly noon. Humidity was high and the temperature was dropping. At this time of year, that usually meant the skies were about to open up. Bilyash wasn't crazy about driving through a thunderstorm. However, traffic was moving steadily and the darkest clouds were behind them. With luck, they would reach their destination before the deluge began.

Meanwhile, Angie was not in a talkative mood. She had turned her head and was staring sombrely through the passenger's side window. Did he really want to know what was on her mind right now? Bilyash opted for no. He turned on the radio to fill the silence between them and focused his thoughts on the road ahead.

By half past the hour, Poochie was dozing, Angie was yawning, and Bilyash was waiting for the light to turn green at Sheppard Avenue. He'd lost sight of both escort cars several blocks earlier. Growing more uneasy by the second, Billy fished blindly in his pocket for his phone.

"Here," he said, unlocking it and dropping it in Angie's lap. "Find Dr. de Maur in my contacts and send him a text. Let him know where we are, and ask him where the hell *he* is. And don't be polite about it."

She did as he asked.

Several seconds later, Maury replied: *Waiting in a driveway, south of the intersection. We've got eyes on you, never fear.*

His jaw muscles working, Billy tightened his grip on the steering wheel. Maury had been against this plan from the beginning. Now the paranoid on the team was telling him not to be afraid? Yeah. Like anyone in their right mind was going to believe that.

Forty-five minutes later, the sports car was slowing down at the foot of the entrance ramp to the parking garage beneath Billy's apartment building. Maury's car was right behind them. There was no sign of the Buick.

Keep going...

The anticipated thunderstorm had apparently passed north of the city. However, another was on its way. As he lowered the driver's side window to swipe his key fob and open the entrance to the garage, Bilyash could practically smell the rain waiting to fall.

The metal panel door lurched into motion, taking forever to slide upwards. He sighed inwardly. It was going to be one of those days. The elevator would probably take its sweet time too.

Maybe it would be better to take the stairs...?

At last the opening was tall enough to accommodate a vehicle. Bilyash put the car in gear and drove it slowly down the ramp, into the dimly-lit interior of the garage. Poochie raised his head, remaining quietly alert, as Bilyash crept along between two rows of parking spaces, several of them empty, then made the turn past the pedestrian exit at the rear and approached his own numbered spot. He glanced off to his left and saw the door descending again, and Maury's car pulling into an empty space on the other side of the garage.

It was going to be a race. Assuming a worst-case scenario in which the concierge was actually Ellsworth lying in wait for them to return, one minute was how long it would take him to get downstairs and intercept them once he realized who they were. Therefore, they had to rendezvous with Barron's team and be going up in the elevator in fewer than sixty seconds.

Billy finished parking the sports car and reverted his face back to one the Yeng would recognize, then grabbed his go-bag with the gun and extra bullets in it, all while trying to ignore the whirlpool forming in his gut.

"Ditch the wig and sunglasses, grab Poochie, and quick-step over to that column," he instructed her tautly. "And pray that there are three strangers holding the elevator for us."

There were. Full body transformation was an intensely private process and therefore out of the question, but Maury, Gershred, and Barron had been able to shift their facial features and change their clothes during the drive to the city. As the steel door swooshed shut and the elevator car began its ascent to the fifth floor, one of the men consulted his wristwatch.

"Forty-five seconds," he said in Gershred's voice. "Not bad. Now, assuming there's a Yeng in the basement who knows where to find the generator that powers the elevators, it should take another forty-five for him to unplug it."

The display above the door was flashing floor numbers. G... 2...

"Wait a second!" Bilyash said. "How do you know all that?"

...3...

The response came in Maury's voice. "We've known it for years. Every apartment in a medium- or high-rise is a potential trap. Did you think we were going to let you move into this building without checking it out first?"

...4...

"But—"

With a lurch that nearly buckled Bilyash's knees, the car stopped moving. Half a breath later, the interior of the elevator was plunged into darkness. Bilyash shifted to his Nash'terel eyes. Angie was standing across the car from him, staring sightlessly ahead and struggling to hold onto Poochie—who, he belatedly recalled, was scared of the dark.

"Billy?" There was a note of panic in her voice.

"Ssshh!" said Maury. "Just sit tight. We figured this might

happen."

Something crashed overhead. Bilyash looked up in time to see a pair of legs disappear through a square hole in the ceiling. Whoever they belonged to then reached back in to help one of the other Nash'terel clamber up.

"Oh, hell," Angie muttered. "Monsieur Poochadour just peed on me. I'll need to change my clothes."

Unsurprised, Bilyash glanced over at her, noting the dark streaks down the front of her slacks and the smell of urine in the air. As much as being in the pitch dark frightened this little dog, hearing strange noises in the dark evidently terrified him even more.

"Okay, we're ready for you," Barron's voice called down.

Together, Maury and Bilyash were able to pass Angie and Poochie to him through the escape hatch before climbing out themselves. That left the car below them empty but still dark. Gershred stood half a floor above them, ready to pull them up and through the elevator door he and Barron had pried open.

In short order, everyone had been evacuated to the corridor on the fifth floor and from there to the interior of Billy's apartment, where Angie made a beeline for the washroom.

"Okay," said Barron, "from the security cameras in the corridor outside, the concierge will have figured out by now where we are, and that we're making a stand here. If we weren't, we would have headed back down the stairs immediately to escape."

"So this is no longer a Yeng trap," Bilyash said. "It's a Nash'terel trap."

"That's right, kid—and once the Yeng arrive, it will be a battlefield," Gershred confirmed.

"And until that happens...?"

"We wait."

While Angie was cleaning herself up, Maldemaur took Bilyash aside. "That face has served its purpose, Billy," he said. "It's time to choose another identity going forward. There's going to be a battle here tonight. We don't know exactly when, but the apartment will most likely be destroyed, and Billy Ash will die. So I strongly recommend that you and Angie make preparations to hit the road. Pack whatever you value and can carry, and do it now, while you have the chance."

"And Poochie?"

"If the dog survives and Pyotren doesn't, Armin can change your poodle back into a Chihuahua."

Chapter Twenty-Two

———◆———

Changing identities and going on the run were unfortunate facts of Nash'terel life. Since becoming Maldemaur's apprentice, Bilyash had had plenty of practice at filling a suitcase in haste. By now he could do it in less than five minutes.

He finished putting his bag together while Angie was in the washroom. When she emerged, he took her into the bedroom and explained the situation.

"Will I need another makeup job?" she asked.

"There won't be time for that. In any case, it will be dark outside, so your Mary Jones disguise should suffice," he told her. "You'll be travelling with Ken Smart, a crackerjack auto mechanic and reformed car thief."

"Ooh, a checkered past. I like it." She gave him a grin that made his heart turn over.

While she was packing up her belongings, he went into the washroom to shapeshift into Ken. The first time he'd worn this identity, he'd been going through a James Dean phase and had turned himself into a sullen-eyed young delinquent. But Angie didn't need a "rebel without a cause" right now. She needed someone whose appearance would make a killer think twice before attacking her. Someone quiet and menacing like James Coburn in *The Magnificent Seven*. It took his essence a few minutes to sort everything out, but eventually he was wearing a composite face that he felt gave off the right vibes.

Then he stepped into the bedroom, where the sight of his new form brought Poochie to his feet. Abandoning his favourite towel, the dog trotted over to sniff Ken Smart's ankles. Then he let out a huff, sat back on his haunches, and deliberately turned his head away.

Evidently, this shapeshifting thing had lost its novelty. Either that or he was miffed at having to remain a poodle for so long.

Angie closed her valise and gave Ken an approving look up and down. "Not bad at all," she remarked. "Are we ready?"

"Almost." Hurriedly, he tucked in his shirt. He found his cache of IDs in the concealed pocket of his bag and swapped out William R. Ash for Kenneth Smart in his wallet. Finally, he took out the pistol Pyotren had given him and laid it carefully on the bed, alongside the extra magazine of bullets. The apartment wasn't a large space, and too many combatants in tight quarters was a recipe for chaos. Ken and Angie had been ordered to shelter in the bedroom, defending themselves however they could from any Yeng who made it past the three Nash'terel in the living room.

"Billy, the food!"

The cooler they'd purchased earlier was sitting half-filled just inside the kitchen door. It needed to be in the bedroom with Angie and their luggage. As Bilyash was crossing the living room to fetch it, the faintest odour of rotting fish stopped him in mid-step.

It was coming from the direction of the hallway. The others had smelled it too and were moving into position around the door. Maury put a silencing finger to his lips and gestured to Bilyash to move back to the bedroom. For several long seconds, motionless and with nerves taut as bowstrings, they waited.

Meanwhile, Poochie had picked up the Yeng scent as well. He slipped through the bedroom door as it was closing and raced into the living room. His ears were pointed forward, his teeth menacingly bared. Cursing inwardly, Bilyash chased after him and scooped him up.

In that moment, the dog became a writhing bundle of teeth and claws, yapping and howling hysterically. It was all Bilyash could do to hold onto him. And then...

Without warning, the floor dropped from beneath his feet and Bilyash found himself flying backward, just as the recliner rose up and hit him, hard enough to knock the air out of his lungs and most of the thoughts out of his head. All at once the room was full of dust and splinters. They hung suspended around him for what seemed an endless moment, giving his sluggish brain time to recognize them as bits of wood and wallboard.

The Yeng had just blown up his front door.

Fuck!

Bilyash landed, gasping, on the floor, next to the leg of his overturned sofa. Immediately, Angie was beside him, urging him back onto his feet.

This was wrong. She was in danger. Poochie was gone and there was no time to search for him.

Silencing her protests with a look, he pushed her back through the bedroom door and slammed it shut. They were under attack, and Bilyash had a job to do: defend that room and the female inside it with the most effective tool at his disposal.

The air felt full of sand. It burned his eyes. He blinked hard, forcing them to stay open as he backed up to the door, spread his arms wide, and commanded his essence to form a magnetic field around his body. Meanwhile, squinting through a film of tears, he was just able to make out a form lying motionless on the carpet before him, and several more bodies squeezing one by one through the newly-made hole in his living room wall.

Bilyash had no idea how many Yeng there were in total. The first one to enter the apartment was covering the rest by randomly firing energy bolts into the haze left over from the explosion. Lamps and ornaments exploded *ba-BOOM* into puffs of dust that further thickened the air, until nothing was discernible beyond the margins of his shield but the sporadic flash of an ion beam slicing across the room.

His magnetic field was holding strong. Bilyash forced himself to remain calm, taking courage from remembered voices as he held his ground in front of the bedroom door.

"As long as he can throw up strong shields, he'll do all right."

"Magnetism is defensive, so shields are your department..."

...and heat was offensive, Jake had said. Offence and defence were a team.

"Whatever you do, don't split up the team!"

As if in answer to his thought, Gershred let out a battle cry. Barron's angry shout soon followed.

And then, all hell broke loose. Bilyash was struggling to breathe and straining to see as energy streams and thrown heat bombs pelted past him in every direction, looking like glistening fish in a milky pool. He was drowning in noise. Smoke alarms were shrieking. Poochie was wailing in panic. Weapons fire sizzled and screamed all around him. And underlying this hellish, inescapable racket was a persistent clamour of raised male voices...

...minus one.

Bilyash's heart leaped up into his throat as, with a start, he realized whose voice was missing. He swept his gaze across the floor in front of him and found the same dark, unmoving form as before.

Maldemaur.

Bilyash knew what he had to do. It wasn't something he'd practised. He had no idea whether he could even produce a field of the necessary magnitude, let alone maintain it until the danger was past. But he had to try.

Swallowing hard, he stepped forward, grasped Maldemaur by the ankles, and dragged him over to the bedroom door. Then the apprentice spread his arms again and poured as much of his essence as he dared—more than he knew was wise—into the magnetic field he'd created, expanding it to encompass the light lord as well.

Almost immediately, Bilyash's limbs objected to this rapid outward rush of his life energy. Gritting his teeth against the pain of cramping muscles, he stood fast. As one minute and then another passed, he could feel his strength ebbing, and an urgent need to feed taking its place. He denied it, refusing to leave his post a second time.

A searing heat ignited in Bilyash's feet. It crept steadily upward, consuming his ankles, then his calves... He swallowed hard, knowing that he couldn't hold out much longer.

Then he felt a tap on his shoulder, and a pistol appeared as though by magic in front of his face. When he hesitated to grab it, it smacked him on the cheek until he did.

"Cover me!" Angie cried behind him.

Next thing he knew, she'd grappled onto Maldemaur's arm and was struggling to pull him to safety in the bedroom.

Defence without offence will fail every time.

She had to have known that open door would draw attention, now that the cloud of dust was settling. The increased visibility let one of the Yeng find a target. Bilyash watched with mounting horror as the assassin looked directly at him, then pointed his ion weapon at the Nash'terel lying unconscious on the floor between his feet.

"Esstateh'mesh ma—!"

All by itself, it seemed, Billy's gun came up and fired, *pop-pop-pop*. It halted the Yeng in mid-curse, throwing him back against the wall with a hand clutched to his shoulder.

Bilyash didn't dare turn away from the battle. Keeping his shield in place, he bent and grasped Maury's other arm with his free hand, then pulled upward with all his remaining strength. Together, he and Angie were able to drag Maldemaur halfway across the threshold. The older Nash'terel had reverted to his true form. If it repulsed her, she didn't let her feelings show. Instead, she thrust her hands under his armpits and continued pulling him inside.

"I've got this now," she said grimly. "You just block the door until I can close it."

It was easier said than done. Bilyash's shield had come under too much fire. It was dissipating, taking his essence along with it. He could feel his bones shifting as his true form emerged.

The sensation of being burned alive reached his belly. If he didn't feed within the next few seconds...

Somewhere far away, the battle continued to rage. Bilyash tried to retrieve some of his essence, tried to call out to Angie, but it was too late. As the last of his strength left his body, the world shrank rapidly to a pinpoint and winked out.

Eyes shut, Bilyash could feel the icy pain of essence flowing along his limbs like a spring-melt mountain stream. There were soft cushions beneath him and a weight on his chest, and something wet and rough was stroking his face. And grumbling.

He knew that voice. It was Poochie.

Just like in a Terrence Macy movie, the Chihuahua had apparently come through it all unscathed.

Bilyash cracked his eyelids open and saw a pair of soulful doggy eyes staring down at him.

"*That's* more like it." Bilyash struggled for a moment to place this second voice, then recognized it as well. It was Barron's.

"You had us worried for a bit, but you're going to be okay, kid," said Gershred. "It's over. We got all four of them, and Maury will be all right too, thanks to your quick thinking."

"Four of them?" Bilyash croaked. "Again?"

"Ellsworth and the concierge, plus two more. Can you sit?"

"Get off me, Poochie."

With an indignant huff, the dog hopped down to the carpet. Two pairs of hands pulled Bilyash's upper body erect, then turned him ninety degrees and leaned him back against the sofa.

Maury came to stand over him, wearing Albert Einstein's face like a mask. "That was the most reckless, irresponsible—"

"—*courageous* defensive tactic I've ever seen," Barron cut in. "This kid can fight beside me any day of the week."

As the infusion of essence reached his brain, Bilyash's thoughts sprang into sharp focus. There was only one place that life-saving boost of energy could have come from.

"Angie!" Glancing around, he made an unsuccessful effort to

get to his feet.

"Whoa! Steady there!" Gershred advised. "She's all right, Billy. She's asleep in the bedroom."

"And the baby?"

Maury's features softened. "The baby's fine. Even in the womb, a Nash'terel has strong survival instincts."

"How long was I out?"

"You've been wearing your true form for about an hour," Barron replied. "I wouldn't try shapeshifting for another hour at least."

"The Council has a hate-on for you, Billy," Gershred said. "They've put a target on your back, and the fastest way to remove it is for Billy Ash to die."

"I know. Uncle Maury told me already."

"And that's why you switched to a new identity. Okay, good. Fortunately, only four Yeng might have seen your new face and they're all dead. And just to seal the deal, Pyotren and Jacomin have staged your fatal car crash. What do you think of this?" Gershred opened an image on his phone and bent to show it to him. Pyotren had done a masterful job of impersonating Billy Ash as a mangled corpse. He looked perfectly grisly.

...which was fine for a Nash'terel who could transform into a whole other being at will, but not for a human who was pregnant with a Nash'terel child. Not even a shape lord could give her a fresh start at this point.

"Does Angie have to die too?" Bilyash wanted to be angry if the answer was yes, but that required energy, and right now just sitting there and speaking words was taking everything he had.

"Of course not," Maury assured him. "The story will be that you were alone in the car at the time."

Bilyash groaned inwardly. Great. Angie's car was now a twisted wreck. Good luck to whoever had to break the news to her about that...

"Once the word gets out," said Gershred with a grin, "the entire Canadian movie industry will be mourning your untimely demise."

"No, they won't. They know I'm a special effects makeup artist, and they'll realize it's a hoax."

"Actually, we've got that covered as well," Maury interjected, "by way of a medical examiner I was friends with back on RinYeng."

"Besides," Barron added, "humans are *ristima*. They follow the noise. Tell them anything loudly enough and often enough and they'll believe it, regardless of what their own senses are telling them. They'll insist that the sky is green and the grass is blue, even while they're standing in a meadow."

Bilyash looked up at him. "Are you sure Ellsworth is dead?"

"Absolutely," came the smiling reply. "You're free and clear, kid. Vicky will be happy to hear that there are four fewer Yeng on this planet, and we can start making plans to train our Nash'terel army. And I'd be honoured, young Bilyash," Barron added, "if you would be the first to enlist."

Bilyash pictured Angie lying on the bed, a peaceful expression on her face as she replenished her essence.

He was tempted to accept Barron's offer on the spot, but if he did it without consulting her first, there would almost certainly be hell to pay.

"I'll have to get back to you on that," he demurred, glancing around him.

The apartment was a mess. The living room had been

demolished, and most likely the dining room as well. Furniture lay tumbled and scattered, some of it in pieces. Dust and debris had settled everywhere. Bullets, heat bombs, and weaponized ions had gouged and scorched the walls and left his favourite chair a smouldering ruin. Thankfully, except for a crimson smear behind the Yeng that he had shot in the shoulder and some fat red drops on the dining room floor, there was almost no blood.

Improbably, the telephone had remained untouched. It chose that moment to ring.

"Hi, it's Pyotren," said a familiar voice. "I'm downstairs with Jake and Armin and the concierge is MIA. Buzz us in."

The Yeng had not only planned their trap well, but by arranging for the fifth floor to be unoccupied, they also made it possible for shape lords Armin and Pyotren to repair the damage to Billy Ash's place, erasing all outward evidence of the battle that had caused it.

While they were working on that, heat lords Barron and Gershred, with assistance from heat adept Jacomin, took charge of the four Yeng bodies, removing and incinerating them while they were still fresh.

As soon as Bilyash had recovered sufficiently to resume Ken Smart's appearance, Maldemaur drove him, Angie, and Poochie (once more a Chihuahua) back up to the safe-house, this time with all their luggage and pet supplies and the cooler of food. It was understood that they would be staying there for at least another week, until the apartment was once more pristine and ready to be lived in.

A couple of days later, Bilyash was sitting on the easy chair, watching Angie snack on cubes of raw steak and feeling a strong sense of déjà vu. It would have been nice to wake up and discover that the events of the recent past had been nothing more than a bad dream, but he knew they hadn't. And he still had a decision to make.

The minutes stretched out.

Finally, he couldn't stand the suspense any longer.

"Barron called me again this morning," he said. "He's going back to B.C. tomorrow to set up the program and he wanted to know whether I would be part of it. I told him it all depends on you, and that he would have my answer after we'd discussed the matter. I know you wanted time to work through the bad memories, but I was wondering..."

She paused, then put her plate down on the coffee table. "Forgive me."

Again?

"Forgive you for what?" he asked tautly.

She lifted brown eyes brimming with sadness to his face. "I wasn't completely honest with you earlier. You once told me that no matter how you looked on the outside, you would always be the same on the inside, and I believed you."

"Because it was the truth, and it still is," he said, frowning.

"And I want it to keep on being the truth. But this program of Barron's is military training. Military training changes people on the inside, Billy. It makes them see the world differently, and re-evaluate relationships. When I say I don't want to lose you, what I mean is that I don't want you to stop being the man I fell in love with. I can handle just about anything, but not that."

Tears were thickening her voice now, and trickling down her cheeks.

She has no idea how young you are, said Jake's voice inside his head.

Bilyash slid off his chair and onto his knees in front of her. Taking both her hands in his, he gazed up into her eyes and said, "Angie, this is something I really need to do, for both of us. And maybe it *will* change me. In fact, I hope it does. I want to grow into my responsibilities as a parent. I want to be able to defend my family. But I swear to you on the ashes of my own parents, the love I have for you will never alter, never lessen, and never die."

Her lips curved into a shy smile. "That sounds almost like a wedding vow."

"Till death do us part," he confirmed. "Actual death, not faked."

"And Billy Ash is really gone? No more magical makeup mojo?"

"I'm afraid so. You're stuck with the guy with the checkered past who knows a lot about cars. Kenny Smart, at your service."

Her smile broadened. "Then, once my conditions are met, I guess we're going out to British Columbia."

Wait. Conditions?

"Let's begin with the replacement car Pyotren owes me," she said.

Bilyash stifled a sigh. It was going to be a long day.

Epilogue

———•———

Two Months Later

Early September in Collingwood was sunny and warm, the air gently stirred by a breeze off the water of Georgian Bay. It was a perfect day for a small social gathering on the paved backyard patio of Maury and Shred's new home. All the guests were able to fit their folding chairs into some part of the shade thrown by the umbrella crowning the circular glass-topped table, where bottles of wine and an assortment of fancy cheeses sat within easy reach.

The get-together had been Shred's idea. Humans had short lifespans, encompassing a limited number of momentous events, so they regularly celebrated and memorialized each one. However, the Nash'terel lived for up to six thousand years. Such things as birthdays and anniversaries became commonplace relatively quickly and therefore tended to slide past unremarked.

An alliance between former enemies, on the other hand, was noteworthy enough to merit recognition. Gershred had therefore issued invitations to a party in honour of the newly-forged business partnership between his partner and Barron's mate, Maldemaur and Vincaspera respectively.

That wasn't the only thing they could feel good about right now. Barron and Shred's operation hadn't only avenged the murders of the Earthborn, it had also plugged the information leak to RinYeng, thus preventing untold numbers of future Nash'terel deaths.

"As of five o'clock p.m., three days ago," Shred announced, raising his goblet in a toast, "every Yeng on the Council is now being impersonated by a shapeshifted Nash'terel assassin, thanks to the graduates of Barron and Vincaspera's very special training program. To the long overdue purge of the Council!"

"To the purge!" repeated the others, raising their wine glasses as well.

To make things more interesting, Shred had also decided that this should be a costumed event. He'd instructed everyone to come wearing their favourite shape.

No charred body had been found in the basement of Maury's previous home, so Doctor Malcolm de Maur, the middle-aged man he'd let his neighbours glimpse occasionally while he was living there, was still a viable identity. Maldemaur had decided to keep this name and form for now.

Before his tragic and untimely death on a side road north of Toronto, Billy Ash had sublet his apartment to Kenneth Smart and his girlfriend (the proud owner of a red sports car). For the party, however, Bilyash had resurrected Auntie Min and her billowing daisy-printed skirt.

Vincaspera had flown east from Vancouver to finalize the Middlevale deal, a partnership between herself and Maldemaur to finance and maintain both the town and the soon-to-be-constructed military training compound near it. Vicky Spears had darkened both her auburn hair and her skin colouring but otherwise remained the same as she'd been before Lilly's death—tall, slender, and strikingly beautiful.

Her mate Barron's favourite shape was the one he wore into battle. No surprise there. Powerfully built and granite-featured, he looked like an action hero figure come to life.

Shred had reviewed his repertoire of identities and settled on the one that had given him the greatest satisfaction—Lieutenant Clifton James of the Royal Army Corps, aka Field Marshal Montgomery's double during the Second World War.

Along with her *dashkra* pendant, Angie was wearing the only shape she possessed, and it was becoming awkwardly large in the belly. But that wasn't the only reason she was having difficulty sitting comfortably in her lawn chair.

Vincaspera had been staring at her in puzzlement, visibly struggling to place her. Then something evidently clicked into place in Vicky's mind. Eyes wide and both eyebrows elevated, she shot upright in her chair, planted her wine glass firmly on the table top, and declared, "Maldemaur, you've been keeping a secret from us!"

He gave her a look of innocent bewilderment.

"Now I understand why you insisted on including that condition in our partnership contract," said Vincaspera. "Angelina is not Nash'terel. She's a human from Middlevale."

This was news to Barron. He'd paused with his wine goblet halfway to his mouth and was staring at Angie as well. Clasping a protective hand around her pendant, she tilted her chin and stared defiantly right back at him.

So did Bilyash, Shred noted approvingly. The kid had evidently foreseen the possible need to protect his mate and had chosen Minerva's shape with that in mind.

Normally, an apprentice didn't dare to challenge an elemental master. However, Min was a formidable figure, her face and bearing warrior enough to give even a master pause—and a second's hesitation was all Billy would need to tip the scales in his favour in a confrontation.

With luck, it wouldn't come to that today. This was a social gathering, after all, and there were other masters present to defuse the situation.

"Actually, Angie is part Nash'terel," Maury replied, "and so is every other living member of your cult. You hybridized them when you injected your own DNA into them to speed up the experiment. The blood ceremony we conducted with that stone proved it."

Tapping her chin with a thoughtful index finger, Vincaspera leaned back in her chair, recalling. "Of course. Yours was the family that left us right after we banished—"

"It wasn't banishment and you know it," Angie said deliberately, now levelling a hard-edged gaze at Vincaspera's face.

Frowning, Bilyash laid a hand on Angie's forearm and leaned forward, his mouth open to speak. Before he could say a word, however, Vincaspera batted the provocation aside.

"And now you're carrying Bilyash's child?" she gushed. "A Nash'terel child? How wonderful! How far along are you, my dear?"

Angie paused, then replied grudgingly, "Three and a half months."

Turning, Vicky exclaimed, "Maldemaur, do you realize what

this means? A hybrid pregnancy lasting into the fourth month! It's unprecedented! And my work made it possible."

Shred felt his stomach drop as he realized: Vincaspera couldn't have known what she did about hybrid pregnancies unless she'd experimented with them in the past. He didn't want to contemplate what that might have involved, or what her final goal could have been. He only knew that leaving Angie at Vicky Spears' mercy right now would not be a kind thing to do. Judging by the narrowing of Minerva's eyes and the way her lips were compressing into a hyphen on her face, Bilyash had been thinking the same thing.

"You mean your *cheating* made it possible, Caspera," Maury corrected her.

"Let's not dredge that up today, shall we?" she said. "After all, an imminent birth is cause for rejoicing. Have you picked out a midwife? And where were you thinking Angelina would live while her mate is training at the compound?"

"We haven't made up our minds yet about that," Bilyash cut in firmly. "Angie and I have come to an agreement. Once we know what our options are, we'll discuss them together, and then Angie will make the final decision. She's more than capable of choosing what would be best for her and the baby."

This reproof barely registered. Vicky furrowed and unfurrowed her brow, then said breezily, "Of course, a mother always knows best. And I would therefore like to make you an offer." Without waiting for his reaction, she turned to Angie and continued, "There are two apartments above the storefront in the building Barron and I own, on the second and third floors. We're renovating the one on the third floor while we live on the second floor. The work should be finished in the next couple of weeks.

You and Bilyash can move in right afterward."

"How much would the rent be?" Angie inquired.

"No charge. You would be our guests. That way, when Bilyash is at the training compound, you won't be left all alone. You'll have your privacy when you want it, and we'll be just upstairs if you're in the mood for company or if you need help with something. As well, I can contact the midwife who delivered Lilly to monitor the pregnancy and attend the birth of the child."

"And will I get to keep it?"

This question, spoken so softly, landed with the force of a physical blow. Vincaspera recoiled from it, her face losing several shades of colour as her expression shifted from indignation to wounded sorrow.

Belatedly, Shred realized how little time had passed since Lilly's murder and how raw Vicky's pain still had to be.

"Of *course* you get to keep your baby," she said, her voice barely a whisper. "What kind of monster do you think I am?"

Shred stepped in before Angie could deliver her next salvo. "She knows, Vicky," he said. "About us. About the Nash'terel. Bilyash has told her everything."

"I see. And because of my past transgressions, she expects the worst of me, just as you and Maldemaur do," came the stiff response. "Tell me, then," she added, her attention still focused on Angie alone, "what sort of help would you accept from me?"

Angie thought for a moment. "I like the idea of having the midwife, and Ken and me having our own place together. What I don't like is being pushed into a relationship I don't want. I didn't like it when I was fifteen, and I won't stand for it now."

"So you're not interested in the apartment, then?"

"I didn't say that. A landlord doesn't have to be a friend—they just have to respect boundaries. Draw up a lease agreement specifying a reasonable rent, and after seeing the apartment for ourselves, Ken and I will discuss whether we want to sign it or look elsewhere."

Angie turned and stared a prompt at Bilyash, who had sat watching this exchange with great interest and was now leaning back in his chair, nodding his head.

"Sounds like a plan," he remarked evenly.

Clearly, the adult in this relationship had taken charge, Shred mused. It boded well for their future together.

Meanwhile, Barron had put an arm around his mate's shoulder. "Vicky?"

Vincaspera's *hainbek* was pressure—telekinesis, the humans called it. After Lilly's murder, she had gone berserk and used her talent to trash the apartment. Now a human test subject had put Vincaspera in her place, and Shred wasn't the only one holding their breath, hoping the patio furniture wouldn't go flying.

For several heartbeats, there was silence. Then, at last, Vicky let out a martyred sigh. "I'll take care of it as soon as we get home," she said.

She wasn't happy, but she wasn't deadly either. Not deadly was good.

Gershred's relief was short-lived, however. There was another problem, one that he hadn't let himself consider earlier and that Angie knew nothing about.

Assuming that the child was born healthy and aged at the Nash'terel rate, it would require constant care and supervision for the first fifty years of its life. Unless being part Nash'terel endowed the Middlevale humans with greatly extended lifespans, Angie might be dead and buried before her son or daughter even learned to walk. And then what?

"Don't be glum, Gordie," said Barron, clapping him on the shoulder with one hand and recharging both their wine glasses with the other. "We've done a good thing. All that data the Council gathered about us is now being guarded by Nash'terel who will keep it secure from prying Yeng eyes on both sides of the rift, and our Earthborn will have champions to protect them while they're learning to defend themselves. After all, they're the future of the Nash'terel on this world." He raised his glass. "To the Earthborn?"

Gershred couldn't argue with that. He touched the rim of his goblet to Barron's.

"To the Earthborn," he replied, adding silently, *and their offspring. May the universe grant them good fortune.*

Arlene F. Marks has been writing since the age of 6, and she has no plans to stop. A veteran teacher of the craft, she has authored two popular literacy programs for the classroom. Her short stories have appeared online and in print, notably in an anthology of reimagined fairy tales, *Grimmer Tales Volume One*. She is also the author of the Sic Transit Terra space opera series (from Edge Publishing) and *Adventures in Godhood*, her first of several recent releases from Brain Lag Publishing. *The Bloodstone*, the sequel to *The Earthborn*, will be released later this year. Arlene lives with her husband on the shore of beautiful Nottawasaga Bay, where she spends time exploring imaginary worlds, collecting interesting-looking owls, and dreaming of one day having a tidy, well-organized office. www.thewritersnest.ca